THE**INDEPENDENT**

Daley,
My very best
to you!

Rich M[...]

January 22nd, 2017

Eastside Gent Press
Austin, TX

This is a work of fiction. All names, characters, places, and incidents are the products of the author's imagination or are used factiously. Any resemblance to current or local events or to living persons is entirely coincidental.

Charles Krauthammer statement in Chapter 35 as quoted in Common Ground: How to Stop the Partisan War that is Destroying America (2007) by Cal Thomas and Bob Beckel and the Wall Street Journal August 29, 2012. Reprinted herein with permission granted by Dr. Krauthammer

Facts quoted in Chapter 35 from Wall Street Journal article April 21, 2014, pg. PA13. Maranto and Crouch and Chapter 37 adapted from Wall Street Journal Sunday May, 17, 2014, pg. C3 by Micklethwait and Wooldridge

Cover Design by Douglas Brown

Library of Congress Cataloging in Publication Data
P S 3 5 6 3 M 4
ISBN: 978-0-9915630-1-2

Printed in the United States of America
by Lightning Source

Books by Rick McGee

Yardstick: A Life Measured

THE INDEPENDENT

a novel by
Rick McGee

Eastside Gent Press

For Sonya

Introduction

Another One in the Slammer! The headline screamed at me, and a lot of others in the state, making us feel like fools all over again. We set the record long ago for most governors in the pen, locked up as felons who stole for a living. And now, we were extending our streak, another bad guy going to jail after taking his due from our piggy bank to buy stuff he didn't really need. It made me angry, hell it made me irate and I tossed the paper aside. When will we learn to elect someone who cared more about getting their job done than getting ahead? It was easy to blame the pols and chalk them up as the bad guys because that's what they proved to be, on a regular basis. It had become all too predictable, elect a new governor or congressman then place your bets on how long it would take for the truth to come out. I put down a sawbuck at the office on 13 months for our current governor, might as well make a dollar with these odds. It was never a question of guilt or innocence. Guilt was a given, the only variable at play was the amount of time.

Many people started rationalizing things, saying to themselves then to others 'he could not help himself, the temptation was too great'. Yep, the heart of Mayor Daly was still beating right alongside a guy named Capone and all the other criminals who brought infamy to our city and state. In a state accustomed to honoring bad guys, some thought we should throw a ticker tape when another governor moved on down the road, just a stone's throw away. We liked to keep a close eye on our former governors as they ate three squares a day and slept on a hard bed. Well, the beds weren't that hard; actually they were comfortable, damn confortable.

The governors were not alone in the muck. The truth is our state was not very good at electing honest pols. I could look at the other side of the coin and proclaim we excelled at electing felons. There's the ticket, something we were good at, actually great at, maybe the best in the world. We were the greatest ever in electing governors that went to jail. Now, that's a bumper sticker.

If we looked in the mirror and had an honest chat with the voter on why we kept electing the bad guys, we'd come to the conclusion it was our own fault. There was no one else to blame, not with the streak we had going. We were way too consistent in the outcomes we engineered at the voting booths on election days. Four of the past seven governors had been sent to jail, a market leading ratio, no other state came anywhere close. None even tried.

I let the anger pass, then wondered, what are the criteria to be governor in a state where the odds favored felons? Heck, it seemed anyone could do a better job for the people than pols who deceive, steal, and lie for a living. Maybe even I could do a better job?

The last whistle blew for me a couple years back and I needed to call a new play. There was still some time left on my clock and I wanted every minute to count. Many say I left the gridiron at my peak, the national championship in the rearview mirror just a few short years ago. Coaching had been good to me and I felt rested after taking a year away from the pressures it brought. It was time to write my next chapter and apply myself, perhaps one last time. Congress needed a kick in the rear and a former football coach might be just the type of person to perform that task. From the chair on my porch with a cold beer in one hand it was easy to see politicians were not earning it. The only thing that seemed to matter was getting the vote and a return ticket to office.

Mount Rushmore need not worry about today's politicians. Chisels were down, stored away for the duration. It would be years, decades, likely longer before this country felt a politician had earned respect, trust and attained hero status. Some felt the bar was too high to climb the mountain, but the truth was easier to assess. Our pols had more important matters to tend than taking care of the folks. It was so easy to understand what motivated pols these days. The old adage, "follow the money," told us all we needed to know. Campaign managers rated higher status than policy professionals and controlled large budgets and talking points, the real tools of the trade. Any outlet with a microphone or pen got fed, and fed well, by the campaign guru who told the pol what he or she needed to think and say. The realization finally hit me... hard! Campaign managers were running our country. "Damn, how did we let that happen?" I wondered aloud.

Unfortunately, a new governor had just been elected, a missed opportunity until he too gets caught in the cookie jar. But the Senate race was on, an open seat that would be another layup for the Democrats. The Republicans would put up a warm body so it appeared they were making it a race, but we knew it was only a sham. Maybe it was time for an independent to run, someone who cared about two sides of an argument. I had built a career based on earning trust, commanding respect, leading diverse groups of people and molding them into a team with common goals. Players and coaches earned their positions every day on the field, in the locker room, the classroom and anywhere we went. Could I apply my skills and experience as a football coach to the aisles of Congress? Did I have what it takes to be a politician? Did I have that kind of game?

These questions bounced around in my head as I opened another beer and tried to drown out random thoughts, but one central theme kept haunting me, kept returning to the forefront of my mind. The critical question in front of me was one I had faced time and again with my players: Could I make a difference in people's lives?

It had taken a while to realize my true purpose and the yardstick I used to measure success. I was built to help people, to motivate, to inspire, to develop a path forward. Sure I had failed and failed often, mostly when the person I tried to help didn't care or didn't try. I learned to let those losses go rather than pile up. Instead, I spent my time with the other kind of people, those willing to sweat, unashamed to cry, ready to bleed if necessary. My wins gave me satisfaction as they carved a positive route in or out of the game. I had learned a great deal about people over the years, how to break them down, build them back up, and most of all, how to create a unified team from disparate individuals that represented all walks of life.

When I looked at Congress with a critical eye I did not see anything positive and I certainly didn't see many people earning it. Most of their time was spent in campaign mode, bending facts into talking points that were spewed on TV, in the press and across social media. Political fact checkers were busier than ever but no one seemed to care when pants were on fire or Pinocchio's piled up. It was expected. It was war. It was Washington D.C. But the real measures, the ones that mattered, the yardsticks that told us how the folks were doing, spiraled downward with no positive outcome in sight. The number of people on the dole continued to rise as full employment and wages tumbled, sapping the spirit and pride of too many.

Could I make a difference in people's lives? I didn't know for sure, but I had a gut instinct that I could do better, a lot better than those already in office. In our state, the bar was low—damn low. My first goal was to convince the voters I was a better choice than the felons they usually elected.

Bob Newton a United States Senator? Hmm, I had faced much tougher odds on the football field. Now was the time, now or never.

Chapter 1

The Debate

"**M**y opponent has no experience. Period. He does not know what it takes to write a bill, much less get one passed."

That sounds about right, I thought to myself. *What am I doing here anyway? I could be drinking a cold one and watching a game.*

The emcee or host or referee, whatever the right title, prompted me. "Mr. Newton, do you care to respond?"

I looked at my opponent, the other candidate, and saw her bracing herself for some retort, a witty reply or an attack on her personage. Instead I simply answered the question. "She's right, I do not have any experience as a politician."

The audience quieted and waited for more. They were used to long winded exposes from the pols who ran for office in this state, heck across the country. My short quips might not go over very well with all these professionals.

"Mr. Newton, would you like to expand on your answer? You still have 50 seconds remaining on the clock," the moderator said.

There he goes again, reminding me to take more time. Why would I take more time, it would only bore the audience to make up a longer answer than needed. "No thank you. My answer was pretty clear. You can give my opponent more time, she has a lot more to say than I do."

That comment drew some laughter from the crowd and a scowl from my opponent. The emcee just shook his head, probably thinking I was blowing my big chance. He did not fathom why a candidate would cede any time to the other guy, or in this case the other gal. Real pols were supposed to steal time from each other not gift-wrap a few seconds.

The debate was taking place in an old theater that seated about 2,500 people. The house was full this evening, every seat held a body and some had two as mothers and fathers brought an extra. Each of the candidates stood tall behind a lectern with ample room for notes if one desired. I left my papers in the hotel room. My team thought it a rookie mistake and they worried I would forget my lines. I had been pumped full of facts, figures and quotes for the media as most pols are during debate prep. But that was not my style, I thought it weak to refer to notes and memorize rehearsed lines. I had absorbed as much as I could and would go with my gut the rest of the way. The host, Adam Jones, a news anchor from Chicago, was seated in front of us, a long table his home with a computer, stacks of paper and a bunch of colored pens. *What are all the pens for?* I wondered. His back faced the 2,500 strong most of the time.

The host gave one last shake of the head then moved on. "Our next topic will be abortion and a woman's right to choose.

7

Each candidate will have 90 seconds to state their view and then another 60 seconds to respond to their opponent. Congresswoman Smith, your turn to go first." He eyed me closely and I thought, *Here we go, a juicy topic early in the debate that will surely liven things up in the arena. Who are the people that attend these things anyway?*

My opponent went on a long-winded rant about the "War on Women," whatever the heck that meant and insinuated I was part of the problem, part of the scourge or the plight that attacked women. Where did all this negativity come from? Why did she think I was such a bad guy? Oh yeah, I was bad because I was not a Democrat, not a liberal, not from her side of the aisle. Maybe I was bad because I was a male. That seemed unfair, but it did enter my mind as she kept ranting.

"Time," said the moderator.

"We will win the war on women …

"Congresswoman Smith, your time is up."

"…And ensure birth control is freely provided to all."

If there was a war on women I know which side to be on. It was an easy call. In my experience, women were smarter, stronger, tougher and also softer than most men. Hell, the men I knew were a bunch of lazed ex frat boys who played ball. They belched and farted their way through school then found some job in the corporate world where they belched and farted some more.

We all knew women were the better sex; they called most of the shots, at least the important ones. They decided things in the home, in the bedroom and in the kitchen. Women ruled how and when we slept, ate and enjoyed ourselves. Men were happy with the simpler things in life. If a man could control the remote and large screen TV in his man cave life would be good. Throw a beer fridge in that man cave and life was great.

Why were women taking so long to rule the world? How come they have not taken over yet? It never made sense to me why women were all too often relegated to the back seat of the car or the back of the line, any line. Women accepted way too much. They accepted a man's right to rule his castle, his kingdom and all the citizens in his domain. What crap. Men were scared shitless that women would someday figure out they were the smarter sex and destined to take the reins. Most men just hoped it did not happen on their watch.

But it was coming and it was coming soon. I could sense it, feel it in my bones, I knew it to be true. Women make better leaders, better CEOs, and better politicians. But not today, not this election, not this time. While my opponent was most definitely female, she was schooled in the black arts of traditional politics where a black belt was earned by keeping your job, not doing your job. And she had been keeping her job for far too long. It was time for her to go down.

"Time. Mr. Newton, you have 90 seconds."

"What's the question?"

"We are on abortion, a woman's right to choose."

"Yes, I know. What is the question you'd like me to address?"

"Can you state your opinion on abortion please and a woman's right to choose?"

The body language from this guy screamed at me like I was back in grade school and not paying attention in class. How did he know?

"I am against abortion."

The audience stirred, especially the female attendees including Amy, my wife, and Taylor, my daughter. That's where I wanted them, on the edge of their seats, ready to launch at my throat, fangs and claws poised to strike. Two more seconds and I would remove the tension and provide them some relief.

One, one thousand, two one thousand.

"And I am for a woman's right to choose."

The emcee or host was at a complete loss, his hands covered his head as he stifled a scream. Just like the Sisters from Immaculate Conception where I went to grade school. They never got me either, but I sure got them, more than once. The audience sat back in their seats, uncoiled from their striking positions, yet ready to pounce again if warranted.

My opponent was one of the old guard, if you count thirty years in political office as old. Actually, she looked pretty good to me, especially behind the lectern when her torso twisted, allowing her skirt to reveal those long legs, honed by hours at the gym. *How am I supposed to compete with that?*

She dove in for the kill and stole more of my clock time, which was fine with me. "My opponent wants to keep women in the dark ages, in the kitchen wearing an apron with a baby on one hip and another on the tit. Women need to rise up and take charge of their lives, their careers and let the man of the house do some of the cooking and cleaning and caring."

Wow, that was a good one. If we were at the bar, I'd buy her another round for that comment, especially the part about the tit. Could I get away with saying something like that? I needed to respond to the crap she kept making up and wondered where she got her material?

"I don't know about this whole war on women thing, I'm not sure who started it, and I'm not sure who's even in it. But I have been fortunate, even lucky, to have a couple of great teachers about the issues important to women— my wife Amy and my daughter Taylor. They're both sitting in the first row."

My opponent gave me some time; well actually it was a rope with a noose. She encouraged me to continue by staying quiet for a change.

"If there indeed is a war on women, I know which side to be on." I gave a head nod and smile to the two women in my life and the audience got a good laugh.

"Let me explain. I do oppose abortion and believe most people in this state and country feel the same way. Abortion is the exception not the rule. And as a general rule, I agree with most churches that abortion is the killing of an innocent child."

About half the audience was satisfied, the other half looked downright angry and moved toward their launch positions again.

"But, and it's an important but, I do not believe the State should oppose abortion, and I believe there are exceptions when abortion may be the best option. The state must respect a person's right to choose, to make decisions for her life, for her body. The State must make room for exceptions, not have stringent laws that deny a person's right to pick their own path. We have debated abortion in this country for decades and we have landed on a reasonable set of laws. We should let this topic rest and focus on other things where we can make a difference, where we can impact people's lives in a positive way. There are more important things we can focus on than trying to gain an inch in either direction on abortion. Let it rest."

My opponent did not have a retort. She spent all her time on those inches, pushing and pulling the rock back and forth and back some more. She made her career on gaining a bit of ground against the Satans across the aisle. Every two years offered another chance to inch up the hill, so long as she kept getting re-elected to the House as she had done the past nine elections.

The debate moderator would not let this topic go and pressed forward.

"Congresswoman Smith, what is your retort, I mean response, to Candidate Newton's position?"

She was stuck. Did she agree with me or not?

Tick tock. Tick tock.

Why do pols have so much trouble with straightforward questions? I could see her head spinning, trying out various answers in her mind, and weighing the odds of retaining or losing votes. Come on, Nancy just answer the question. Tell the voters what you think, how you really feel. Tell them the truth. I don't know why my subconscious was rooting for my opponent, hoping even praying she and I could have a conversation. Yeah that's it, a simple straightforward talk without any darts or jabs. Now that would be a change for the better. Come on Nancy.

Tick tock. Tick tock.

"Mr. Newton cannot avoid the War on Women. He has no solution, no stance, no voting record on this or any other issue. How can we trust what he says? Women will no longer tolerate the backward ways my opponent stands for. We will not allow my opponent and his party to take away our birth control."

My whole body sighed. I was not surprised, just disappointed at the customary rant from Nancy. When in doubt, evade the question, juke the moderator and attack your opponent. Her approach was probably some tactic from chapter one in the handbook on how to campaign effectively. The book titled something like *How to Win Elections by Slamming the Other Guy*. It made her look tough when she was on the attack, I guess. I thought it made her weak, it was clear to me she was not answering the question and that's weak, damn weak. Yet she got some applause anyway. Not for a good answer, nope that wasn't it. She got applause for the attack, for showing she was tough and would not back down against the enemy.

The moderator seemed pleased and wiped away a grin. He did not care about facts or positions; he just wanted action, a fight amongst the candidates, something to drive the ratings and his personal status. If he could make the candidates look bad, then he looked good. It usually did not take much, just get the pols talking and they will eventually back themselves into some corner then come out swinging against the other guy or gal.

But I had no intention of playing his game, not one bit. I would get elected…or not…based on truth, facts and policies that I wanted to enact as a United States Senator. It was time for change, real change, and I was taking one shot to make a difference. I would not be a traditional pol, I wanted to shake things up and throw out as much of the old guard and their practices and processes as I could. I might get hurt along the way and my family might get embarrassed, but we were ready, or so we thought.

I rewound the last comment from Nancy in my head. She had shifted from abortion to birth control and blamed my party. *Hmm, that was a mistake.* "Mr. Jones, if I may. Congresswoman Smith is once again using false facts to fit her talking points." I looked over at Nancy and felt the daggers penetrating through my eyeballs. She would beat me in a stare down, no problem. "Nancy, which party are you referring to? What party do I belong to that is taking away your birth control?" I waited for the answer everyone knew was not coming. She had slipped and attacked me as a Republican, her usual enemy. A few seconds of silence so the audience could see Nancy hesitate, was priceless.

Then I continued to twist the knife in her abdomen. "And

let's add a touch of truth to the discussion. No one is taking birth control away from anyone. Isn't that right, Nancy? It's really a matter of money, who pays for the birth control, not whether someone has access or not. That's the real truth right, Nancy? Who pays the $9 per month for birth control?"

The moderator had enough and went in for the save, as my opponent did not want to engage further. "Time," said the referee.

Nancy recovered with a shot across my bow. "Bob, are you volunteering all males to pay for birth control and be the responsible gender in a relationship? Or do you want to keep saddling women with the cost and the burden as you men have done forever?"

That was a good shot, touché Nancy, touché, I thought to myself.

Abortion was not my issue, not by a long shot. I would not campaign on abortion, would not create messaging around this particular issue, but I would let people know where I stood and how I would vote. They deserved to know. My energies, time and resources would be invested elsewhere to make the greatest impact I could in the time allotted. I had a fixed time schedule to accomplish things, important things, and meaningful legislation. I was on the clock; a self-imposed, one-term clock that gave me six years to get something done. Six years was not very long, but to me it was a lifetime. It was just about the same amount of time the doc said I had left and I intended to use every minute.

The debate was becoming a bit of a bore, at least to me, and I went on the first of many short daydreams, back to high school and the gridiron that helped shape me.

Chapter 2

Mark

*Z*ip The tight spiral went fifteen yards to the right sideline into Mark's outstretched hands for a first down, but he did not get out of bounds and precious seconds ticked off the game clock. The first half was winding down and we trailed by three after an uninspiring thirty minutes of play. If we could score on this last drive, Coach might lessen his rage in the locker room. *Nah, not much chance of that*, I thought, but still I had to try.

Ten of us ran to the ball and lined up for the next play, a spike to stop the clock. But ten was one short of the required eleven as Mark trudged into position too late. The yellow flag hit the ground and we went back five. The clock had begun anew and nearly ran out as the ball hit he ground, one second remained. The stands were full, although the rain poured down as family and friends squeezed us in on Friday nights. Our field goal kicker was not the best, but he always gave it a good boot. He ran onto the field and readied himself to tie the score. His kick was high and straight and looked good from the sidelines, where I watched his ball, but fell two yards short as time ran out. The loyal crowd showed disappointment on their faces and most kept their hands in front blue jean pockets. They knew Mark had cost us three points and an easier halftime rant from Coach.

I looked at Mark and shook my head as he walked off the field while the rest of us jogged into the warmth of the locker room. Mark was my guy, my best friend and something was wrong, very wrong. He usually inspired the team with his hustle on and off the field. I pulled Mark aside before we entered the sanctuary, the football locker room. Once inside, it would be Coach's altar and he would pour some Holy Hell on our heads for the way we performed in the first half. We knew we deserved it, but we still wanted to avoid it.

"Hey Mark, what's going on man? You're not yourself. I know something's troubling you. What is it?"

Mark looked like a grey ghost that had not slept in a long time. His blank face stared off in the distance, his mind far away and certainly not focused on the game.

"Mark, wake up, snap out of it. Let me help you."

Mark blinked a couple of times and seemed to get some focus back in his eyes. "I don't know what to do."

"Whatever it is, we will get through it together. Now tell me what's going on so I can help you."

Mark stared off in space; he was back in some kind of trance that kept a tight grip, tighter than Mark could fight. I grabbed his arm and raised my hand toward his face thinking a good slap would do the trick. I hesitated just for a second and Mark slipped away. He did not move hard or fast, he just sulked away, shoulders down, head bowed low. It was the saddest thing I had seen in a long time. No way was Mark making any more catches on the field today; he had bigger problems on his mind, much bigger.

We got beat up at half time by an upset coach and beat again on the field in the second half. Coach didn't care about the score when he ripped into us. What did matter were our lousy effort, our lack of hustle, and our poor attitude. These things mattered to Coach and they should have mattered more to me. I was supposed to be the leader of the team, the guy everyone rallied behind, the one they looked to for an example of how to act, how to, "behave as a man," as Coach would say. But I wasn't in the mood, not on this day, not when my best friend was stuck in a rut, a rut so deep I was afraid he would never come back. Something about Mark struck a fear in me, I could not put a finger on it, could not describe the feeling I felt. It was something deep and I didn't know what or whom to blame.

After the game I escaped the melee of fans and family and tackled Mark in the parking lot, shoved him into my car and locked the doors. We were going to talk this one through, and I would show him some way, some path he could take to get his act together. We sat in my car and watched the lot clear. One by one, the cars, trucks and buses created more space for the two of us to breathe. The rain began to fall, a soft and steady stream that cleansed away the remainder of our game.

Then Mark told me his story and I sank into the muck with him. I doubted we would ever climb back up into the light of day and realized I now wore the same glassy stare that Mark had on that day.

Mark's mother was pregnant at age forty-five. After giving birth four times, the last one a decade ago, somehow and someway she was with child again. It was not a planned event and in this case, not a healthy one either. The doctor warned it could be life threatening and recommended a quick ending. For some it was an easy call, choose life and move on down the road. Mark's mom was the religious type, the kind who went to church on Sundays, again on Mondays, sometimes Wednesdays, and once in a while on Fridays. She was a regular, a premium client who had a lot of miles in the church bank, but she did not have enough miles to redeem for an easy out. There would be no free ride on this flight. It was going to be bumpy and choppy until the plane landed with a new child in tow. Mark's mom chose life for the unborn and hoped and prayed she would be around to see the show.

Mark's mom went into the hospital the night prior to our game, her last wish and the last words Mark would hear his mom say were, "Play for me son. Play for me."

A week later she died, the baby too. Mark often reflected back on his mom's last words and wondered if he misheard her. Maybe she really said, "Pray for me. Not play for me." The distinction was small, just one letter different, yet the meaning changed from day to night, or night to day. That one letter stole Mark's innocence and prevented him from having a life, well an enjoyable life anyway. The letter r destroyed my best friend.

I did my best to console Mark while we downed a six-pack of Bud Light. The liquor storeowner did not card me that evening; he knew the reason and need for the brew. I met him around back and vowed not to return. "Keep it to six then take him home," was all he said.

I learned the price of religion that night and the cost Mark's mom was all too willing to pay. It was her right and we all respected her for it. Too few were willing to make a life stand for something they held so dearly. Mark's mom always stood tallest among the parents in town. She taught with her words and behaviors, easily separating right from wrong, truth from lies, and fact from fiction. She showed us more than told us and we loved her all the more for it. But the cost was not just hers to bear, Mark also carried the weight and still does to this day. I debated her choice with myself time and again but could never figure out if she was right or wrong. That wasn't the point. The thing that bothered me most was she did not believe there was a choice in the matter. That was the hardest pill to swallow for Mark and those around who watched him sink deeper and deeper into the muck.

Years later, I ran into Mark at an Irish pub near our old neighborhood. It was the kind of place where most men sipped on a whiskey as their Guinness was slowly poured from the tap. The pub brought the drinks and the clients brought the stories, a fair deal all around. We had not kept in touch and had grown apart as many high school friends do. I sat on a stool by the bar, as was my custom, and saw him playing darts with money on the line. He looked at me and gave a grin then threw a bullet for the winning score. Mark scooped up his greenbacks then walked to the bar to have a pint with a buddy. We shook hands and hugged it out as the memories washed over us. We rewound some tapes of our favorite games and told some tales about the girls we knew and wondered what they were all doing now. I bought more pints and we had some laughs until Mark got quiet. We both knew what brought the quiet, though we hoped it would have stayed away a bit longer.

"She said pray for me that night. I now know it for sure," Mark said.

A tear ran down my cheek faster than I could wipe it away. But I didn't care if anyone saw it. I cried for Mark, but I also cried for myself. Mark's mom was also my mom. She had "adopted" me long ago when we were just kids. She knew the bond between Mark and I was tight and would grow tighter. She even called me son in a playful way that only a real mom can. Mark and I had grown apart because it was too hard, too painful to remember. We did not fight it. We just paid; then paid some more. Year after year we paid a high price for her "decision." The high price we paid was our friendship. The bond had been broken and could not be fixed.

We downed our beers as the silence lingered, neither of us wanted to go, yet knew we soon would. I watched the clock on the wall tick a few seconds and then felt Mark stir in his seat. He wiped his cheeks with the back of his hands and rose to say goodbye. We shook hands for a long moment and looked each other in the eye. No words were needed as we went our separate ways, again.

Chapter 3

The Debate

"Mr. Newton you have 60 seconds to reply," said the moderator.

I didn't really have a reply for him and thought some silence would be the best play to make.

"Sir, do you have any response to Congresswoman Smith?" the moderator asked.

I looked over at Nancy, then out at the audience, and wondered how we could make any progress if all the pols remained glued to their positions. Every politician had market research and factoids to back up their stance on any issue. They knew which angle to play and which offer to make for any voting segment. Running for office had become more science than art these past ten years. Each message had been vetted with voters through surveys, focus groups and market analysis. Each word and syllable was weighed on the voting scale—the only measure that mattered. So what if the factoids weren't exactly true? Just use the data to back up your view and get the votes. So what if the voters did not really understand the issues? Keep to the message, secure the vote and move on. That's what really mattered, get the vote today and figure out how to rule later when fewer people cared. False facts had become a politician's best friend. I watched the clock tick down to 30 seconds and said, "No reply, sir, I believe we covered that topic well enough."

The moderator sighed then signaled time had expired. That was my cue to respond after the clock hit zero as was quickly becoming my norm. "I believe Congresswoman Smith is correct. Women do bear the heavier burden when it comes to birth control, no argument from me on that point."

The moderator was not a happy camper and waggled his finger. Like that would stop me. I turned to face Nancy and said, "At least we are now talking about the reality, about the truth. The birth control issue, if there is an issue, is about money and who pays the cost. It's not about access, so let's remove all that smoke from our discussion, no more false facts Nancy, no more talking points, no more war on women. Let's just talk to each other."

The audience was rather quiet and the females were not smiling. It was time for another sound byte. I peered out at the 2,500 strong and said, "I want to make it as easy and inexpensive as possible for the women in this country to obtain and pay for contraception—not abortion pills, if that's the choice they want to make."

Many of the females sat forward at the unexpected words coming out of my mouth.

"Females do carry a higher burden than men, a much higher

burden. Nancy, I believe we should thank women not punish them."
I looked out at the audience and said, "Thank you, ladies."

The audience stirred.

"Including birth control with insurance benefits is more than okay with me, and if my male counterparts think about it for a second or two, they will agree."

I looked over at Nancy and saw her nails carving grooves into the wood lectern. *Should I stop here and take a small win or go long*, I asked myself. *Hell, I came to play.* With my gaze still on Nancy I said, "Rather than talking about the false war on women, we should be talking about the many battles that women fight and how the U.S. Congress can help."

Boom. The audience stilled and Nancy glared at me.

"Time!" said the referee. "Time, Mr. Newton."

I nodded my head up and down once. It was indeed time to move on as I saw a lot of the 2,500 heads do the same. The moderator shuffled some papers and struck a paper on his desk with the red pen, again. *What's with the red pen?* I wondered to myself. "We will now discuss gay marriage. The same rules apply on time, and Candidate Newton you are first up," said the moderator.

"What's the question?"

The moderator shook his head sideways for a couple of seconds then sneered. "Please state your position on gay marriage."

Another juicy topic, important to a lot of people and for good reason, money was involved again and that motivated folks. There's a lot more than money involved of course, but in the end, it really is about money.

"To me, marriage is aligned with religion and the church, whatever religion and church you belong to. My church believes marriage is between a man and a woman; I have learned and lived that creed all my life. It would be disingenuous for me to say otherwise."

My opponent stood a bit taller, her hands were turning red as they gripped the lectern with all her fury. She was a spring all coiled up and ready to pounce. But I had fifty seconds remaining and this time I intended to use them.

"That said I believe our country has not been fair to gay people. We have given marriage and married people an unfair economic advantage. There are tax benefits for marriage, property rights are more easily transferred if you are married and healthcare is more easily administered if you are married. I could keep going, but you get the idea, married heterosexuals have an unfair economic advantage over gays who are unable to marry and that is wrong."

The audience had been rustling, eagerly waiting the beat down that my opponent was ready to deliver. Now they quieted, ready to hear more. Many looked disappointed, perhaps confused that I was telling them what they wanted to hear. *Huh? Why be disappointed that I agree with you, why not give me some props for that?* The political system had trained the voters well. I wondered if Pavlov was looking down on our system and smiling.

Undeterred, I dove into the deep end of the pool. "I believe the State must support gay unions and remove the unfair economic advantage enjoyed by married people. It would be too hard to reverse engineer all the policies and laws at the state and federal level that provide financial advantage to marriage, so we should not even try to unwind decades and centuries of tradition. Instead, each state, including this state, should advance the cause of gay couples by supporting civil unions and bestowing the same rights and protections to gay unions as we currently provide to heterosexual unions."

Half of the audience applauded, much to the dismay of the moderator and my opponent, who shrunk back a few inches.

"Keep Church and State separate and remove the unfair advantages in our laws. Get married in your church, and get the same economic advantages for all types of unions from the State."

This time, one half of the audience stood and yelled their support for my comments. The other half was still absorbing my short speech, unsure if they agreed or not. Much like my opponent, I could see them weighing things in their heads, looking for the political angle. There's always an angle from the pols, one way or the other there's an angle. And for every angle, there is some new way to raise money. Politicians in this country have become slaves to the money that feeds their campaigns and puts their butts back in power. The cycle repeats itself again and again, angles to money to power.

It was time for the punch line, the tidbit for the media that shortened everything to a headline or a quip, and I was going to give them another one.

"Our country is better when there are more families, more homes filled with people who care about each other. We are a lot worse off when families break down." The audience was feeling a positive vibe and hummed along with me. "The way I see it, supporting gay unions, gay marriage, whatever the right term, is also supporting more families." I heard a few yells. "Gay marriage equals more families, and I certainly support that." Boom. Another sound byte delivered. That's when the applause got loud, again from about half the audience.

From the frown on my opponent's face I could tell her thunder had been stolen, swiped away by a rookie. She was playing the angles in her head again, and I hoped it hurt. The clock showed ten seconds remaining, time for one last sound byte or two.

"Is there anyone in the audience or on television who does not support families? Do you believe the pols in Washington have been helping or hurting families the past year, the past decade, the past three decades?"

Three more seconds. "When you cast your vote next month, I challenge you to ask yourself one question, just one question. And then vote with your gut."

"Time", said the moderator. The audience was still. They wanted to hear one more quip from the independent candidate. They wanted to know the question.

"Are you voting for the families in your city, in your state, or are you casting your vote for the lifelong politicians who live in Washington, District of Columbia?"

"Time, Mr. Newton."

"It's time to change the old guard and their old tricks and get our country back, get our cities back, our neighborhoods and communities back."

"Time, Mr. Newton."

"Throw out the Washington politicians and their policies that have ravaged the family structure in this country."

Applause broke out in the arena along with a few hoots and hollers. Not everyone was clapping, but a lot of them were and many stood tall, no longer contained by their seats. This time I welcomed the release of tension in the room and did my best to look stoic, poised, and as much like a leader as I could. I stood on my toes and nodded my head in appreciation. I wanted to look to my left at my opponent but dared not shift my eyes from the voters. Not now, not when they were starting to understand my message.

"Time, Mr. Newton. I said time!"

I stole back some of the time I had given away previously and hoped it was used wisely. The moderator was not happy, hell he looked a bit angry, but what did I care? He kept trying to apply old rules and old ways that no longer fit. He stood for the status quo and it was time for him to go as well.

My communications team had to like that one. Not only had I eaten more time on the clock than allowed, I had pivoted away from gay marriage to families and then to bashing the pols in Washington, District of Columbia. I think that's the word the communications team used, pivot. But this was not just any pivot. It was a double pivot, and I could almost see the smiles on their faces. They had trained the football coach to pivot during a senate debate. Now that was something.

Gay marriage was not my issue either. Sure it was an important topic and many across the country were rallying behind the cause, which I fully supported. Some argued there were not many gay people in the country, why bother? My usual retort was, "There aren't many Jews in the country either, or the world for that matter. Should we stop supporting the Jews?" The other tactic I liked was playing the "Did you know" game—usually at a bar or a party. For example, "Did you know Gary was gay?" Or, "Did you know the school principal was gay?" Or, "Did you know the baseball coach, the bartender, the fireman, your neighbor were all gay?" Most of the other players in the game had no clue who was gay and who was not. It was revealing, even humorous to witness the shock on their faces, especially when I told a few white lies about who was gay. That was not my fault; it was the beer, always blame the beer.

The entertainment value of the gay card game was high and I liked being entertained. Gay marriage was not my issue because there were other ones more important to me, closer to my heart and my passion. And I was on the clock. No one knew about the limited time remaining on my life clock, no one but the doc and me. Not even Amy.

As the audience continued their applause, I looked out beyond the moderator and stared at some of the many faces in the crowd and saw Toby in the second row. He gave me a wink and a broad smile, knowing I welcomed and needed both. I returned the smile as my mind went back in time to high school and the day Toby helped me become a man.

Chapter 4

Toby

Boom! Toby could punt the ball. He kicked the heck out of it and even placed the ball where he wanted, often inside the five-yard line. He was the best darn punter I'd ever seen. It's not often we get to see an expert at his craft, up close, every day. And Toby was indeed an expert at his craft. He would boom punts all practice long and keep booming 'em after the other players went home and the lights went out.

Toby had a lanky frame, tall and lean, with arms and legs that stretched for miles and then some. He could have played basketball or volleyball or almost any other sport in high school, but he loved football and the challenge it gave him. As a punter he stood out from the rest. He performed his feats about fifteen yards behind the offensive line, all alone, much like an opera star, much like a diva. He only needed the snapper to send a tight spiral through his legs into Toby's hands, and then the rest was up to him.

Boom! Another rocket launched into the air fifty yards downfield.

When Toby connected on a perfect kick, the ball would soar high and far down the field of play, not returnable by the opposing team. Usually, the punt returner waved his arm and settled for a free catch, after watching the ball for nearly five seconds in the air. It was an awful long time to wait as every head in the stadium went slowly up then slowly down. Five seconds seemed an eternity as the crowd hushed and the punt team barreled downfield like a thundering herd. Most returners reluctantly surrendered, waved their arm, caught the ball and flipped it to the referee. It was a complete waste of a play for the opposing team and the talents of an elusive runner with quickness and speed.

On occasion, the return man would make a mistake and take a needless risk by making a catch without waving the arm. When the ball hit his hands the herd was all around, swarming then launching at his legs and chest—anything that attempted to move. A second later, the return man would be at the bottom of a pile with a half ton on top, sometimes without the ball that bounded away when the herd struck. And that was the goal, all part of Toby's plan. Frustrate the return man and tempt him into a dumb error that could change the outcome of a game.

Toby was good. He was smart, and he was damn good.

Toby was also gay. He tried to hide his truth but it got out, as secrets often do. His fears were misplaced, as the guys in the locker room did not seem to care. Well, most of them did not care or at least not show it. They placed greater value on Toby's foot than any other body part. Toby's foot won a few games each season and winning football games was indeed more important than just about anything else. That was fine with Toby. He wanted to be judged by his performance on the field, not his desires outside of the game.

But his coach cared. The special teams coach cared a great deal. He felt it his duty to show how much he cared whenever he could get away with it. Bad jokes and gay slurs were often hurled at Toby as he kicked the ball on the practice field. One particular practice was pure hell for Toby. It's a day I'll never forget.

"Come on you pansy, kick with a straight leg," Bubba yelled.

Coach Bubba laughed at his stupid joke. He railed on Toby and would not let up. We all called him Bubba because he was fond of saying, "I'm just a country boy." Besides, his real name, Kyle, did not wear well on his 290-pound frame. Bubba seldom saw his shoes as his small feet worked over time to carry his bulk around the field.

Shank.

Toby let Bubba get under his skin and shanked a ball down the right sideline about twenty yards away, an irregular kick for an expert.

"Get this diva a skirt!" Bubba gurgled.

Toby refused to look at Bubba and signaled for another ball.

"Damn boy, if you can't handle a little heckling on the practice field how you gonna do out there in the real world."

Shank.

Another bad punt, this time down the left sideline about fifteen yards. Toby hung his head but refused to look at Bubba.

"Will you look at that? This feller can't handle the pressure. How you gonna handle those big gay boys when they pull your pants down and waggle their weenies at ya? Huh? You ready for that kinda pressure? Are you feller? Oh I get it now, that's the kinda pressure you like. Oh yeah bring on those big boys, those hunks of beefcake. Our feller here is ready for some manly friends, some good ole gay boys."

Bubba would not let up. The shanks gave him more fuel to rub it in Toby's face, but only at arm's length. Bubba was too scared to get close to Toby. He was frightened some of the gayness would rub off on his redneck fat ass.

Toby called for another ball. This time he caught it and just held onto the football. He did not move forward, did not punt the ball. He just stood there as if he was waiting on something. And then it came.

"What's a matter gay boy? Can't ya get it up? Can't ya kick that ball? You should be a real pro with balls, huh? All that playing around with balls is how you get your jollies. Isn't that right, gay boy?"

Toby turned to face Bubba who was about twelve yards away. Then he raised his arm in a fluid, fast motion and threw a dart right at Bubba. The special teams coach did not react very quickly, it was a bit difficult to shift all that weight even with a bullet on its way. The spiral spun toward Bubba's head and hit him in the bridge of his nose. A bulls-eye! Bubba went down with a yelp, a girlish cry, and there was blood everywhere. Toby had busted Bubba's nose.

I hurried over to Bubba and looked down at him on the ground blubbering away. "He broke my nose. That gay son of a bitch busted my nose. Oh man, it hurts," wailed Bubba.

Bubba tried to get up but fell backwards and rolled around on the football field. "I am going to kill that pansy ass! Where is he?"

The QBs and ends were working on timing passes nearby

and we had seen the whole thing. Our head coach missed practice this day, the first time in eight years. He was attending to a sick mother and we all feared the worst. His absence allowed Bubba to reign over the team and he had taken full advantage, until the dart crashed his face in.

I moved closer to Bubba and stood over him. It was time for some leadership and as the starting QB it was my job. I removed my helmet and glared at Bubba as he stuck out his hand for some help. My instincts took over and I swatted his hand away. I was straddling Bubba now, towering over his largesse as the entire team circled the two of us. It was a sight seldom seen on the practice field, the coach flat on his back and the QB on top. The players remained quiet; none offered encouragement, not a single word was spoken as they inched closer to the action.

Bubba and I glared at each other, waiting for someone to make a move. Finally, Bubba had enough and pushed on my legs to get some room. I did not cede any ground, not to Bubba, not on this day. The circle of players tightened around us and helmets were removed.

"Bubba, it's a shame you fell and broke your nose."

"What? That's not gonna fly QB. You saw the whole thing. That gay bastard threw a football at me and broke my nose and he's gonna pay. I'm gonna whip his gay butt; now get outta my way."

I squatted down, my feet tucked under Bubba's armpits and my butt on his chest. It was an awkward position on the fifty-yard line of our practice field, a place where grass seldom grew. Coach Mac molded boys into men on this field, mixing mud and turf with passion and spit. He molded me and there was not a chance in hell I would allow Bubba to disgrace this place any longer.

I leaned into Bubba and stared into his eyes so my message would not be misunderstood. "Bubba, here's how this is going to work. You will apologize to Toby for the insults and slurs and you will forget about your broken nose."

"No goddamn way, QB. Not gonna happen. I'm gonna have some butt, even if it is gay butt. He's all mine QB. He's all mine! And quit calling me Bubba, you call me Coach. Got it!"

We were nose-to-nose as Bubba realized he would not escape and finally stopped squirming. "Bubba, you don't deserve to be called coach. You don't deserve to be on the same field as Toby. The way I see it, you have two choices. One, you become my enemy in which case I will make it my mission to get you kicked off this team and out of coaching…forever. Or two, you apologize and never…and I mean never… hurl an insult or slur against Toby or any other player you believe is gay. You are an embarrassment to our team and to the coaching profession."

The sunlight went away as the circle tightened again and the players' cast their shadows across all of Bubba. I let the silence hang, wondering what Bubba would do. By this point, I really didn't care which choice he made. Making Bubba my personal pet project was something I was finally prepared to do.

Chapter 5

The Debate

"Mr. Newton?" asked the moderator.

"Ah, sorry. Yes, I am definitely here with you, Mr. Jones."

"The clock is running, Mr. Newton."

He was always reminding me about the clock, as if I didn't know what's going on. As if I didn't know how much time remained on my clock. The doc had said, "Maybe five or six years," maybe that long. And then he said, "Get your things in order." I knew how much time was on the clock and did not need any damn moderator to remind me.

"Mr. Newton, are you going to answer the question? The clock is still running."

Oh that clock. "Sorry, what's the question again?"

His whole body slumped, this time his frustration was earned. I was the bad guy and it would probably happen again.

"We are on immigration. What is your view of immigration reform? Do you have an opinion you'd like to share?"

Now he's being sarcastic. It was one thing to not like me very much; it was another to show disrespect, especially in front of a large audience.

"Tony Blair, the former Prime Minister of the United Kingdom once said, "a simple way to take measure of a country is to look at how many want in…and how many want out." *That was my pivot.*

"Folks, that's the only good news. Sadly, immigration is a perfect example of political calculation and how our country's leaders fail to lead. Rather than crafting solutions and debating ideas with some sense of urgency to solve an important problem, our government representatives placate voters with tough talk on TV. They have no intention of rolling up their sleeves to do some real work, not when an election is only a year away. That's too risky for today's politician. In football we had a simple phrase for this behavior. We called it, 'playing not to lose,' instead of playing to win. When a team plays not to lose they are admitting defeat and only delaying the inevitable loss."

Heads were nodding in the audience. They knew, they understood, they agreed that too many pols were playing not to lose their seat.

"We are a nation of immigrants and most are proud of their heritage. However, too many of us have forgotten where our forefathers came from and the hardships they endured to migrate to our great country. We have forgotten because we are spoiled. We don't have empathy for future immigrants, nor do we enforce our laws. As a result, we have chaos and confusion, the usual results of our Federal Government in charge. When there is chaos and confusion, we have political fights. Both sides of the aisle are dug in and no longer interested in sound policy. Nope, sound policy is now less important than beating the other guy or gal. Getting a political win, or a good sound byte in the media, or better yet, denigrating the competition and making them look bad is the real goal of politicians in Washington."

I let things settle for a moment. I was preaching and needed to get back to talking, to having a conversation. People were tired of sermons full of talking points, recited like hymnals in church. I looked out at the audience and shifted my approach. It was time to ask a question or two.

"Why do we allow twelve or thirteen million people to labor in our country illegally?"

Pause. One, one thousand, two one thousand.

"At what point do we send them back, or welcome them in?"

I looked out at the audience and felt the stillness in the room. It was unexpected. They had been restless during the other debate topics but not this one. It dawned on me their guilt had taken over. Not a soul in the room could avoid it, and many felt shame and embarrassment. Most everyone knew, or at least interacted with an illegal immigrant, some of us each and every day. The best way to get my message across was to make the audience squirm and take advantage of the guilt.

"Why does our president use false facts to make us feel more secure about the border? Deportations are up dramatically because border turn-backs are now counted as deportations." I shook my head in a display of disgust. "False facts mislead us into believing the Federal Government is doing a better job protecting the border when in reality it's a dam ready to burst."

I took another short pause. "The sad truth is the politicians on both sides of the fence are abusing immigration as a topic for selfish reasons. One party views illegal immigrants as a voting block, just another segment in their marketing plan that requires a message and an offer to entice voters at the poll. How sad is that? The other party is no better. All they see is a tall fence with armed guards and drones along our southern border, and a one-way ticket home for most of the thirteen million. Then they can puff their chest and cock their rifle and feel safe." Pause. "What bullshit."

The moderator woke up and waved his finger at me.

Crap, I just swore on TV. Ames is gonna kill me later.

The moderator waved his finger at me, again.

If they can't take a joke then ... nah.... I decided not to finish the thought in my head because something else bad could slip out of my mouth. I moved on. "In the meantime, the thirteen million toil away farming our fields, doing our laundry and mopping the office floors." I paused here for an important moment. Most people thought of immigrants as the low rung on the ladder of life. Too few remember or even realize most of us are descendants from immigrants who earned their way up that same ladder. "You know folks, the thirteen million might have started out with a pitchfork or a mop, but many of them have the smarts and the skills to climb a rung or two or even more. Just like our parents or grandparents or great-grandparents may have done before them."

I did my best to make it personal for the audience so they could not hide from the truth, from the reality of our situation. Now it was time to attack the pols. "And the politicians in Washington go on the Sunday TV shows and spew their talking points. When the national media has beautifully cited their well-crafted messages, then it's a good day in the nation's capitol. That's the measure of success. Talking points delivered like a Sunday sermon with flair and printed above the fold in the *New York Times.*"

Fifteen seconds remained. It was time to wrap. "Do you believe our values as a nation end at the Rio Grande?"

I looked out at the audience and let that question settle in. There was some squirming going on.

"President George W. Bush asked that question years ago and we still hide from it today. "The solution is not that difficult. We created this mess and we need to clean it up. Build the fence where it makes the most sense, deploy the drones and troops and close the holes in our border. Then clearly communicate our borders are closed and we will enforce our laws. That's step one."

Keep it simple, I told myself, *real simple, step one, two and three.* "Step two is to register the thirteen million so we know who they are and issue green cards to those who have no criminal record, so they have a legal status, but no vote. The Democrats don't get a voting block and the Republicans don't send anyone home."

"Time. Mr. Newton, time."

"Neither political party can claim victory, they both lose. But the thirteen million people can attain a sense of belonging, a sense of security and some peace. The thirteen million get the opportunity to climb the ladder, which benefits all of us."

"Time."

"Step three of course is to let all illegal immigrants apply for citizenship through the normal process. Get in line with everyone else and follow the rules. It will take years for them to attain citizenship but it will be fair to those who have entered our country legally."

"Mr. Newton Time."

"A simple three step plan. We should enforce our own rules, remove the confusion and chaos and welcome the thirteen million. That's on us. It's about time we answered George W. Bush's question with a plan."

"Time! Damn it! I said time!"

The moderator just lost it. Keep the grin away I told myself. No smiling, not now. Keep it back, doo da doo doo. Keep it back doo da doo doo. It helped to hum the street tune from Rocky and I don't know why. *Doo da doo doo.* I adapted the lyrics a bit, but it worked and the grin stayed away. My mouth and chin never quivered so much. *Doo da doo doo.*

Immigration was not my topic either and that was not my best speech. It wasn't my topic, but it was personal. I delivered my message with some passion, which I surely felt mostly because of Jesse.

Chapter 6

Jesse

I had never seen cleaner floors. They sparkled and made me feel guilty to step on them. Every Monday morning our office floors shined a light. It was noticeable. Someone took a lot of pride in their job to make these floors shine, and that someone was Jesse.

Everyone loved Jesse, including me. He was a perfectionist at his craft and we were his witnesses. He got up early, went to bed late and never sat down, never took a break, never understood the word rest. Jesse was born without a pause button. He swept, mopped, cleaned and did everything else to keep our football house in order, no small task at a major university.

Jesse wore the same cap everyday. It nearly matched our school colors, which was his intention. It was off by a shade, maybe two but no one cared. Jesse honored the team he loved and we adored him for it. He tipped the cap on a regular basis, just a short up and down with his right hand. The left hand usually held a tool of some kind, an instrument of his profession. He seldom removed the cap from his head, not for me and not for the players. He only removed his cap when a lady graced his hallways and there was no mistake as to who owned those hallways. They were Jesse's halls and when a lady walked by, Jesse would remove the cap from his head and bow. Not a full bow, more like a half bend with his head up and his smile warm. Jesse was all class all the time.

I found him one day in the equipment room fixing some gear. He did not notice me walk in, I rarely entered the room and he had no reason to expect me on that day. It was a dark room with rows of shelves that held pads and gear. There was one desk in the corner with a small lamp and that's where I saw Jesse. I hid by the door and watched as Jesse worked some magic. It was not his job to tend the gear and it only took me a few moments to realize it was his passion. He worked with such care and precise movements it made me think of a Swiss watchmaker. And then I saw it. Jesse wore no cap, his bald clean-shaven head reflected the light in the room and I was mesmerized.

One of our assistant equipment managers had quit a few days earlier with no warning. He just up and quit and left the place a mess. It was always a mess, but even worse now. In less than two days Jesse had things back in order and sparkling just like the floors in his hallway. Jesse was in his element, his craftsmanship and his passion came together in our equipment room and it shined. Jesse wore a broad smile as he brushed and groomed and snapped and melded the football equipment in place.

It did not take me long to put two and two together. I wasn't the sharpest coach in the tool shed, but I was a quick judge of people and knew in that moment Jesse would be our new assistant equipment manager. Then I learned he was an illegal immigrant and my plan came crashing down around my head.

It started with a conversation with the Athletic Director. "Willy, I'm hiring a new guy to replace Hank the old assistant equipment manager who left us in the lurch last week."

"Sure, Bob, whatever you want to do is fine."

Willy, or "Big Willy," as I liked to call him, was the Athletic Director, my boss and a good buddy from back in the day. Willy used to pour my drafts at Graham's Bar on campus and never took a dime. He knew I couldn't afford it and it was a good business decision to keep the QB in the house. The owner had issued very clear directions on that score as he made his return on all the hangers on.

"Who are you hiring, Bob? I'm just curious."

"Jesse, the maintenance worker. He's been taking care of things and all the kids like him. He's actually very good with the equipment."

"Bob, have you checked into his background, talked to his employer, made sure he's not a felon. Have you done your homework?"

Leave it to Willy to get to the nasty side of things. The lawyer in him was ever present, although he did save our butts now and then.

"Of course, Willy. It's all checked out and wrapped up with a red bow."

Willy raised an eyebrow and tilted his head—body movements only he could make that challenged what I said. Somehow he always knew when I was skating around the edges of the rink.

"Bob, are you ever going to get with the program and call me by my first name like all the other adults around here?" He was grinning now but I knew he was also serious. "Willy it's just not gonna happen. I have not called you Tom in years and I have no intention now or tomorrow or next week."

"Yeah, that's what I thought. Now get outta here; I have real work to do."

I left the office and called Alice, my assistant.

"Alice, we need to check into Jesse's background."

"You talked to Willy didn't you?" Alice chided me. While Alice worked the phones, I called Jesse into my office, a place he had been before but always alone. Knowing the background check was a mere formality I went into open field ahead of my blocking and offered Jesse the job. I was eager to see his face light up, to see his smile at the prospect of fulfilling a dream. And honestly, I wanted the feel good moment, the glow, which I felt I deserved. It was selfish and egotistical, but I had earned it. I was doing a good deed, helping another man take a step up the ladder.

"What do you say, Jesse? You ready to retire the mop and help us with the gear? We'd love to have you on the team."

Jesse sat still and stared at the ground. He did not want to sit, but I had insisted and it was my office. Finally, Jesse raised his head. His eyes were wet as he looked into mine. He glanced around the room at the pictures and mementos I had collected over the years. He cleaned and cared for all of it, and I could tell he took as much pride in the school and football team as I did.

"Mr. Coach, I love my work and the school."

He always called me Mr. Coach. I stopped correcting Jesse after a few years realizing there was nothing I could do to change him.

Jesse raised his right hand and tipped his cap, a good sign. "Mr. Coach, is it possible that I could have the equipment job? It would mean so much to me, to work with you and be close to the players. It would…it would…it would be a dream come true."

I smiled at Jesse and patted myself on the back with a large invisible hand. The feel good moment was nearly here and I was tingling all over. "Yes Jesse, it's more than possible. The job is yours," I said with pride. "Alice is talking with your employer, just a formality. Once the background check is complete then we can make it official."

Jesse's shoulders slumped a little.

"It's okay, Jesse. Give me a day or two. That's all it should take, just a couple days."

"Thank you, Mr. Coach. Thank you." Jesse rose and turned to leave the office. After a step he turned back around and gave me a half bow. He gracefully removed his cap, and I never saw such a beaming grin from the man before.

Jesse had finally removed his cap for me. "Okay, Jesse, Okay. Get on outta here. Alice or I will be in touch soon, very soon."

The feel good glow did not last long. Alice learned some things and it was not good news. Jesse worked *off* the books for a company the university contracted to maintain the infrastructure of the school. He was assigned to the Athletic Department and had been working here for the past fifteen years. Jesse supported a family, a wife and two sons, ages 13 and 12, both born in town. Jesse had no criminal record of any kind and was a devout Catholic, very active in the church.

"Why off the books, Alice? What does that mean?"

Alice was perhaps the most efficient person I had ever known. She seldom hesitated, there was too much to do and she always got right to it. Alice was a perfect balance for me. She made me look good, even organized.

"Alice? What are you not telling me?"

Alice gulped. A slight movement in her throat and the gulp had cleared. A flash ran through my head and I knew we were about to have an uh-oh moment. *Damn.*

"Jesse is an illegal immigrant. That's why he's off the books."

"Illegal immigrant. Ok, what do we do about that? It can't be that hard to fix. What's the plan?"

Alice moved forward in her chair to deliver the bad news. "Coach, Jesse is considered a felon. He broke the law by illegally entering our country and could be deported back to Mexico."

My insides melted. "Well what's the fix for that. Let's make him a citizen or something that is not illegal. Jesse has been around here for 15 years, he's not just a janitor he's part of our family."

"It doesn't work that way, Coach. The university can't and won't hire illegal immigrants. Jesse would have to return to Mexico and get in a a very long line to apply for citizenship. It would take years, maybe longer."

"What about his family? The two kids were both born nearby. Are they illegal too?"

"No. Both sons are citizens since they were born in the United States. But the parents are both illegal and at risk of deportation."

Alice and I dug and dug and dug some more. We could not find anyway out of the tunnel that had closed around us. A week went by and we had not called Jesse. I wanted to keep working on the issue, find some solution, something or anything we could do. But the good deed glow had burned out, as we could not do a darn thing. And then things got even worse.

The contractor feared retribution from the school for employing illegals, although everyone knew what was going on, everyone but me. They were going to fire Jesse, or the equivalent of firing someone who's not on the books. They did not want to fire Jesse but the university lawyers got involved and threatened to pull the contract because the contractor employed illegals, which of course was against the rules. No matter that everyone knew the rules weren't followed. It was okay so long as no one talked. *Just keep quiet and don't tell anyone and it will all be okay. Yeah right,* I thought. *Okay for everyone but Jesse and people like him who want to move up the ladder, just one rung up the ladder.* It was a mess, a complete mess and entirely my fault.

"What have we done, Alice?"

Alice was the loyal type and always had my back. She knew some tricks and played them whenever Coach needed some slight of hand. But in my office when the two of us huddled, she abided by my rules: Speak truth and only truth.

Alice shook her head but did not say it. She did not correct me with words; her look was all that was required.

"Sorry, I meant what have I done."

Alice moved us forward. We needed to salvage the situation. "Coach, we need Big Willy."

I cracked a grin, the first in a long while. Alice never called Tom, the Athletic Director, Willy—much less Big Willy. But this time she knew we needed a hammer with some force behind it, and Tom's nickname said it all.

"You're right, Alice. We need all of Big Willy and then some."

Big Willy pulled us out of the crapper and got things almost back to where they were. He never said, "I told you so;" he did not have to say it. We both knew I was to blame and though my intentions were good, I had screwed up big time. Willy caught some flak from the administrators who balked at the whole illegal immigrant fiasco. He calmed everyone down and did what he could to save the situation.

Jesse kept his job and shined the floors and we hired someone else to manage the gear. A few weeks later, I saw Jesse mopping the halls and a nice lady walked down the aisle. I hid behind the corner and watched her go by as Jesse paused and waited for her to pass. That's when my feel good moment turned into a nightmare as Jesse's cap stayed on top of his head. I had finally found a way to change Jesse. The man would never be the same.

Chapter 7

Stevie

I looked to my left, past Nancy and saw him hiding behind the curtain that struggled to contain him. It was a big curtain that could have circled around my mid-sized frame a few times. I thought of myself as mid-sized, maybe large, but not too large. Though to be honest, I had some trouble hiding the beer gut, now and then. Some men took pride in their paunches as if they had been earned from sixteen-ounce curls. I tried hard to balance the intake with gym workouts, which was a bit challenging on the campaign trail. I stopped comparing myself to Stevie and saw he was signaling to Nancy with his fist. It looked like he was punching something or pretending to punch something. It was clearly a signal to hit me in the gut. Nancy shooed him away with a few flaps of her left hand but he would not leave, not until he received the acknowledgement he craved. Finally, Nancy gave the up and down head nod, in ultra slow motion. It looked as if she had succumbed and admitted defeat.

Stevie nodded back and gave one last air punch that was emphasized with a grunt and a sneer as he looked over at me. The puppet master was pleased and wanted his target to understand the blow was coming and would bring some pain. It would be a low blow, that's the only kind of punch he threw. The campaign manager stood at attention and drooled in anticipation. He would soon witness the famous football coach collapse to the floor, his manhood afire from the cheap shot. Nancy's campaign manager wrote the book on dirty tactics and tricks. His formula was more like an attack plan, a frontal assault on the opposition. Votes were all that mattered and facts seldom entered the picture.

He had a winning record and expected to add another W when this campaign ended. That's all that counted to campaign managers like Stevie, get the W at all costs. Then, he would take his tricks down the road, destroy more reputations, make up more lies and count more W's. Policies seldom mattered to people like Stevie, they only served as appetizers for the real entrée: the opposition. Stevie's cauldron was custom built with a set of wheels to easily move from one campaign to the next. It burned hot and it burned often, leaving a pile of ashes in every town he worked.

I did not care for Stevie; hell, I hated the man, and I never used the word hate, well not until I got into politics. It was not difficult to fathom why Nancy hired Stevie again. She wanted to win and gave up some of her soul to get the Senate seat she so desperately needed.

The sad reality is that I liked Nancy and had voted for her years ago when she was young and unsoiled. We knew each other once, though that was a while ago. Nancy stood tallest among the newly elected as she moved onto Washington, a short decade after college. Then she landed in 'the circle', surrounded by greed and corruption and became a different person. She was not innocent, she wanted to join the club, be part of the in crowd and manipulate the system for personal gain. Her initial craving was not money or power much unlike her colleagues. She wanted respect and thought a congressional seat sated that desire. Nancy wanted to set an example for other women and place a marker for young girls to follow in her footsteps. That's what earned my vote and affection back in those early years.

She was one of the good guys but somehow lost her way and now had to rely on scum like Stevie to get her throne, a U.S. Senate Seat. Nancy looked over toward me. Her posture was perfect, her nails manicured, hair coifed, her outfit shaped perfectly to her body. She struck the pose of a smart and determined woman, someone I once wanted Taylor to look up to. But her eyes were sad, they seemed to plead with me to drop from the race, run away from the debate, cede the throne and evade the sucker punch. It was coming and coming soon. Her eyes did not want to hit the low blow but the puppet master controlled her arms and Stevie was ready to launch the attack.

As I wondered about the sucker punch coming from Nancy, I thought back to the day when Stevie took over Nancy's campaign.

*****

"There he is, the best football coach in Illinois history!" Smirked Stevie.

"Hello, Stevie."

"Coach, great to see you. Bring any film for us to watch?

Maybe that championship game, huh? We'd love to break down some game tape, see you in action."

"Sorry Stevie, no game film today."

The big guy sighed as his shoulders went up and down, then let out a grunt from his head moving sideways. *Like I'm supposed to entertain this lard ass*, I thought. We were in Nancy's hotel room, a large suite that wrapped around two, maybe three corners of the building. She stood in the far corner and looked out at Lake Michigan, one hand on her left hip and the other holding the cell phone to her ear. Clearly Nancy or Stevie or both opted to spend their ample campaign dollars on a few luxuries, whatever it took to maintain the image they projected to the voter.

"What are you doing here, Stevie?"

"Coach, I am here to run Nancy."

"You run Nancy?"

"I run her campaign. I am Nancy's campaign manager."

I put my hand out for a good shake then felt his sweaty palm on mine. He felt like a fish, all slime all the time. Not much had changed with Stevie, not much at all.

Nancy walked over and saved me as I wiped my hand on my trousers. *Note to self: get pants cleaned.*

"Bob, it's great to see you."

She looked great. Her face lit up the room as everyone stopped for a moment, all eyes on Congresswoman Smith. Her dress held on tight to the curves of her finely trimmed body and her heels had long stem spikes, as usual. She was a sight to see after all these years and my eyes gave me away as they took a few seconds longer than necessary to capture the scene. "Nancy, hi. It's been too long, always good to see you."

Our hands clasped then we moved in for a quick hug. It was

never a fake hug with Nancy; she was much like Ames, my wife. Nancy gave a warm embrace to those she cared about and luckily that still included me.

The room cleared, leaving the three of us, Nancy, Slime Guy and me. Paul, my campaign manager burst into the room a minute or two later. He always seemed a step behind.

Nancy gave Paul a warm smile but Stevie and Paul did not shake hands, they barely acknowledged each other. We were huddled to finalize the debate rules the two teams had been working on for a few weeks. We were done ten days ago until Stevie showed up to run Nancy. Then all hell broke loose.

Paul had a stack of papers and passed them out as we took our seats on the plush couches. This was to be a quick review, a final pass and a decision made by the two principals. Stevie grabbed his handout from Paul and held it out over the table that separated the opposing teams. Then he whipped out a lighter and lit the handout on fire. He chuckled as the flame grew and then he tossed the burning trash toward Paul whose face went white.

My eyes moved from the flame to Nancy but she would not meet my gaze. She stared down at the table and her body went rigid. Her hands lay still on top of her knees as they touched together. She was playing her part, acting out her role, ceding the scene to Stevie. The whole thing had been rehearsed, planned well ahead, a surprise assault by Slime Guy. Stevie was definitely running Nancy, no question.

Paul recovered a bit and doused the flames with the ice water in his glass. "What the hell Stevie, we agreed on the debate rules last night!" Paul said.

"Nah, I changed my mind Pauli. We are starting over."

Paul wanted to hit Slime Guy but I reached out my hand and

gently but firmly held him back as I rose to a standing position.

"Nancy." I looked at my opponent.

Nancy kept her head bowed, her eyes somewhere on the floor, counting threads on the ugly green carpet.

"Coach, over here," Stevie said. He moved his left hand back and forth, inviting me into his web.

There was not a chance in hell I would give him any recognition, not after the orchestrated stunt he'd just pulled. "Nancy, your boy is misbehaving and he's your problem. You can put together the next draft of the debate rules and we'll take a look when we have some time. Your ball, Nancy."

Paul was still clenching his fists, but he realized I was leaving the room and followed me to the door.

"Walk away Pauli, keep on walking. This is not your last whipping," Stevie yelled.

I stopped at the door and took a breath. Most times you just let the bad boys act out their rage and pay them no attention. That's what they crave, attention. My head yelled, *Let it go coach. Let it go.* But my gut yelled to smack the bastard. Give him a crack on the head that he'll remember for a while. *Let it go or smack the bastard? Let it go or smack him?*

Then my ego got involved and whenever ego gets in the middle of things it's an easy call. *Smack him yelled my ego and gut,* as they outvoted my head, two to one.

I returned to the table where Nancy remained still. She was a mannequin, ready to be placed in the storefront window. At that moment I pitied her, she was no longer the Nancy I had known, respected and admired. She had become a politician who would sell her soul for a seat at the table. She knew exactly the type of person she had hired to run her campaign. Lighting Paul's handout on fire was only a signal that the real fight would soon begin and Nancy was fully prepared to torch anything and anyone who stood in her way.

I shifted toward Slime Guy for the first time since he burned the handout and saw him snickering, enjoying the moment. He was here to play some ball.

"You know, Stevie, I believe there is a flicker of fire in those ashes." I eased over to the table and picked up the pitcher of ice water and with both hands threw a wave at Stevie. He was not fleet afoot, not by a long stretch and the water hit him on the chin and washed over his suit. A bulls-eye! I half expected, ok hoped was more like it, the water to melt the jerk, but my hopes were dashed as he slithered to the bathroom to grab a towel.

A few drops splattered on Nancy and gave her a jolt. She stood as Stevie roared and threatened his revenge. "Enough," said Nancy. "Enough."

I stared at Nancy, my former friend and hesitated for a moment. The polls and all the analysts had her well ahead of the newbie, yet she hired Slime Guy and I finally understood she was making it clear who ran whom. If she had to play some dirty pool to win the votes, so be it. If Slime Guy was the best trickster and could teach her how to hit below the belt, bring it. In hindsight I was not surprised, not one bit. Nancy had warned me long ago there were rules to be followed and rules to be broken. "Just don't get caught out in public with your fly open" was an expression she liked to use. The suits always laughed at that joke until they realized Nancy seldom wore a fly.

"You want to play ball? Fine. Game on."

Paul and I left the room as his eyes thanked me for throwing the wave of ice water on Stevie. I put my hand on his shoulder as we made our exit. "Is this normal behavior for a campaign?"

Paul looked at his shoes then at me. He breathed in deep and said, "It's normal for Stevie and anyone he works for."

"Yeah, I was afraid you might say something like that. We need a new game plan that works under a different set of rules."

Chapter 8

Low Blow #1

"What are the traits we should look for in our U.S Senators? I am often asked that question in regards to my opponent when I travel around our state. Sure people remember Coach Bob winning one championship game, but does that give him the credentials to be a United States Senator? Does it even give him the credentials to be up here on stage?"

Hmmm, I wonder where this is going, I thought to myself.

"How has football prepared Coach Bob for the U.S. Senate? For one thing he did make $3 million per year the last five years of his contract. That's $15 million in just five years time....$15 million!"

So that's where she is going. My earnings?

"Our beloved Coach Bob who won a single championship game in all those years was in it for the money just like all the other coaches in college football. Do you realize the football coach makes more money than a tenured professor, more money than the Athletic Director, more money than the Provost, and more money than anyone else in the University System by a very wide margin?" Nancy shook her head sideways and showed as much disdain as her twisted neck would allow. "Yes, Coach Bob was victorious in one big game and for that he walked away with millions that he now uses to finance his political desires."

The moderator nodded along just like the audience. Money always gets their attention and I had made a ton of it.

"Let's set the money aside for a moment, after all we are a capitalist society. Well, at least the top 1% is capitalist. The rest of us scrape and claw every day of the week to put food on the table and a roof over our heads. Not the 1% though, they use their millions to buy a U.S. Senate seat."

Nancy was baiting me, but I was not hungry. Her comments were hardly worthy of a nibble. She looked over at me with a dare on her face then served up some more meat. "Other senators have been wealthy, Coach Bob is not alone in that regard, but rich men before him put in their time to learn how our political process works. Rich men before him had voting records, governing experience, and strong community backing."

She had the audience's attention.

"What does Coach Bob bring to the table? He took over the coaching reins of a top school in our state, recruited players with questionable backgrounds and was suspended for violating NCAA policies."

So that's where she wants to go. I should have guessed.

"The people I meet in my travels ask about policies, the health of our economy, how we will create more jobs, provide better education and continue to support those in need." Nancy slowly scanned the audience from left to right. "And then they ask me how can a football coach, a suspended football coach who was investigated for running a sordid program, have the leadership qualities needed to solve our societal and economic challenges."

Nancy turned to face me. "They wonder if a suspended football coach can even understand the issues that normal people face every day."

Boom. Low blow delivered like a true politician. Slime Guy must have been very proud of her delivery, I thought.

Nancy shifted toward the audience and I could not help but notice those long legs again. They looked much the same as the night they were wrapped around me. I shook my head to clear the memory banks but not before a quick video of that night ran through my mind.

*****

I sat in my favorite stool by the bar and signaled Willy to pour a draft. Everyone on campus knew this was the QB's stool and few dared take a seat. It was made of oak with a curved back that was well worn and fit like an old boot. I worked hard to carve the shape of my butt into this stool and wondered if I should leave it behind or take it home as a souvenir. My four years were nearly over and the stool had become a good friend. Willy obliged as he always did and slid the suds in my direction. Five seconds later, I gave the high sign again and Willy slid another brew. I downed half the glass in a single gulp and saved the rest for a second, maybe two.

"Bartender, hit me."

Willy was talking up a pretty lady, but somehow made a graceful exit and grabbed my empty glass. As he poured a third beer, we both noticed the girl had faded away into the crowd.

"Damn Bob, she got away."

Willy laughed and I snorted. We both knew he wasn't going to score, but hope is an eternal flame that burns in all college boys. I grabbed number three and sipped more brew as Willy stood nearby and tapped his fingers on the bar. "What's going on, Bob?"

"It's nothing, Willy, nothing man."

"Alright, the tap is off until you share."

"Willy, I'll buy the damn beer, just keep it coming."

That's when Willy knew something was very wrong. I had not paid for a beer in nearly four years of college. The QB drank for free, that was our deal and I certainly held up my part of the bargain.

"Ok man, its your funeral."

Damn right it's my funeral, I built the box, dug the hole and dove in for a long sleep. Shit what an idiot, I thought. *How could I screw up the best thing I had going?*

My head was feeling light as I looked around Graham's for a familiar face, any familiar face. I saw her across the room surrounded by three Pikes, not my favorite fraternity. Nancy looked good. She was built for tight blue jeans and heels and she knew it. She flicked her hair with her right hand and raised her head enough to peer over the crowd. *Too funny*, I thought. She was surveying the scene for more fertile ground. The poor Pike boys were toast; they just didn't realize it yet.

I kept my gaze on Nancy and she saw me looking her way. She gave a smile with a slight tilt of her head then raised her eyebrows and looked for some encouragement. I was considering my options when my head signaled yes with an up and down nod before we could all vote. Then Mr. Ego awoke and said, *Hell yes*, while my gut clenched.

Nancy got the signal and made her move. She faked right then turned a full circle and moved left. She eluded two of the dudes but the third grabbed her arm and blocked her path. Nancy tried to yank her arm away but the Pike held on tight. I expected her to look to me and plead for some help but she had other plans in mind. Those spikes weren't just for play. She let loose a full kick to the groin and the Pike went down. Nancy kneeled and whispered something in his ear and then poured the rest of her drink on top of his head. The golden liquid drenched the fallen dude and went down his shirt, but he didn't budge. The Pike was not taking anyone home tonight; he was probably hoping to walk again some day.

Holy crap, I thought. *Note to self: don't piss off Nancy.* Then I looked up and she was standing right in front of my stool. I looked her up and down and all around and let out a mighty whistle inside my head. The jeans were black and skintight while the spiked heels screamed some red. Her blouse was tucked tight inside her jeans, showing off a toned body. Her lips always seemed puckered and ready for action. *Holy crap, what am I getting myself into?* I thought.

"Hey Bob, you drinking all alone, darling?"

Wow! That was a question with some double, maybe even triple meaning. *This girl did not fool around, or did she? Well, we're darn certain going to find out*, I said to myself.

"Hi Nance, yep I am all alone tonight and for a bunch of nights to come. Have a seat."

I looked over at Willy and signaled for two beers. His mouth was open and his eyes went wide as he mouthed 'no way' to me. I nodded and mouthed back 'yep' and that's when Willy knew Ames and I were no longer a couple. I did my best to bury the split deep in my memory banks so I could concentrate on Nancy.

Nancy knew better than to ask about Amy, she got the only answer she needed. The QB was flying solo and she wanted a ride. We downed our beers and made small talk while the Pikes made their way out the door. I closed my legs as the injured dude was helped out of the bar, it was instinctual, and a defensive maneuver I hoped was unnecessary.

Nancy noticed the reflex moment and giggled, though her eyes seemed like daggers to me. Nancy was armed with a bunch of weapons. I was going to bed this girl tonight, but my eyes would be open the entire time.

We snuck into Nancy's place since she liked the home court advantage. She went in the front door and I climbed up the fire escape around back. We met at a locked window that she quickly opened and hurried me down the hall to her room. We passed a girl who scurried away and turned her head to avoid eye contact. She was well trained and knew not to say a word. We stumbled into the bedroom and Nancy hit the lights. Her blouse hit the floor and my belt soon followed. She wrapped one leg around me as her back leaned against the door and I noticed the red spikes were still on. *Were they weapons on standby or for personal pleasure?* I wondered.

She reached forward to undo the leather straps on the heels and a flash hit me. "Leave them on."

I could not tell if she smiled or sneered, it seemed a mixture of the two. The only thing I knew for certain is we were going for that ride.

Luckily for me, it was a brief encounter, a one-night show, and the details never to be revealed. Once in a while I'll watch the replay in my mind, shake my head and rub my thigh to relieve the imagined pain. It was real pain on that night long ago, the kind of pain that feels good in the moment but feels bad the next morning.

Ames and I made up a few days later. She forgave me for being a stupid, silly, selfish college boy who spent more time with the guys than his girl. Thank God she was the better man and kept us together through some rough patches. Neither of us said a word about our short time apart. I often wondered if Amy found out about Nancy, but I never had the courage to ask. In some ways I got less stupid over time.

*****

The moderator glared at me as if it were his responsibility to say next question. I guess it was. He picked up a red pen and made a slash on his paper. *Hmm, I wonder what that meant?*

The clock had 50 seconds remaining, precious time to make a witty retort or better yet, hit back with a low blow. The moderator remained quiet and searched for his next question that allowed the silence to envelop me. He was probably hoping I would take a hit with the audience. Instead, I cleared my throat and said, "You know, if we want to speak the truth about our earnings, then we should talk about all of it, not just my salary from football."

Nancy had no idea where I was going and that was the point.

"My wife and I file our taxes together, jointly. Over the past five years she did very well. If memory serves, Amy made more than $250,000 per year on average, from her real estate career. Amy is one of those one per centers, I guess.

The audience hummed their applause.

"And better yet, Amy made a lot more money than I did

during our first seven or eight years of marriage before our daughter arrived. She's the one who put our food on the table and kept a roof over our head as we slowly crept up the economic ladder of opportunity that our country affords all of us."

I glared at Nancy and used some telepathy that I bet she understood completely. *Come on Nancy go ahead, take on Amy. I dare you. I double dog dare you. Ames would chew you up and spit you out.*

I locked onto my wife and said, "My wife, Amy, is a shining example of a smart, strong and successful woman, who sets the right example for young girls in our country."

Amy winked at me and mouthed, "love you, babe."

I hoped the audience and everyone on television caught my inference. Amy was also the example for girls to follow, not just the congresswoman.

The audience liked my last comment and Amy's reply, which was shown on closed circuit television around the arena; they applauded.

There were twenty seconds left on the clock and I decided to use them. If you have some momentum then keep going, and I definitely had some *'mo' on my side.* Bringing Amy into the equation always gave me some 'mo'. "I want to amend my earlier statement about Congresswoman Smith." I turned to face her and said, "She is definitely qualified to be a United States Senator. That is, if you want the same type of Congress we have today, a Congress that can't get anything done; a Congress that does not know a thing about teamwork; a Congress so dug in on their points of view they don't try to listen to a different argument."

The audience leaned forward in their chairs, happy to see entertainment hour had arrived.

"If you want the same results we've been getting the past

five years, ten years, then please vote for my opponent."

That got them going, now there was applause and they wanted more.

It was getting warm in the arena so I took off my jacket and set it on the floor. I didn't remember we were on TV and forgot we were in a formal debate. I just behaved naturally, like I was back in the coaches' meeting room. "If you want change, then I say throw them out; throw them all out and let's start over with a new team. Let's clean out and clean up Washington!"

The referee jumped in at that point and said, "Next question. Err, I mean time!" The moderator stared at me unsure of his next move then a flash hit him and he seemed ready to give me a whack. "Candidate Newton, please follow decorum and keep your jacket on. This is a United States Senate debate, sir, not a football field."

Slap delivered. The audience gasped and Nancy hid a laugh.

"Well sir, maybe we need less decorum around here and a lot more truth. Let's remove some of the suffocating formality and have a conversation."

He just stared at me and wondered who was in control. I did not behave like a "normal" pol, whatever normal was for someone who ran for office. The silence gave me an opening and I took it. "Shall we talk about the elephant in the room, or rather the elephant that my opponent keeps hinting at?"

Nancy bristled but signaled she was ready for a fight.

"I have spent my career in football at the high school and college level, where I had the privilege of working with, learning from, and teaching young boys how to become men. There are numerous metrics we used to measure our success. Clearly our win-loss record was the most visible and perhaps the most important to our fans, alumni and the media. And being truthful, without a winning record I would not have lasted very long as a coach. But it's the other yardsticks that mattered just as much to me. Our graduation rate for example was always tops in the conference and in the top 25 nationally."

The clock had run out but I was on a roll and the moderator and Nancy likely figured I was about to commit political suicide on stage with all this football talk so they let me continue on. What the heck, the voters needed to know what they were getting and I was surely going to tell them.

"Most important to me and the other coaches was helping our players establish a life plan after the last whistle had blown. Every plan was unique, none more important than the other. This is where we spent our time and how we judged our performance when behind closed doors where truth matters and headlines don't."

I looked directly at my opponent across the stage. "Nancy you ask what do I bring to the table? What can a college football coach possibly do to help our state and our country?"

I turned to face the audience. "When I look at the state of our union I see a broken team; a divided house; a crumbling, ineffective and inefficient system. I see a governance model with no leadership, where people take pride in making the opposition look bad more so than making the country better."

I saw a lot of heads nodding up and down.

"In my experience, the gridiron is almost completely opposite from the halls and aisles of the U.S. Congress where facts don't matter, teamwork doesn't exist, and nothing gets done."

I looked out at the audience and realized this is what they came to hear. They wanted to understand how and why a football coach could make a difference in the U.S. Senate.

"I think Congress can learn a great deal from someone with

a proven track record in helping people move forward in life. As you mentioned earlier, many of our recruits came from the streets, from poor crime ridden neighborhoods. We also had kids from money, those one-per centers—as we call them today. On the field we mixed black, white, brown, poor, rich and every other color and background you can imagine. We all came together under one roof with a common goal and a team-based measurement to gauge success. We did not allow any "aisles" to split us apart as our Senate does today. We believed in each other and supported each other."

It was time for a breath or two then I started again. "I am proud when I watch some of them play in the NFL on Sunday afternoons and Monday nights. Well actually, nearly everyday of the week these days."

The audience laughed a bit.

"I am proudest when I see former players succeed as lawyers, doctors, business executives, architects, artists and small business owners. You can look on my website and see the countless names of former players who support my candidacy and the successes each of them have become. I learned from those players and they learned from me. It's time we called a new play in Washington, and I suspect a successful football coach who measures life beyond wins and losses is just as good, if not better, than anyone else."

I faced the audience and said, "Folks, I learned to attack my coaching job with a mixture of passion and spit. Well, I see a lot of passion from the politicians in Washington—a lot of negative passion aimed at the enemy who is anyone across some infamous aisle. But I don't see any spit. I don't see anyone getting it done down in the trenches, doing the hard work to create and pass laws that make a difference in people's lives.

The silence in the arena filled the air. No one moved.

"I'm reminded of a quote from a congressman and former football player, who I always respected. Jack Kemp said, "People don't care how much you know until they know how much you care."

I ignored Nancy and Mr. Jones and remained glued on the TV camera. "What do you say, folks? Do you want more of the same negative passion or do you want someone who will care enough to bring some spit to Washington?"

The audience did not hesitate and let out a loud roar, obviously they liked football and were indeed tired of the gridlock in Washington. I guess they understood what I had meant with the word spit. I was not sure how easily that would translate from the football field to the aisles of Congress. It seems the voters understood the basics pretty darn well.

I picked my jacket up off the floor and thought about tossing it to Amy in the audience, but put it back on instead. The moderator was right about decorum and I had made my point. There was still some room to put a red ribbon on this episode so I moved us along by saying, "Next question."

Then I went back in my mind to college where it all began.

Chapter 9

Nancy

The morning after my one night with Nancy required some strategy. I awoke with one dead arm, a throbbing thigh, and a pounding headache. Other than that, I felt great. My head and thigh let me know it would be a while, perhaps a long while before they were back to normal. But my dead arm could be solved a bit easier and quicker if I could just move Nancy to the other side of the bed. She wore no clothes and I admired her curves, they were still in all the right places. I glanced up and down her lines and said, "Wow," a few times, then did a quick check and found I was bare butt as well. *Oh man,* I thought to myself, *should I rally for round two or get out of dodge?*

I blinked my eyes a few times and looked around. It was a good room with a bookshelf, small desk and chair the only furniture other than the bed. Books and folders were neatly stacked and two prints stole a bit of wall space. Dresses, blouses and jeans were neatly hung in the closet with plenty of air between each garment. Nancy valued organization and simplicity.

The debate ensued as my head and gut went back and forth and back again. My heart did not participate in the discussion; it was still stuck in a rut. My pounding head was beating my gut instinct that wanted a replay. *What the heck?* my gut thought, *might as well dive in again and remember the details this time.* But my headache was deemed a higher priority and we began the extraction from Nancy's bed. That's when Mr. Ego stood tall and took over.

Thirty minutes later, Nancy was asleep again but this time on the other side of the bed. It took a special maneuver at the end of our coupling. I used a half nelson wrestling hold to stick the landing so Nance ended face down and a body length away. Now I could finally make my escape, though there were a few more body parts in pain. *Damn.*

I made my way home across campus, replaying the tape of last evening's performance in my mind. Each time the tape ended Mr. Ego hit rewind and we all watched the show again and again and again. I walked up the steps to the fraternity house with a limp and made my way downstairs to the kitchen for a bite to replenish some energy. I was tired and hungry. It was Sunday and the donuts had just been delivered. Once in a while a guy would get lucky and arrive home just in time for fresh baked goods on a Sunday morning. It was a beautiful thing, calories be damned. After a couple, well let's say a few chocolate donuts were snarfed down with hot coffee I found my room and plopped into bed, hoping and praying to not rise again for a week, maybe two.

It felt like ten minutes but had been ten hours when Kevin busted into my room with a spry smile on his face. "Dude, what happened to you last night?"

"Go away, man, leave me be."

"Willy said you left Graham's a bit early."

"Yeah, I hit the library now get outta hear."

"And Willy said that five minutes after you left the bar Nancy followed in hot pursuit."

"Willy is making up stories. He must have been drinking last night. Just one beer and you know what happens to Willy."

"How many times did you hit that library last night, Bob? Huh, how many times?"

I punched Kevin in the arm and rolled over my sore thigh. "Oh man, that hurts."

Kevin giggled like a little girl. He got the answer he was looking for and finally left my room.

I hope he keeps a lid on. Five minutes later the phone blared in my ear. "No! Go away!" I screamed.

The phone rang and rang some more. It would not quit, so I picked up the damn thing and barked out a very weak, "Huh?"

"Bob, it's Nancy."

Mr. Ego rallied and we were sitting tall in bed. "Uh, Nancy. Uh, what's up? I mean, how are you?"

"We need to meet. You free now?"

For the first time in history, my head and gut beat back Mr. Ego and we decided not this time. *We are not rallying again today.* "Nance, it's probably not a good idea."

I just called her Nance instead of Nancy. She might take that the wrong way like it's a pet name or something. Damn.

"Last night was great and this morning too. But that's not why I'm calling. We need to meet and meet soon."

Uh oh, what the heck does that mean? I wondered. "Ok. I gotta take a shower, give me an hour."

I crawled to the bathroom on Two East and was serenaded by Kevin strumming his guitar.

"Strings, what are you doing in the bathroom, dude?"

Strings was the nickname we called Kevin. He ignored me and continued to play. I did my duty and enjoyed the tunes, though the companionship in the bathroom was more than a bit strange.

On my way out I looked at Kevin and said, "When I get married you are playing at the wedding."

Kevin looked at me and gave a nod then went back to his music. He was in the zone and when he got in the zone there was not a thing that could break his trance. The boy could play and I just booked a freebie for the wedding. *Wedding?*

As I made my exit Kevin looked up and said, "It's the acoustics. The bathroom has the best acoustics." Then he went back to strumming and singing and I just laughed.

Nancy and I picked a place on the edge of campus where we hoped no one would notice us. She looked great as usual. She wore tight green pants with black boots and an open V-neck top that kept going and going. *Oh man, this might be painful, I* thought. *Note to self: Nancy is not wearing spiked heels but she is wearing boots. I wonder which hurts more?*

"Hi darling. How are you feeling?"

Darling? Holy crap this could be a bit rough. I raised my eyebrows and bent my head sideways, trying to send Nancy a signal that I had no idea what she meant.

"Sit down, Bob, and remove that worried look. I got my nails done today but they won't strike if you're a good boy."

Yeah right, they struck a few times last night, I reminded myself, *more than a few times.* Her nails were long and chiseled, much like the rest of her. *Note to self: behave, beware, and be ready.*

Nancy looked at me and smiled. I had no idea how to read her smile and that may have been the point. She had the upper hand and would let me know the play when she was ready. "I've got big plans with my life."

I nodded and bet she sure did have some big plans; then I wondered if those plans included me.

"We had our fun last night, QB, but that's all it was. Just some good ol' fashioned fun between a couple adults."

My whole body sighed as the tension released and was blown away from me by the wind.

"Besides, you belong to Amy and I'm not one to steal another girl's guy."

"Ames and I broke up the other day."

"You don't get it. Amy knows she has to let you loose, even if for just a little bit, to see if you return to her. What better time than senior year in college to set you free. Knowing Amy, she still has a rope around your neck. I was the lucky girl who found you during a break."

"So she's testing me?"

"Yes, darling, she is testing you. And you will most certainly pass."

"I will? How do you know?"

"Bob darling, we had a great time last night. But this morning when you were uh, shall we say sober, you weren't saying my name honey."

"Oh geez, I'm sorry, Nance." *Damn, I said Nance again.*

"Forget it. We would never last … though …"

It took me a few counts to notice Nancy stopped talking. *Damn.* I slowly turned my head to face her and tried to give a warm smile. My body throbbed and pleaded for a nap. "Go ahead."

She hesitated. I wanted…needed to hear more. *Come on Nance; finish your thought. Tell me more!* I yelled inside my head.

Everything slowed down and it was already slow from the prior night's events. Nancy batted her eyes once, then twice, and breathed in a deep gulp of air. "I sure would have enjoyed trying, QB."

My jaw sunk low and my mouth sat ajar as I readied a reply to Nancy's surprising confession. She was a tad faster and placed two fingers on my lips to keep them sealed and said, "Shhh." She brushed my hair back and looked deep into my eyes.

Nancy controlled this game and decided to punt on third down, or was it second. I felt respected and cheated at the same time. *This girl is made of something strong.* The moment passed and Nancy's eyes watered, yet no tears flowed. She was trying to open herself up to me but it was a struggle. Something held her back, kept her in check. She let out a deep breath of air along with a whole body shrug and moved on. "I will ask you for something."

My heart pounded a little stronger. What is she going to ask for? I wondered.

"I want your vote. I'm running for President of the student body and I want the QB to vote for me and tell all his friends."

I had forgotten Nancy was a junior and had another year in school. "Student body President?"

"Don't look so surprised. I'm just getting started, there will be a lot more votes down the road, and I expect you to be there."

"A lot more votes?"

"I'm going to be a congresswoman, and maybe a governor or a senator one day. And I'll need people like you and all your friends behind me."

I saw a good deal of her behind last night and smiled at the thought. Nancy knew I was drifting, probably knew where to and gave me a slap on the knee to bring me back.

"Hmmm, Governor Nancy. I can picture you sitting at a large desk with those red spiked heels resting on top."

"You sure didn't mind me wearing them last night."

The memory finally reached my brain. "Oh yeah, I do remember those spikes now." I shook my head and mouthed 'wow' to Nancy. She raised a couple of eyebrows then her face went rigid. She clearly wanted to close the deal. We were reaching the end of our chat and we both knew it was time to go. Nancy moved us along. "Now don't let Amy know I gave you back so easy. It could have been one hell of a fight."

Nancy giggled and I knew she was poking me again, this time figuratively. Our serious moment had passed and she moved us along with some laughter.

"Amy? Shoot, I'm not telling her a darn thing."

"Do we have a deal? I get your vote and support and we both keep last night to ourselves?"

I looked at Nancy from head to toe and the important parts in between. Then I stuck out my hand and said, "Deal."

Nancy had better ideas and moved in close to seal our deal with a kiss that gave me the tingles. It was a long, slow, deep kiss that left a lasting memory. She sure could kiss.

After a few moments we parted and Nancy said, "You're going to think about me, QB, and when you do, I hope you remember our one night together fondly. I know I will." She got up, walked away and never looked back, not even once. I watched her for a while and felt somewhat heartened when I noticed a slight limp. Nancy and her boots faded away into the late spring day.

I sat on the bench a few minutes longer to enjoy the memory. Nancy and I were done, our single fling behind us. Yet, I sensed we would intersect down the road perhaps more than once. My right hand began rubbing the pain in my thigh, and I turned around to head back home to Amy.

Chapter 10

President Nancy

Nancy carried the female vote by a wide margin and about half the males, although not that many cared enough to vote. I did convince a third of the football team to rally and Nancy appreciated the support.

I don't remember her platform and hardly saw her after the election. It seemed mostly a ceremonial position; something to put on the resume with flowery words about leadership experience and skills gained. Nancy knew the angles and played them well. She got the resume adder and moved on down the road.

We ran into each other a few years later at a bar near my hometown. She was standing on the other side of the room surrounded by three guys in suits. The suits were outgunned and outnumbered; *they just didn't know it yet*, I thought.

I sat on a stool by the tap and sipped a brew and saw her

peering over the heads of her troupe. The stool was made of hard wood and let me know it would take some work to break it in. I would not commit to regular visits unlike my college days, but I showed up often enough to have a decent relationship. Nancy made eye contact and her face lit up as a flash went through my mind. *Oh no, one of those dudes is about to get whacked and he's gonna regret it.*

Nancy made her way over without any incident and gave me a warm smile. "Bob, darling it's really you." She pulled me up out of the stool and gave a quick hug and peck on the cheek. "I've missed you, QB."

"Nance, it's good to see you, too." I noticed my right hand instinctively move toward my thigh and redirected it to my front pocket. There was no pain to tend and we did a quick vote to make sure there wouldn't be in the morning. If you are keeping score, Mr. Ego abstained.

"Are you going to buy me a drink, darling? I'm empty and need to escape those boys in suits for a while."

I laughed and shook my head. "Some things remain the same, huh, Nance?" I knew she liked it when I called her Nance, so I gave her the small pleasure.

A booth opened up and we settled in for a memory stroll that didn't take very long. I seldom used a booth as it boxed me in much like defensive ends tried in my glory days. I preferred the open range the bar stool offered, and a quick exit or escape from a pursuer was always on my mind. It was a darn good memory and I may have blushed as Nancy kicked my leg. After a short recap of our college tryst our discussion turned to the present and got a lot more interesting.

"How are you, QB? Are you enjoying coaching?"

I sipped some suds and eyed Nancy. *Was it time for some truth talk with a former fling from school?* I asked myself. There was something about her that drew me out, made me want to do better, and reach that next level. She stoked my competitive fire and I don't know why. Sure she was attractive and smart, she still had those curves in all the right places and knew how to show them off. It was something else with her, something deeper. I wanted to perform at my best when around Nancy and I am fairly certain she felt the same. That's when the flash hit my brain. She approached me at Graham's bar that night three years ago so we would always have that connection. We were on the same level that night and for some reason, she wanted me to know it.

The realization brought a grin to my face. "It's good. I love being on the field and getting paid to toss the ball around. What's better than that?"

Nancy grinned and did not flinch when she batted my return back quickly. "Come on, I bet there's something going on beyond just playing a game. Give it up, QB."

There she goes, stoking my competitive flame. Nancy knows how to get underneath the camouflage. "Ok, ok. Yeah I love coaching, really and truly love it. The first year or two was a bit rough. I was naïve in the beginning and thought the job would be easy. It was hardly going to be much of a transition for me, going back to my old high school as a quarterback coach."

Nancy nodded her head, letting me know this was the conversation she wanted us to have. *Keep going, QB,* she said with her eyes. *Keep going.*

"The thing is I am darn lucky to be working for Coach Mac my old high school coach. He's an artist on the field with the players and in the backroom with the coaches. He has helped me see things I never saw before and is showing me how to teach, not just coach. He molds boys into men and helps them build a path after the last whistle has blown."

"What is it about Coach Mac that inspires you?" She dug deeper and I knew she would keep digging and digging until she was satisfied.

"I guess the best way to say it is Coach Mac motivates the kids and the coaches with a mixture of passion and spit. Meaning, he gives us reason to be encouraged, to stretch for goals, to reach for our dreams. Yet at the same time, he keeps it real, down to earth. Everything about Coach is tangible. It's easy to understand his morals and you know damn well when he is upset. He can deliver the most meaningful locker room speeches to fire up the guys before a game and get it done in two minutes or less. It's incredible what I am learning from the man."

Nancy nodded and smiled. "Tell me a story about your Coach Mac."

"Huh?"

"How does he mold boys into men? How does someone do that…in high school?

"A story, huh?"

"Yes, one story."

I searched for a story, one story to sum up the most instrumental person in my life. One story. Mac had a lot of wins and championships but that's not what separated him from the pack. *One story…hmm…got it.*

"It's a short story about a player named Stanley."

*****

"Stanley was a loner. He was also a big kid—extra large times two in all the wrong places. The other players needled him endlessly and called him all kinds of names, none of them very creative. Coach had a policy that anyone who tried out and got through two weeks of summer practices made the team. He did not believe in cutting people who worked for it. The odds were low for Stan, but with Coach Mac he had a chance. At the end of each practice the players ran two laps, sometimes three, around the field then sprinted to the fifty-yard line to hear a short pep talk from Mac.

"Stanley had a tough time with that last lap and especially the sprint on hot days. Seventy players ran in a herd while Stanley waddled alone a few hundred yards to the rear. He seldom finished in time to hear Coach. Since he was last, he also got stuck carrying in the practice gear. I was sure Stanley would give up or pass out, but he kept plugging away each day. After the first week of twice a day practices, Stanley began closing the gap. He made it around the field a few steps faster but not in time to hear from Mac. On the eighth day, Coach finished his talk and sent the kids to the showers just as Stanley made it to midfield. The kid was worn out physically and emotionally, he had just missed his goal and I thought he might break down. Coach looked at Stanley and said, "Take a knee." All the coaches stood there with Mac and Stan, unsure what to do. Mac was giving Stanley a breather because another rule was everyone had to run off the field and there was no way Stan could make it, not without some rest. After a few minutes of heavy breathing the only sound, Coach reached down to pick up a tackling dummy, threw it over his back and ran off the field. The other coaches got the clue and we cleared the gear as Stanley ran empty handed. On the ninth day, Mac gave a longer pep talk than norm and Stanley heard about half. On day eleven, Mac moved the huddle to the end zone to cut off the sprint and Stanley took a knee with the team. On the fourteenth and last day of summer practice, Stanley beat two kids around the field. When Mac sent the players to the showers Stanley ran with his peers for the first time. He stopped about halfway, turned around and ran back to help the two slower kids gather up the practice gear. Coach stood there staring at Stan, hands on hips and nodded his head up and down a single time. I never saw a bigger smile on a player than the one Stanley wore that day.

"Stan didn't ask for help, didn't look for special treatment. With a few subtle moves Coach gave Stanley all the encouragement needed to earn his place on the team. The name-calling ended as Stanley received respect and made lifelong friendships with the other kids as they ran laps together around the field."

*****

"Hmm, it's a good story, short yet sweet for a football coach."

"Well, I would hardly say sweet when it comes to Coach Mac."

We sipped our drinks and knew it was time to shift our chat. Before I could serve up a question for Nancy she dove in with another of her own. "Who are you voting for in the upcoming election?"

I had not paid much attention to politics at the time. Ok, I did not pay any attention and had no idea who was even in the game. "Er, you'll have to help me a little bit. Who's running?"

Nancy gave me a figurative slap on the head with her grimace. "Bob, I'm working on Congressman Vaughn's campaign. He's a brilliant man who stands for things I believe in. You really must meet him and more importantly, vote for him."

"Congressman Vaughn?"

"Yes, QB, that's your congressman and the reason I'm here in town."

She wanted me to ask what she and Vaughn believed in. I could tell she was dying for that lead in so she could launch into a diatribe to educate the football coach. My beer glass had been drained and I glanced at my watch. If she wanted some softball questions then I was going to need more beer. Nancy picked up the cue and said, "My round. What can I get you?"

Nancy leaned over just enough for me to catch a glimpse. Mr. Ego got back in the game and announced his presence but my head, gut and heart anticipated the awakening and pounded him back down. Nancy awaited my reply. "One more draft for me."

She scooted out of the booth and was accosted by the three suits on her way to the bar. They surrounded Nancy and blocked her path. *Silly boys they have no idea who they are messing with*, I thought. I settled in for some entertainment and wondered how she would tame this new set of pups. A short video of the spiked Pike raced through my mind and my whole body shivered. I watched with great anticipation, but Nancy did not raise a leg to kick a suit in the groin. Those college bar skills were not needed with the suits. Instead, she deftly shifted two out of her way with a gentle hand on each shoulder. The pups were mere pawns on the board and Nance moved them along when she was ready. Ten minutes later, she returned with my beer and a fancy drink with some fruit for herself.

"Here you go, one draft beer for the coach." Nancy liked to serve, but only to people who could hit the ball back. So far I was getting aced and needed to put the racquet on the ball. She took a seat and stared at me as her red lips remained sealed.

"Okay I'll take the bait. Why are you supporting Congressman Vaughn? What makes him so special?" I shifted around to get as comfortable as possible, thinking we might be here a while.

"Bob darling, as you boys say in Chicago, we are on a mission from God." Nancy removed her jacket and settled in to educate the coach. Just as she began, one of the suits waddled over. He carried some pounds in all the wrong places and his belt put up a mighty struggle but failed to hold the rolls at bay.

He wiped his brow and leaned over Nancy's shoulder, "Nancy, you coming back soon?" The suit focused solely on Nancy as most men would so I did not feel slighted. The better man in me stood up and put out a hand for a welcoming shake that was ignored with a sneer and another wipe of the brow. His hand was too busy for a shake and he clearly looked down on Nancy's guest. Maybe it was my attire, the usual mix of blue jeans and t-shirt in school colors worked for me most days of the week. His suit probably cost a month's salary, especially if the tailor charged by the yard.

Nancy noticed the snub and rose above it. "Stevie, I'd like you to meet a dear friend. This is QB, I mean Bob. We are friends from college and he coaches at the high school nearby."

"Bob, this is Stevie, a colleague of mine on Congressman Vaughn's campaign staff."

I stuck my hand back out to appease Nance and Stevie did the same. Thankfully, he did a quick wipe so the greasy palm wasn't ringing wet. Still, he felt like a fish.

"A coach?" Stevie asked.

"Yep, that's me, Coach Bob."

Stevie eyed Nancy with raised eyebrows, clearly wondering why she was wasting valuable time with a lowly high school football coach. Before he could make a quick exit, she put her hand on his shoulder and pressed downward so Stevie would take a seat, just like a well-trained pup in Nancy's house.

"Stevie, Bob and I are discussing Congressman Vaughn's platform. Why don't you help me outline for Bob what we are working on and why it's so important?"

Nancy had pressed some button and Stevie was off to the races. He loved to perform in front of Nancy. I don't remember much from that initial baptism. There were a lot of big words, a lot of numbers, and too many laughs at their own jokes. I failed to comprehend much of the content and my interest in their endless topics waned as I prayed for rain, prayed for relief, hell I prayed for redemption, anything to get me out of that booth. After an hour, Stevie was losing steam and began to wrap up.

"In summary, Reagan is running up the deficit by spending more on defense and stealing from social programs that help the poor. It's irresponsible to spend the country into needless debt and record high deficits. It's heartless to cut monies from those who need it most and at the same time enact tax reform that lines the pockets of the rich who don't need it. The man is out of touch with the people, out of touch with reality and still living on some movie set in his mind."

Stevie had finished but I had no idea how to reply so I just asked some questions, some simple questions. "Why does Reagan feel we need to spend more money on defense?"

That got Stevie's motor going again. "He's a cowboy, an actor pretending to be a cowboy is more like it and spending a ton of money on military toys is a game to him. It's just a stupid, selfish and expensive game. He wants more toys than the Russians and if he can show the commies the U.S. has a bigger stockpile then he wins."

Stevie sat on the edge of his seat with his jacket off and shirt-sleeves rolled up to his elbows. His whole body was moving back and forth in a jerking motion.

"Are you unafraid of the Russians?"

He looked at me with contempt. "It's a stalemate. We got nukes, they got nukes and no one has an itchy trigger finger, yet. The more we spend, the more they get nervous the more they spend. It's a vicious cycle that repeats again and again as the weaponry piles up and up. It's a foolish game with no good ending and Cowboy Ronnie is getting his jollies while our country suffers."

Man, this guy is a piece of work. He was in attack mode all the time. I nearly ordered a rare steak to throw on the table just to see how Stevie would react. Instead, I plodded ahead with another question. "Do you believe the Russians can keep up with the U.S.? I don't know the details very well, but we have much better technology and better weapons, right? Why not beat them in the arms race and help ensure our country and the world are safe?"

I was out on thin ice now and felt I was defending President Reagan, but it was the only play that made any sense with Stevie on the attack. This was not a conversation; it was a wrestling match to see who would get pinned first. I looked to Nance for some relief.

Nancy interjected, "Stevie is just saying we spend too much on defense and as a result we are going into debt and starving the many programs for the poor and needy. He's not saying to stop spending money on defense, just dial it back and spread the wealth."

"Hmm, how many social programs do we have?" I asked.

Dead silence.

Stevie pounded the table and his face went rigid. It just locked up and I could tell his teeth were grinding. He finally spoke, "It's not the volume of programs that matters, *Coach,* it's the amount of money being siphoned away into Reagan's toy box."

Stevie emphasized coach with a derogatory sneer, making it clear he had superior knowledge over the high school employee. The ladder rungs were being measured and Stevie had himself far above the high school coach. That much was clear as he gave Nancy a wink and nod of the head, acting as if he had just pinned the best athlete at the table.

I thought to myself, *Nancy and especially Stevie have spent more of their time attacking Reagan and the Republicans than advocating their own policies.* I had no idea who was right and who was wrong, neither political side appealed much to me at the time. But it's always easier to criticize the other guy than come up with your own plan. *What the heck,* I thought. Let's have some fun and see how far I can push this guy. I gave him a nickname in my head, *Slime Guy. Ok, Slime Guy, here's a turd in your lap.* "How do you know which social programs are working and which ones aren't working?"

Nancy and Stevie looked at each other. It seemed they seldom were asked simple questions about their programs, in particular how they operate and whether they work.

"Bob, what we are saying is the social programs could be more effective if the republicans shifted more money to them rather than spending the money on defense," said Nancy.

This was getting repetitive and a bit boring. Blaming the other guy was the easy way out. I never allowed the players to blame the outcome of a game on the referees or our opponent. Players knew I held them accountable for our performance on the field. The other guy did not matter. "Hey, I'm just a high school football coach, what do I know."

Stevie smiled as if he had won the match and pinned the coach. *No chance, Slime Guy,* I said to myself, get ready, here comes the zinger. "There's just one thing." I took a sip to make sure I had their complete attention. "You didn't answer my question."

Nancy and Stevie looked at each other then back at me. "Huh, what question?" asked Stevie.

I looked at them both and saw Stevie wipe his brow. *Got 'em.* I took another sip of my beer. "I understand your larger point about shifting monies between defense and social programs. What I am curious about is how you measure the effectiveness of the various social programs. What's working and should be continued, maybe receive greater investment and what's not working and maybe should be discontinued?"

Nancy frowned and Stevie put his head down on the table, which is where I thought it belonged for the past hour. Clearly they were tired of being asked questions.

Nancy shifted gears. "Why do you think the social programs in our state are not working? You seem to have an attitude against them without any facts to back it up."

Huh? The tide in our discussion had turned, now I was suddenly the bad guy and only because I asked a few questions. *Is this how politicians work? The best defense is a good offense?* "I don't know much about politics and I certainly have no facts about the social programs in our state. But I do have a story, if you two are interested?"

Let's see if they want to hear something real, something at ground level right around the corner from the bar and our happy hour. Will these finely dressed political animals spend any time listening to a lowly football coach? I wondered.

Stevie looked at his watch. He was fine spending time with Nancy and me so long as he had the microphone. Nancy grabbed Stevie's wrist, patted him gently on the forearm and said, "Sure Bob tell us a story. Let's see what you got."

Atta girl Nance, atta girl, I thought. The real Nancy was still in there somewhere, although I was very worried she was being shaped and molded by the wrong kind of people.

I took a big gulp of beer, sat forward in the booth and told them about Rodney.

Chapter 11

Rodney

"This new play is going to work, I told myself as I paced up and down the sidelines. It had better work was more like it. We were down by five points with a minute to go in the game. Jerrod was behind center, a junior QB in more ways than one. He had the skills and the smarts and was starting to find a groove as our new leader on and off the field.

"The play was highly dependent on Rodney our fullback. He had the responsibility to block anyone who blitzed the quarterback. We kept Rod back in anticipation of an all out rush to ensure Jerrod would have time to make the throw and have a chance to win the game.

"When I rewind the tapes in my head and watch this play, it always moves in slow motion. Even if I press fast-forward, the play unwinds in a plodding manner, each player trudging along with heavy feet. The football gods wanted me to feel some pain each time I saw the rerun so they made sure it took a little longer.

"Jerrod took a clean snap from center and setup in the pocket. He moved confidently and looked in control. The primary receiver separated himself from the defensive coverage as our 'pick play' worked to perfection. Jerrod cocked his arm and took dead aim as the linebacker made his move and exploded through an open gap. I looked at Rod and made the calculation in my head. We were in good shape, possibly great shape. Rod would make the block and Jerrod would have plenty of time and space to make the winning throw. I was feeling good and began to put a W on the board in my mind. It would be our first win of the season after two tough losses. We needed the win; I needed the win, the whole town needed to see a damn W."

I took a sip of my brew and saw Stevie look at his watch again. I thought to myself, *if you're that bored and have other pressing matters then get the hell out of my booth, dude.* Nance saw my grimace and smiled at me, offering encouragement to continue the story.

I continued on. "Rod was a step slow and the linebacker timed his leap well. He deflected Jerrod's pass and the ball went up in the air and came down in another defender's hands. The interception sealed the game and the W in my head turned to an L, our third in a row."

Stevie rolled his shirtsleeves back into position and put on his jacket. "Nice story, Coach; sorry about the loss. Nancy you ready?"

Nancy knew I had only delivered the opening chapter of the story and realized it was time to let Stevie escape. "Stevie you go ahead," she said.

Stevie took a few seconds to wiggle out of the booth as neither of us offered a hand. The slime from our first shake held me back and his disdain for a football coach prevented him from doing the same. I watched Stevie waddle away wondering if he was the norm for a politician and the career Nancy chose.

"Sorry. Stevie is a brilliant political strategist but he does need to work on his social skills."

"His social skills? What are you doing hanging around people like that?"

She chose not to answer and waited for me to move on. Instead I downed my beer and looked in her eyes, as no words were needed to send the signal. Nance ordered me another brew. "Where is this story going?"

I thought to myself that this was not a bad afternoon, now that Slime Guy had made an exit. I was drinking for free—just like at Graham's bar on campus and Nance was looking good. Mr. Ego raised his hand to request another vote and everyone else hesitated. *Uh oh.* I went back to my story.

"Rod was a step slow that day and it cost us the game. As I watched the tapes again and again and again, it was clear Rod had time to make the block. Then it began to dawn on me that Rod was a step slow too often. He was a talented athlete and a starter on our team, but there was no good reason for him to miss that block, no good reason that I could comprehend.

"A few days later I saw Rod in the lunchroom, sitting alone in a distant corner. The first bell rang and the kids scurried along to class, everyone except Rod. He sunk low to the ground, hid under the table and waited for the room to clear then crept behind the serving counter. I walked silently to the back wall so I could steal a peek, and my gut clenched as Rod stuffed lunch scraps into his jacket pockets. I told my feet to step it back quietly and carefully, but they were nailed to the ground unable to respond to my command. The second bell rang and my left foot awoke and kicked the nearby table. Rod kept working through the clanging bell but froze when he heard the table screech along the tile floor. I hit the ground with a thud and hid from sight as Rod made his way to the door. He did not look back, not even a quick glance over his shoulder. He did not seem to care about the lunchroom intruder. Rod had more important things on his plate."

"I called Rod into my office the next day for a talk. 'Rod, have a seat.'

"He sat in a worn out chair and tapped his foot on the floor. It got louder as I finished some work. 'Rod, thanks for coming in.' His eyes pleaded with me to keep our chat short as the floor in my office took a pounding from Rod's foot.

"'Rod, I'll get right to it. You are not getting the job done on the field, not playing at the level I know you can play. You're a step slow Rod and we can't win ball games when our fullback is a step slow.' Rod's foot slowed a beat but each hit on the floor got heavier and louder. " 'What's going on Rod?'

"Rod eyed me and shook his head back and forth.

"'Rod, I'd like to help you but I gotta know what's going on.'

"This was not going very well. Rod sat rigid, defiant in his chair as I waited for a sound. The heck with the old adage, first one who talks loses. We were not in a negotiation. I was trying to help the kid and had to make a move.

"'Rod, it was me in the lunchroom yesterday.' Well there it was, the truth out in the air sitting in the space between us. What's the kid going to do now I wondered? Come on Rod, give me something, anything I can work with.

"'Coach.' Rod breathed in deep and started again. "Coach, I'm hungry."

"The kid is hungry, what does he want from me a candy bar? I wondered. Rod could tell I did not understand what he was trying to say. 'Coach, I'm hungry all the time.'

"'What do you mean 'all the time' Rod?'

"'Coach, I don't know where my next meal is coming from.'

"This coach got taken to school that day. Rod lived with his mom and sister in a building that pretended to be an apartment. We walked up a few flights to see his place as the elevator had given up a few years ago. Carrying people up and down had proved too much of a burden and the gears ground to a halt from a lack of grease. The refrigerator blew hot air and the furnace spit out some cold. If they could only swap some parts things might have been different. Rod's mom was not home, she seldom made an appearance and when she did show, it was to lay on the couch and wait for another episode to pass. That's where the grocery dollars went, up her arm or in her leg; there was always a vein to carry the gold.

"Rod gave me the nickel tour since a dime's worth was not necessary. I shook my head more than once but held my thoughts inside. The place was strewn with clothes and grime ruled every corner. Garbage cans were full and I noticed an empty laundry basket in a closet. The kitchen counter was not visible as every size and shape of can, bottle or pizza box had it covered. There was nothing good to say, not a damn thing. I grabbed Rod and moved us toward the door. It was dinnertime, and I knew one football player who would eat well that night. We sat in silence as Rod ate for two people, maybe three. He was accustomed to food coming his direction in peaks and valleys and while tonight was definitely a peak, Rod had to plan for the low tides ahead.

"I began my calls the next morning, but it did not take long to figure out there was little I could do. It seemed an obvious thing to a naïve football coach. We were spending government monies to buy drugs rather than food, and two kids went hungry, as their mama got high. You'd think it would be easy to find someone in charge who cared, who wanted to fix the situation, wanted to get involved. I never felt so alone in my life and began to comprehend how Rod felt. I finally understood why he was a step slow…always a step slow."

I stopped my story and breathed in deep then exhaled long and slow and wondered how Nancy would react. Would she be surprised? Would she care? Would she know what to do?

"What did you do next?"

"I did the selfish thing. I made sure Rod and his sister had a good meal on Thursday nights."

Nancy signaled she didn't get my drift. "Why Thursdays?

I stared at Nance for a few seconds and knew my confession would soon be complete. But I also knew it would not make me feel one bit better. "Because our games were on Fridays, and I wanted Rod to have a good meal the night before."

Nancy opened her mouth but did not know what to say. We sipped on our drinks and looked out into space, neither of us knew where to go next. Even Mr. Ego waved a goodbye.

Nancy picked herself up off the mat and rallied for one last round. "Did you find out anything else about Rod's mother, or his father?

"Yeah, I kept looking into things, made a few more calls, even went back to Rod's home to talk with his mom. Rod's father flew the coop a couple years earlier and never looked back. It seems he had more important matters to attend to rather than rearing his two offspring. We found some help for Rod's mom, but she kept going back on the dope so the professionals moved on.

They could not waste limited resources on a druggie who would not help herself. The checks kept coming and she turned them into gold and no one could or would stop her."

The silence returned and we finished our drinks.

"I don't know how Rod's story compares to others, and I am not indicting the system because of one experience. My gut tells me that Rod's situation is not unusual. I think there are a lot of hungry kids at schools all over Chicago who don't know the next time they will eat. It's more than a sad situation and I have no idea where to go for help."

"That's why Congressman Vaughn wants to put more money into programs that will help Rod and his family."

"I don't know if lack of money is the problem. Remember, Rod's mother gets money; she just spends it on the wrong thing. I honestly don't know if throwing more money at this thing will do any good. There's a fundamental gap where people like Rod and his family fall through the cracks. I certainly don't have a ready-made solution for you; heck, I don't even have an idea. I just hope the experts, like Congressman Vaughn, understand it better than I do. Maybe he can figure out how to get food money directly to the kids when their parents aren't getting the job done.

"I am sure he understands." She tried to look confident and overcome the sudden frog in her throat but her body gave her away. That's when I realized she did not understand the problem, did not even know about the problem much less have any idea how to come up with a solution. She bet all her marbles on a pol named Vaughn and was confident he was the answer.

Why are you so confident in this guy? I wondered. I couldn't let it go and asked. "What has Congressman Vaughn done to earn your confidence? Why do you have so much faith in him?"

Nancy swallowed once to steel herself. Two swallows were one too many and would have made her look weak. "Sometimes you just have to go with your gut instinct. That's how you and the boys would say it right? It's hard to describe, but I feel smarter in his presence. He challenges me to be better. That's the best answer I can give you…for now."

Nancy evaded my question and she knew it. At least she had the balls to say so. Her look pleaded with me to let it go but we both knew I would not let it go the next time. "Ok I'll give you a pass, one pass. That's it. Next time I want to know how the congressman is earning it." From my vantage point no politician was earning it as long as kids like Rodney went hungry.

We were talked out and ready to get back to our lives. We eyed each other closely and knew it was time to move on. Nancy broke the silence with a closing thought. "We live in such different worlds. Guys in suits surround me all day, every day and you have jerseys and school colors in your locker at school and probably your closet at home. I think we can be good for each other. You have a street level reality that I need to better appreciate and learn from. And I can help broaden your knowledge on how our state and country work."

I raised my shoulders and eyebrows in unison, wondering where the heck she was going.

"What do you say, QB? Should we get together every now and then to compare our lives and share our experiences? It's not like we will ever be opponents on the football field or the political arena."

I eyed Nancy for a few seconds. She was proposing something that was clearly out of bounds. Getting caught would cost more than a yellow flag and fifteen yards. "Just get together and talk, huh?"

"That's right just talk. No play." Nancy wore a serious look, she seemed determined, perhaps even motivated to keep something real in her life. I figured she needed a viewpoint the suits could not give her. She was willing to work for it, to earn it. *Atta girl, Nance.*

Mr. Ego was bummed though. He knew there was no need for him to rise again, not with Nancy. *What the heck*, I thought, *it never hurts to have a friend. Someone who can help me figure out what to do about the Rods in my life. If we kept things innocent and above board there should not be any penalty to pay. Right?* Plus, I had been surprised, well ok shocked, that I enjoyed the political discussion. It had stretched my mind and tugged my heart. I felt a positive energy from our conversation that day and somehow I felt smarter. My brain was working overtime; it had not been exercised like this in a long while. "Sure, I'd welcome a chat now and then. Let's not make it a regular thing, a once in a while thing would be great."

Nancy and I had shifted our relationship. Our future meetups would exercise our brains and our hearts. My thigh would feel no pain. We both stood and shared a warm hug. Some reunions end in tears, ours started with fond memories and ended in sadness that day. We did not realize at the time our plan would be a roller coaster of emotions for both of us.

Chapter 12

Two Years Later

The phone rang on my desk and startled me. The phone rang all the time just not much after ten p.m. I shuffled some papers and hoped the ringing would stop, but no such luck. "Hello," I mumbled.

"QB, how are you, darling?"

Uh oh, I thought. "Hi Nance, you're calling kinda late."

"It's only ten, a lot of us are just getting warmed up this time of night."

"Well, I'm just winding down and about to head home. It's good to hear from you."

"Don't be a party pooper. I'm not calling about tonight anyway. You free for happy hour on Friday?"

I was considering my options as the seconds ticked off the clock and wondered what would be my motivation for another meet-up with Nancy.

"I'm buying, QB."

Bingo. That brought a smile to my face, free beer tended to do that. "I'm in, see you Friday around five."

*****

She was sitting in a booth all alone for a change, and I scooted in next to her as I nodded to the stool by the bar. It looked jilted and then some. A lady was spinning the stool around not showing much respect. The stool spun and spun some more then stopped to face me dead on. It seemed to mouth two words 'save me'. I shrugged my shoulders and felt a pain in my gut. There was nothing I could do so I moved on. "Where are the suits?"

"Where are your manners?" She leaned over and kissed me on the cheek and said, "I've missed you, QB."

All tease all the time, I thought, *just like back in college*. The girl still had the looks that killed me every time I stole a glance. "Always good to see you." I eyed her up and down and decided to return the serve. "Always good to see all of you Nance, every darn bit."

She liked the compliment but had no intent of playing the game too far. She was here to talk, to share some stories and that was fine with me. It was fun to spar with Nancy about old times, but that's where the times needed to stay.

"Ok QB, what story have you brought me tonight?"

Nancy moved our discussion along quickly, right to the heart of our meet-up. *Hmmm*, I thought, *she might have some news*.

"You know, I need a beer before I can spit out a tale."

Nancy looked for a waitress but none headed our way. She wiggled her way out of the booth and gave me plenty to think about. She returned with two beers much to my surprise.

"I only drink one beer at a time."

"Calm down. Can't a lady enjoy a cold beer now and then?" She sipped on her brew and gave me a smile.

Nancy seemed happier, relaxed and more like the old Nance from school when not surrounded by the guys in suits. The suits weren't good for my friend, but I couldn't push it. She would need to make her own call on that one and hopefully before it was too late.

"That's good with me." We both drank some brew and enjoyed a moment together without any outsiders, without any disruption, and most of all, without Slime Guy.

"Let's change up our routine tonight, lady's first."

Nancy looked ready. She had anticipated my move and quickly parried back. "Lady's first? Okay QB, I'll go. Put your seat belt on it might get choppy."

Nancy had a story to tell. She had been asked by the "party" to run for office and with no hesitation, declined. She was flattered, of course, but did not feel ready, nowhere near ready. She needed more experience, greater knowledge, and honestly, a better understanding of the political system. She had no idea how to run a campaign or how to persuade voters to pull her lever. "Real voters," she said, "not college kids." She was a raw talent with a lot to offer and willing to work for it, wanting to earn it, but wasn't quite sure what it was just yet. College was in the rearview, yet still visible. It all felt way too early, and frankly, she was a bit nervous. Not scared, Nancy was never scared. She was on unfamiliar turf and wanted to get some grounding before she asked the public to take a vote.

The party listened to Nancy's concerns politely and when she finished her rejection they did what parties do. They asked her again, and again and again. The "party" had its mind made up, its decision made, their candidate sat before them. It was a done deal; only the candidate did not realize it. On the fourth request she wilted and accepted. They wore her down with flattery and chicanery. After all, the two went hand in hand with the party. Nancy would run to be a State Congresswoman with the Democratic Party. She would not be the youngest to serve, although she would be the youngest female ever elected if she won. That was something.

"Wow, that's fantastic. I am very proud of you."

Nancy smiled, a generous wide beaming smile. She did not blush, did not bat her eyes, only the smile gave her away. I was still important to Nancy, she wanted to impress me, show me what she could do, make me understand she would be important some day. I already knew all of that of course. Nancy was a very determined individual. It was very cool to know she still wanted my approval.

"When does the campaign begin?"

"Stevie is pulling that together ..."

I interrupted. "Slime Guy?" *I used the nickname I had given Stevie. I gotta remember to keep these things to myself.*

Nancy's face was not shining any longer. "Slime Guy? Come on, QB, that's a low blow and it's not deserved. Stevie is a whiz at campaigns. He's one of the brightest young minds in the party."

"The party, huh? That used to be a fun word, party. Why did you politicians have to screw up the word party?"

I was doing my best to move on from my Slime Guy slip and hoped some bad humor would do the trick. I put my best smile out there and jutted my chin; then I felt the slap on my cheek. It was not a hard slap just a slight touch as Nancy's hand slowly grazed across my face.

"That's for Slime Guy, I mean Stevie." Nancy shook her head left and right at her own slip and we both shared a good laugh.

The music played on and we felt the tune bounce off the walls in the pub. It was one of those older haunts that managed to stay in business as ownership shifted from one generation to the next. The beer was always cold and the grub sated some hunger without any lingering memory the next day. The clientele seemed to get older and younger at the same time, a good mix all around.

I stopped gazing around the bar as the music shifted from one old hit to another and looked straight at Nancy. "Ok Nance, just one question."

She straightened her back and wiped her smile away. Her body language spoke with clarity, "Bring it."

"How will you win?"

She hesitated. We both knew she wanted to say Stevie has a plan but Nancy did not want to serve up a lob for me to crash down upon her head.

Come on Nance, put the ball in play. You know I'm ready to score.

Instead Nancy acted as the better man, downed the rest of her drink and said, "Are you going to keep up or hug that first beer a while longer?"

Zing! She got me and aced a shot past my outstretched racket. Every now and then I failed to remember how savvy this girl could be. I accepted the challenge and gulped some suds then handed my empty glass to her. "I do love free beer."

Nancy repeated the process and returned with a couple cold ones, and we settled back into our discussion.

"I know it's a bit early for you to have a game plan so let's skip my last question...for now. One thing I am wondering though is where will the money come from. How will you afford to pay for your campaign?"

Nancy raised her eyebrows and eyed me carefully. "You're not going to like the answer but here it is anyway. The party. Stevie told me the party will kick in to get things off the ground and help us with fund raising."

"Well that figures. The party has you covered. And what do you owe the party in return? Just what are they expecting from you?"

Nancy was not ruffled at my question and snide reaction. "It's not like that…at least not yet anyway. The best analogy I can think of, one that you would understand, is from college. Joining the party is like joining a fraternity or sorority. It feels right to hang around these people. We have fun together, spirited debates with each other and we believe in the same things. I don't know all the rules yet; I don't understand the norms they follow. That will all come in time."

Good answer, I thought. Anytime you can use a college fraternity or sorority as rationale to backup your moves in life, there are reasonable odds you will have a good time, and possibly a damn good time. Just don't get caught roughing up the pledges or in this case the suits.

"Ok, I'll let this slide. Don't be surprised when I ask you again about those suits. They had their eyes on you last time we were in this place, especially that Stevie character. Watch yourself; I don't trust the suits and maybe you shouldn't either."

Nancy turned serious. "Bob you have no idea how much it means to me that you are concerned. Give a girl some credit, I can take care of myself and this path feels right to me."

That was the second time she'd called me Bob and I had no idea how to interpret it. We sat back in the booth and enjoyed the suds. The vibe in the bar felt good as we allowed a pause in the conversation. For many people the silence would cause an unforced error, a fumbling of words that had little meaning, their only purpose to keep the dialogue moving forward removing the awkwardness in the air. That was not necessary with Nancy, not one bit. I needed every extra gulp of air to ready myself for the next ball coming over the net and I expect she felt the same. Besides, I enjoyed the view.

It took me a few more gulps of beer to find my courage. I finally nodded to Nancy and let her know I respected her choice. In my head I kept wondering, *Of all the jobs in the world why would Nancy choose a role that most people disrespected or did not care about?* "Ok, I'll stop being a critic…for a moment." I decided to switch to serious mode and contorted my face to match my words. "Why do you want to be a politician? I mean, you could do anything and you chose politics. Why—?"

Nancy took her time. It was a life defining question, an important moment in her life or at least in our relationship. The answer mattered. My reaction mattered. She pursed her lips, breathed in deep and sent a hundred-mile per hour serve over the net. "I want to make a difference in people's lives."

The tennis ball came right at my midsection. I thought, *move left or move right just move. Now!* It was too late as my feet stuck to the court and the ball hit me in the groin and all the air was sucked out of my body. I was unable to speak so I listened for more words but she had stopped. *Damn!* The one time I needed her to keep yacking for a while she shut it down and tapped the table with her nails. She wanted the ball returned. Off my racket would have been the customary approach, but I dropped it when both hands went to massage my pain.

Nancy made a simple statement that did not need any

expansion to improve it's meaning. She may have been a bit starry eyed and perhaps naïve, but she was also the smartest and toughest female I knew. Hell, she was the smartest and toughest person I knew, next to Amy.

After a few gulps of air I noticed my glass was at half-mast, the dark fluid still capped by a thin layer of cream-colored suds. I raised the glass, looked at Nancy and said, "Alright, that may be idealistic, but I have a lot of confidence you will indeed make a difference. You just might get my vote. You have a ways to go to earn it, though you took some long strides tonight."

Nancy smiled and sipped some brew.

"Well done Nance, well done indeed. I like that you made them work for it. Tell me one thing, just one thing that will distinguish your campaign from your opponent, whoever that is?"

Nancy paused for a moment. I could tell she wanted to get the words just right. "I want to help girls understand they can do everything a boy can do. I want more girls in college, taking the hard courses, competing for the top jobs, earning the big bucks or staying home with the family. Too often a girl's path is based on limitations. I want to remove the limits."

Ball returned over the net. Her lager still filled her second glass as the first beer went down a bit fast but she responded, gave me a clink and took a large swallow.

"That's a real positive approach at least for half the voters," I joked. I could tell she was holding back. "There's something else Nance, what are you not telling me?"

"Are you insinuating I am keeping secrets…from you?"

"Hmmm, I can tell there's more going on inside that head of yours. You'll tell me when you're ready. I just wanted you to know that I know there's another reason you are running."

Nancy stared right through me. I could not tell if she was sizing me up or testing me. Her eyes were shooting lasers. Finally she said, "QB there's nothing more, no hidden secrets…it's just… it's just that I've had to overcome a lot of challenges to get where I am."

"Because you're female?"

"Yes, simply because I'm a woman. I don't expect you to understand, not completely."

I did not have a reply, not one I had considered or even thought about. I wanted to hear more and waited her out.

Nancy's eyes watered and she looked away.

Geez, what brought that on? I wondered. *Come on, Nancy, let's find out if we are to be friends, real friends. Trust me,* I said with all my might inside my head. *Trust me.* I don't know why I wanted it so much. At that moment my emotions took over. There was no vote— my head, gut, and even Mr. Ego ceded to my heart, which beat a few decibels louder than normal. I felt the sweat on my neck and back.

Nancy turned and looked into my eyes.

Don't blink, whatever happens just don't blink.

She let a tear streak down to her chin where it stayed for a second, then two and three before finally dropping in her lap.

"My brother…my older brother…was the star athlete, prom king, and future leader of the free world. That's how my father saw it anyway."

Nancy let out a deep breath as I rewound the tape in my head. *She said, "was," past tense. That's not good, definitely not good for the brother. Let it out Nance keep going I signaled.* Another deep breath allowed me to blink.

"I haven't talked about Derek in so long."

She said his name, that's gotta be a good sign, right? I never had a girl as a friend before. It was always one word for me: girlfriend. I was on unfamiliar turf and unsure what to do. *Should I hold her hand? Nah, you dummy, just let her talk…like a buddy. A buddy?*

"It was the final home game of Derek's senior season. The stands were full and the crowd seldom took a seat. When Derek took the court as the last of five starters the building shook and everyone screamed 'Der-ek…Der-ek…Der-ek.' I remember putting my hands over my ears as Daddy whistled. I usually sat with my freshman friends and talked through the game, but not this time. I stood next to Daddy and felt his pride pour out. I didn't mind Derek was the favored child, didn't mind Daddy spending all his time practicing shots and doing drills. I knew at that young age my father was living through Derek. It made him happy."

Nancy breathed in deep, and I could tell the bad news was coming next.

"Derek missed his first eight shots and we trailed by ten at the half against a cross town rival. The second half was a different game. Derek was everywhere, stealing balls, grabbing rebounds, and pouring shots in from all over the court. The crowd went wild and the arena got even louder. Toward the end of a close game, Derek streaked down the court with a player chasing from behind. He rose high in the air and it seemed as if he was floating. For a moment, a brief moment, the crowd quieted and held back a roar in anticipation of a slam-dunk. Then the left side of his body contorted and he clutched his chest as the ball and Derek fell to the floor. I remember hearing the ball bounce away until it hit the wall with a thud."

I knew it was okay to hold her hand now and tucked her fingers in mine.

Nancy moved forward. "I made the volleyball team the next year, ran for vice president as a junior and got a few votes for homecoming queen my senior year. I did everything I could…to replace him. It was my turn, I was the only one left."

That's a lot of pressure, I thought. *How does a girl live up to Daddy's expectations and win his approval?* The traditional path would not have worked for Nancy, she'd be miserable and Daddy too.

Nancy was talked out and looked drained. "I don't know if you bring out the best or worst in me, QB."

"Hmm, if you're undecided, I'll take best."

She gave me a sly look and I could see a smile starting to form. We needed a good laugh before we ended this one.

I just nodded and took a note to self: *If I have a daughter someday she's lucky to have people like Nancy paving the way.* For some reason I began laughing to myself and could not keep the giggles back.

"Give it up, QB, what's so funny?"

"I just remembered a political joke someone told me the other day."

Nancy eyed me carefully and said, "Go ahead, make my day."

"The first female president, let's call her Nancy, gets elected president and is spending her first night in the White House. She has waited so long for a female to finally climb to the top of the mountain. The ghost of George Washington appears and Nancy says, 'How can I best serve my country?' Washington says, 'Never tell a lie.' Nancy replies, 'Ouch; I don't know about that.' The next night the ghost of Thomas Jefferson appears. Nancy says, 'How can I best serve my country?' Jefferson says, 'Listen to the people.' Nancy says, 'Ohh! I really don't want to do that.' On the third night the ghost of Abraham Lincoln appears. Nancy says, 'How can I best serve my country?' Lincoln says, 'Go to the theater.'

I deserved the punch in my arm and we both laughed aloud. We clinked our glasses one last time and etched another memory in the back of our minds. There was more truth coming our way, and I did not know if it was the painful kind but had a feeling it would be. We did not keep score of our matches, but I gave this one to Nancy. She had served and volleyed well, although I thought that she should skip the beer next time. That was definitely not her game, but I appreciated the effort.

Atta girl, Nance, atta girl.

Chapter 13

Five Years Later

"I'll get it, Mom. Hello?" I said into the phone.

"QB, how are you, darling?"

There was only one person in the world that called me QB and darling in the same sentence and it wasn't my wife. I was staying with my mom for the weekend as Amy set up our new home at the U, a few hours south. *How did Nancy track me down at Mom's house?* I wondered, but quickly knew it was a waste of time. Nancy could find me just about anywhere.

"Nance it is I, the QB of your dreams back to haunt you." Sometimes words do sound better in your head. *Note to self: stop being cute and get back to being a stud, or better yet just a regular guy.*

"You can't haunt me, dear, but you can buy me a drink. How about tonight at our usual place?"

Tick tock. Tick tock. I did not want to give a quick yes or a slow no. I compromised and went with a slow yes. "Sure, see you around five."

"Bye for now, QB."

I walked into the pub and saw Nancy in a booth to my left and my old stool across the room near the taps by the bar. The debate raged in my head: *Should I slide over to the booth or take a seat on my stool? Booth or stool? Talk to Nancy or chat up the bartender?* I wondered.

It was time to vote. My gut and heart wanted the comfort of the stool and some distance from Congresswoman Smith. My head and feet pointed us toward the booth, but I did not move. We were stuck in the middle of the pub, looking foolish while we all waited for Mr. Ego, who finally obliged with a smile to my friend. Then I saw it: Nancy had already ordered and had my favorite beverage next to her on the table. It was an easy decision after all and we sidled over to the booth.

Nancy stood and greeted me with a warm embrace and peck on the cheek. "QB, it's so good to see you."

"Nance, always good to see all of you, too."

She blushed, which was my intent.

Damn she still looks good. "I see you got me a beer, thought I was buying today."

"Have a seat, there will be plenty more rounds for you to be a proper gentleman."

Nancy was still good with the quips that had double— and sometimes triple meaning. Mr. Ego wilted and went down for the evening. We took our customary places in the booth and settled in for a five-year catch up. I sipped some brew and Nancy did the same as we waited for each other to begin. We hit the table with our glasses at the same time and I bounced mine back up for another gulp. The double sip move worked and Nancy got our evening off the ground. "Ok QB, I'll go first you big coward."

I grinned and sipped some more brew as my beer went to half-mast. *The first one always goes down easy*, I reminded myself then put the glass on the table. *Note to self: slow it down cowboy.*

Nancy leaned forward as her head looked left then right then left again. She signaled to me to lean in as this part of our conversation needed to be guarded from anyone who might be listening. I looked at the Tuesday night crowd, all five of them, and laughed inside my head at the secrecy. Her right boot was well within striking distance so I knew to keep my serious look on the outside.

"What's up?"

"I'm running for Congress."

"Huh, you're already in Congress."

"I'm running for the U.S. Congress. The party wants me to retain the seat of a longtime congressman who is retiring next year."

Wow, Nancy is in the show or whatever cool term they use for Congress. Is there a cool term for the politicians in D.C.? I could not think of one but there had to be, right? She sat there beaming across from me waiting on some kind of reply. I did not need to take a vote or complete an inventory of my emotions. I was consumed, totally consumed by an overwhelming feeling of pride. My friend was on her way, well on her way toward her dream and I was so very proud of her. She had not won, not yet anyway. She had been picked or asked or lobbied by the party, and that was really something. *Now how the heck do I show her how proud I am?*

Before she could show shock or surprise or sadness at my silence I scooted over next to her and moved my head in close to hers. I looked deep into her eyes and my right hand moved to her cheek and caressed her. "Nance, I am so proud of you." I then sealed our emotional moment with a kiss on her cheek and the best hug you can give in a booth not designed for hugs. The whole time I just hoped she knew how much I respected her courage to go for it.

I moved back to my part of the booth after our embrace and went back into QB character. "So, do you have any chance of winning?"

Nancy smiled. She knew I was back in role, back to being her QB. My question had two meanings. First, it was a tease, a negative slam that says 'You got no chance kid, give it up now.' The other meaning was for us to dive in deep and discuss this very cool career challenge in front of her.

Nancy had a good barometer of my insults and barbs and translated me easily. "It's a horse race between me and two others. I'd put the odds at less than fifty percent for any of us. If one of the other men drops, then I have a good chance to win in a shootout."

The girl spoke my lingo. "Why do you win a two-man race?"

Her eyebrows shot up and I realized my error. "I mean why do you win a one-man, one-woman race?"

"Two reasons. The party will back me, and I'll get the female vote."

I looked at my friend and tried to avoid asking the next question. I didn't want to know but I had to know. "Do you have a campaign manager?"

I closed my eyes and braced myself for the reply. *Come on Nance, don't say Stevie, let Slime Guy move on down the road.* My whole body clenched up tight and Nancy knew the reason as she took a deep slug of her drink.

"You know who it is and don't give me any grief. I am here to celebrate tonight not fight about Stevie."

No reply was the right answer as I let the moment pass. It's always easier to drink more beer than engage in a difficult conversation. I moved us in a new direction. " If you win, do you move to D.C. or stay in Chicago?"

Nancy did not hesitate. "Chicago is home for me, always will be. I'll rent a small apartment in D.C. with a roommate and keep my place here."

"Hmm, that must put a dent in the dating scene." Ok, my curiosity got the best of me. *Who was Nancy sleeping with, was she dating someone serious, or was she a loner?* I raised my eyebrows, indicating I knew I was intruding on private territory. She knew whom I was sleeping with though we never talked about Amy.

"It's easy to find a date…but hard to find a good guy. Where do you hide them all?"

"Good guys are everywhere." I looked around the bar to point a few out but failed to find anyone that would measure up.

"See what I mean? You set a high bar, QB." Nancy smiled. I loved her smile and the warmth of her face. Most men I knew would gladly date Nancy but few would keep up.

Nancy stepped in to fill the void. "Your turn, QB. What story did you bring me today?"

I was trapped in no man's land—too close to the net and too far from the baseline. Nancy blew one past me for a winner and now it was my game to serve.

Before I could begin Nancy stepped up. "Yes I know, you'll need another beer to tell a good story." With that, she was out of the booth in a quick second, and I watched the male heads in the bar turn as her hips swayed on her walk to the tap. Yep, it would be easy for her to find a date, just not the right guy.

There was no inner debate on which story to share. I wanted to talk about Cindy. Nancy returned with another brew and readied herself to return serve.

Chapter 14

Cindy

"Cindy was the captain of the girl's junior varsity basketball team I coached in high school, one of numerous jobs I held to earn my keep. Coach Mac didn't have a budget for my football position so he bartered my time away whenever he could to close the budget hole. I never did forgive him for making me 'Driver Bob,' the best darn driver educator in the Midwest. But that's a different story.

"Cindy set the example for other girls to follow and most of the boys could have learned a thing or two if their ego did not interfere. She won more than a few games with her hustle on the court. Cindy dove for the loose ball, boxed out her man and played full out until the last whistle blew. Our games were on Saturday mornings following the Varsity games on Friday nights. It was a tough gig as most JV girls skipped the Friday night parties to be fresh the next morning.

"Around midseason, Cindy was called up to the Varsity team, and I knew the rest of our season was done. We would be without a rudder, adrift at sea and we all knew it. Yet we wished Cindy well because it was her goal, her dream and there was no doubt she had earned it. She played that first Varsity game and played well. Cindy came off the bench, dished out six assists, scored four points and stole a couple balls. Late in the game she dove head first into the bleachers and tossed the ball behind her back to a teammate who scored. The gymnasium roared their approval as the sell-out crowd welcomed Cindy to Varsity ball. Cindy's daring play shifted the momentum of the game and helped the team get a win. I was proud, damn proud of the kid, the girl, the player and our JV leader.

"The next morning came and I dragged myself to the gym. Usually I had some urgency in my step, enough nervous energy for two, perhaps three coaches, but not this day: our first game without Cindy. The team must have felt the same as they dressed slowly and were nearly late for warm-ups. We slogged through some practice hoops as our customary two-dozen fans looked on. They were quieter than normal, they knew too. The horn blew and the game was about to begin as I readied myself to call out the starting five. That's when I heard the roar from the two-dozen faithful. They were stomping and hollering and a few even tried to get a wave going. It was a good attempt but failed miserably as there were more empty seats than full. No matter, we all appreciated the effort though I could not figure out the sudden excitement as I scanned the crowd. Then I looked back at my team and saw Cindy appear in full uniform ready to take the court.

"'Sorry coach,'" said Cindy.

"'You're sorry, kid? What are you sorry for?'"

"'I'm late coach.'" Cindy looked at the other players and said she was sorry to them too. I busted a gut inside as my pride in Cindy grew a foot or two and I forced a tear back from where it came. The kid showed up for our JV game and she came to play. The horn blew and the opposing team went to center court. Our starting five was expected soon and the players waited for my cue. I smiled and shook my head as the players looked at me with hope in their eyes. My usual move was to bust the player, put her on the bench for the duration and they all knew it. It was against the rules, my rules, to be late for practice much less a game.

The horn blasted again and the lead ref blew his whistle. "'Coach you ready to play some ball?'"

"'Yeah, we're ready. We're more than ready.'" The twenty-four fans were still on their feet and we could all feel their vibe. *It's just a JV game*, I reminded myself, *just a darn JV game*. But it was my team and Cindy's team and she came to play even though she still wore bruises from last night. No other Varsity player made an appearance; the JV team was beneath them. They didn't even sit in the bleachers to support their mates. Saturday morning was reserved for sleep and much needed rest from the game and the parties on Friday night.

The hell with the rules, I said to myself. "'Ok team let's get our regular starting five on the court.'"

"Cindy smiled, as did the rest of the girls. Our team, along with its captain, took the court and we all got ready for a good show. The twenty-four fans behind me made the stadium sound and feel full, well not quite full but they gave a good yell. Cindy played half the game as I made sure she got some rest, still she led the team in scoring and assists as she often did. When she sat it was next to me, her usual spot. Neither of our butts saw much of the chair as we were up on our feet most of the time cheering, yelling and clapping for our girls on the court. The other team stood no chance and we chalked up another W, our tenth in a row."

My lips were dry and I grabbed the glass to quench my thirst. Nancy remained quiet as she awaited the punch line. She knew there was more to the story than a tough kid who showed others how to play ball. I took one more sip and started again.

"Cindy was more than an athlete, much more. She had a kind streak that drew people to her. It's a bit hard to explain, but she was the cool kid in the group without trying to be cool. She loved to wear hats but did not flaunt it. Most hats just looked better on her head so she went with it. She didn't walk into a room expecting people to notice, they just did, no matter what she wore or how she walked. Cindy had a presence about her that you sensed and felt. Everyone knew there was real substance in this girl. Part of the reason is she wore a bright smile and she had rap, that's what we called it back then. Rap. If a dude were lucky enough to strike up a conversation, Cindy would extend it and then some. Most guys tried to keep their words few and their hands busy as they hustled girls into the back seat of a car. Cindy unarmed the boys and commanded their respect as they realized an awkward pickup line would never work, not with this girl."

I paused to see how Nancy was feeling about my Cindy story. "Sounds like a great kid." That was Nancy's way of saying, *Where the heck is this story going?*

"I heard from Cindy the other day. It's been eight or nine years and she sent me a letter. Cindy teaches sixth grade math and she volunteered to be the girls' basketball coach. One of her starters showed up late for a critical game and everyone begged for her to play. Cindy deliberated as the ref blew the whistle and called for the starting five. Then she remembered a similar experience that occurred years ago and a coach who allowed the late show to play. The flash jolted Cindy into action and she told the star player to take her seat."

I took a sip as Nancy said, "Hmmm."

"Cindy closed the letter by saying thank you for the lessons and teaching her about life and to play ball. Then she offered some advice: 'Be as tough on the girls as you are the boys, Coach. There's no difference between the genders on the field of play.'"

Nancy purred again and waited for more. I could tell she was expecting a bad news story or a tearjerker about Cindy getting mugged or worse. Her expression said it all, *Where is the societal problem to solve?* "Ok, QB. Nice story, I love this Cindy kid. But where's the problem? What's the issue to solve?"

Nancy didn't get it. Maybe the puzzle was too hard for her, too hard for anyone to solve. I had seen so many sad news stories over the past ten years; so many tearjerkers that needed help and way too many that expected it. Nancy needed someone to open her eyes to see the challenge, perhaps the biggest challenge we face.

I wore my serious mask and looked into Nancy's eyes. I stared as hard and deep as I could then waited a beat, maybe two, and knew she was nearly ready.

Nancy sat forward in the booth tilted her head and signaled for the serve. *Bring it, QB, she silently screamed.*

"There's not enough Cindys."

I picked up our empties and went to the bar as Nancy sat alone in the booth, her mouth agape as the ball went by. I returned with a final round, sipped some suds and noticed Nancy wore a serious look.

"You might need more than a beer, QB."

I steadied myself and took a big gulp. *Are we going back to the dating scene?* I wondered.

"His name is Peter."

I nodded.

"We were with each other for three years. I knew after our second date he was the right guy. We could talk for hours. He would hold my hand when we went to a movie."

I looked at my beer and thought about taking a sip but remained perfectly still.

"Peter arranged a weekend getaway to upper Michigan last summer. It was a perfect place and we both had news to share. He brought the ring and I brought the baby."

Oh no. That's not good. I reached for the beer.

"We had not talked enough…he uh…did not want a family… and I would not…I could not…"

Nancy refused to cry and steadied herself. She looked determined to get through the story, although I knew it was tearing her up.

"We called it quits. I thought it was temporary. I reasoned that we were just angry at each other and it would all blow over. He felt I chose the baby over him, and I felt abandoned. It was a tough place but people work these things out. That's what I told myself."

"What happened?"

"I never saw Peter again."

"What about…"

"The baby? I was going to be wonder woman. Keep the career, have the baby, and do it all by myself. The doctor said it was stress, too much stress. I lost the baby a few weeks after I lost Peter."

"I'm so sorry, Nance."

"It was a girl…and I would have wanted her to be like your Cindy."

Chapter 15

Rosalind

We made a pact at our last meet to reunite in two or three years, however five ticked by quickly as our lives were full. Amy and I were in Michigan. I was the new Offensive Coordinator for the State School with a mission to put points on the board and earn some Ws.

Nancy renewed her congressional seat every two years, splitting her time between home and the nation's capitol.

I was in town on a recruiting visit and stopped by the pub for a cold one. *Just one beer*, I reminded myself as I walked through the door and took a seat on my stool. Mr. Ego raised his hand to ask a question. *Who are you kidding, just one beer, huh? Good luck with that.* I thought it would look a bit silly to argue with myself, at least not until I had a beer—or maybe two. *Mr. Ego was right again*, I seldom stopped at one. If I had, the evening would have been a lot shorter.

I finished the first round then ordered some grub to go with round two. And then I heard it. "Is this stool taken darling?" There was only one person with that voice who called me darling. My quiet night at the bar was done. Nancy pulled me up into a warm embrace and shooed a few suits away. Those damn suits always had her surrounded. "QB, it's so good to see you."

Nancy wore her best smile for me, not the fake one she used with the voters. I was trapped in the bright lights of her pearly whites and stood there like a deer in the middle of the road. It took a moment to snap out of it and deliver my customary line: "Nance, it's good to see you too; good to see all of you."

She knew it was coming yet enjoyed it anyway. Old friends can get away with that kind of thing because the real meaning of a vintage quip is seared deep into our memory banks where only the good things are stored. Nancy flicked back her hair. It was an instinctual move, muscle memory reacting to a moment.

I pulled the stool back for my friend and said, "Let's try the stools tonight, mix it up a bit. That alright?"

"The stool will do just fine. As long as we get to catch up, I'd sit almost anywhere."

I shook my head at the compliment as my mouth formed a grin. "Are those suits going to be ok?"

"Oh, don't get started on the suits; they're big boys and can take care of themselves."

Her quick retort did not bode well for the suits. She released a bit too much emotion with her reply and I tucked the observation away. I bought the beers and we settled in for an impromptu meet-up. We didn't bother to ask each other if we had the time. It was understood. I served first by pretending to ask an informed political question. "Ok Nance, tell me straight, is your boy going to win in November?"

Nancy was surprised, but not shocked at my question. "Don't tell anyone … he's not my guy. He'll lose and might lose big. The Reagan train has a new engineer and it's still going strong. Thank goodness the Democrats have the House and Senate."

So much for Dukakis, I thought.

Nancy continued. "Besides, Ann Richards is 'my guy'. Did you see her at the convention? She killed it, really killed it."

"Yeah I saw highlights of her speech. The lady knows how to deliver a line and rally an audience. The silver spoon joke was a perfect putdown of George Bush and the Ginger Rogers line summed up what a lot of women feel in just a few words. Nicely played." I nearly said more but reeled it in.

"Give it up, QB, don't hold back."

"It's just that if Ann Richards is your guy, I suspect your team will get a lot of good laughs on the campaign trail but you will fail at governing."

"Alright, explain it to me. Why do we fail with Ann at the helm?"

"It's just a feeling."

Nancy sat still for a minute then yelled out. "Bartender, two more beers." She looked at me dead square in the eyeballs and said, "Your serve."

I gulped my beer and prayed for some inspiration, anything to help me get through the next five minutes. The barkeep brought our next round and removed the drained glasses. It was time to serve the ball. "Ann Richards is funny, really funny. People like her dry wit, her humor and her grace. She has such style and is a wonderful communicator."

Nancy waited for more.

"But all her best lines, all of her humor, the vast majority of her speech was based on the negative. She's great at the put down, making her opponent look bad. That's how she got her laughs, by making someone else look bad."

Nancy gave me a *So what?* look.

"It's not hard to blame someone else. It's not hard to poke fun at the other guy or gal, not hard at all. We all learned that in kindergarten. The hard part is coming up with a positive message, a game plan of policies and actions, and a team based approach that includes diverse views and backgrounds. I didn't hear much of that from Ann nor anyone else."

The silence hung in the air between us. I took a sip and another. "I don't mean to beat up on Ann Richards. I think she's terrific and if I saw her in a bar she would drink for free, at least on that night. It's just that I hoped for more, because I agree with you, she's the best bet in your party."

Nancy gulped some air as the wrinkles in her forehead finally receded, but I knew they would be back. Nancy wore a frown when she was upset and the frown brought the wrinkles that usually led to some kind of pain for me. My body cringed. I had become darn good at anticipating the body blow that was surely coming. I hated those wrinkles and the signals they sent.

Whack. She gave me a dope slap across the forehead. *There she goes again with the double meaning, some physical pain along with a message about me being a dope. I get it Nancy, I surely get it, but do you get me?* I wondered.

"Ok QB, give me some facts. Pour some truth out on the bar not just down your throat. Where and how was Ann negative?"

There would not be an easy escape, I thought. I took a sip and another and then one more, looking for courage in my brew. There was none to be had, but I enjoyed the search. I could feel Nancy winding up for another slap as I delayed my response. I did not want any more pain, but there would be some hurt in either direction. If I stayed mum another dope slap was headed my way. If I shared some truth, there could be blood spilled, my blood on the bar. I glanced down at her feet and saw some spikes. *Which way to go? Dope slap to the head or spike to the groin? Slap or spike?*

I made a choice as my knees closed together, the best defensive maneuver I could muster. I had never thought about being a hockey goalie and suddenly wished I had. Those skills might've come in handy. "Okay, here goes. First a confession, I watched some of the convention and saw all of Ann's speech."

Nancy raised her eyebrows. "You surprise me."

I wanted, ok needed to soften her up and I had chosen to tell some truth so might as well let it all out.

"For goodness sakes why would you watch the convention?"

I put my best innocent face on, the one I used to wear in grade school when the Sisters from Immaculate Conception caught me nipping on the wine they used to make the blood. "I was doing some research."

"Research? For what, QB? Do tell."

I reminded myself it was the second serve. My first hit the net so the second had to be in or I faced a double fault. Not a good way to start an evening with Nancy. "I wanted to be better prepared to have a real discussion about politics and the things you care about."

Nancy went red and that seldom happened. Once in a while she blushed in my presence, but that was usually a shade of pink that disappeared quickly. She wore some red on her face and neck for three seconds, maybe four. Her hand reached out and caressed my face. She looked into my eyes and said, "Thank you, QB."

It was a nice moment between friends and so far the "soften up" plan was working, maybe too well. My knees relaxed and opened some space between my legs. *How do girls sit with their knees together?* crossed my mind? Nancy pulled her hand away, straightened her back and let one rip. "Man up QB. Let's hear some truth."

The real Nancy was back and the "soften up" plan was toast. *Crap.* My second serve was in but Nancy crushed it back over the net and it was coming right at me.

"Ok here goes. Ann called Reagan a liar in so many words. I know he's your enemy, but he's also the president and most people respect him and think he's done a decent job."

"Hmmm," responded Nancy.

"She also said the Pentagon makes crooks rich and America not strong—a bum deal all around she said. Perhaps there's some truth in there, but give me some facts, don't call someone a crook without any proof."

"Hmmm," Nancy said.

"'And she said we won't have the America we want until we elect leaders that tell the truth, not most days, every day.'"

There was silence from the bar stool next to me. I decided to wait it out and went to my brew for strength.

"Was there anything she said that you liked?"

"Yeah. She and Dukakis and the Democratic Party don't like debt. They favor balanced budgets and Dukakis bragged he balanced his state budget eight or nine years in a row. That seems practical to me."

"Ok let's turn the tables. What do you think of George Bush and the Republicans?"

Time for a sip… better make it a gulp. "I like Bush. He seems a decent man and he's got wind at his back from eight years of Reagan. It's the safe choice. But…he's more negative than Ann Richards, attacking Dukakis all the time rather than discussing his own plan. That I don't like. It's a weak sign that he's guided more by his campaign team than his own beliefs."

"That's very insightful. How did you come to that conclusion?"

"You know how."

Nancy reflected for a moment. "I haven't a clue."

I moved my stool away from Nancy just out of harm's way, I hoped. "From the suits that hang around you."

Zip. The ball went passed Nancy. She did not even try to hit it back.

"You are a different person when Stevie is around and the two of you go into battle formation, or some kind of attack mode against your supposed enemies."

"Hmmm," said Nancy.

"And I read an article where Bush's campaign manager said something like: 'Republicans can't win in the South on the issues. Instead they have to make the case that the other guy, the opponent is—a bad guy.'"

"Hmmm," said Nancy.

"If you were in a close race, a race so close you could not predict the winner. Would you go negative? Would you attack your opponent and smear him or her rather than focus on the issues?"

Nancy wore her poker face well as the seconds ticked by. "I won't go negative, no way, no chance. I'd rather lose than lie to win a seat. And frankly, I haven't needed to go negative."

I knew more was coming. We both took a sip as Nancy readied her serve.

"Stevie and the party don't hesitate to go negative. They don't leave many tracks so it's hard to pin the blame on anyone and by the time voters figure it out, the election is over and people have moved on. The lies don't matter after the last vote has been counted."

"Hmmm," I said.

Nancy looked down at her shoes, usually that meant a confession was imminent. "The sad reality is that negative attacks work. And in a tough campaign, she who goes negative last usually loses."

"How does it work? How does a candidate win by going negative?"

"You'll have to ask Stevie."

"Fair point. Just tell me a few tactics. What have you seen?"

"Ok, QB. There's the whisper. A lie is created and then spread by word-of-mouth or sheets of paper placed on car windows or some other method. You get the idea. The lie is whispered around the campfire and impossible to trace back to the source."

"What's an example whisper?"

"You might say a candidate's spouse is a drug addict. Or, you might insinuate a candidate is having an affair. Sometimes the whisper lie is put in advertising and spread on TV, radio and local papers by third parties friendly to one of the candidates. It's mostly scare tactics. The campaign that went negative has complete deniability since the third party is doing the dirty work."

"Hmmm. What's another example?"

Nancy sighed.

"One more."

"Ok. This one is more of a slimy campaign trick than going negative against an opponent. One campaign sent fake Christmas cards to an opponent's voting base making it appear they were from the opponent. The cards said the candidate had changed his opinion on abortion just a few weeks prior to the election. The voters were of course devout religious believers so there was a massive uproar that had to be quieted down, which distracted the campaign team at a crucial time."

Nancy could tell I wanted just one more.

"Last one. One campaign hired a telemarketing firm to flood the phone banks of their opponent so they could not call out to reach potential voters the last week of a campaign. It was a close race."

"Why do politicians need to lie and cheat? I don't get it."

"Why do offensive tackles hold? Why do defensive players grab facemasks?

"Hmmm." I reflected a moment and then said, "That might be true but it's not a fair comparison. We have referees and there's a very good chance the offender gets caught and receives a penalty."

"That's true, yet it still happens in football, in other sports, in all vocations. People cheat to get ahead."

"Yes, that may be true, but we have referees and penalties, both are very effective at correcting bad behavior. Who are your referees? What are your penalties?"

"The referees are the press, love them or hate them, and their own built in biases. Penalties? That would come from the court system and the judges. By the time they get involved it's usually too late, way too late to matter."

"So the odds are low at getting caught and even lower to get penalized. Each campaign manager weighs the risk and many determine it's worth it. Why not throw some mud. It usually helps and there's a slim chance of getting in trouble."

"That's right. Unfortunately, that's exactly right and it's getting harder and harder to avoid. Going negative and playing dirty tricks is the norm these days and each cycle it gets worse and more personal. It used to be after an election, all was forgiven. Not anymore. Grudges are built and carried over into Congress, making it harder and harder to work across the aisle with the supposed enemy."

That reality deserved another round. I ordered two beers and we took in the sounds of the pub.

"In football the offensive tackle might risk a holding penalty but there's a high chance of getting caught and there's a penalty paid on the spot. No waiting on a judge until after the game is over. Plus, most fouls are mistakes, unintentional or made in the moment. Very few are pre-planned and they are not personal attacks against an opponent's character, or worse, his family. There's no comparison between cheating in politics and athletics, Nance."

"Hmmm," said Nancy.

"Tell me, why do pols play Jeckyll and Hyde? Why are you Jeckyll on the campaign trail and Hyde after the votes are tallied?"

"Would you prefer us to be Jeckyll all the time?"

"I'd prefer you not allow Stevie to tell you what to do." *Uh oh, that was an opinion to keep to myself.*

Whack. I was just out of reach for another dope slap so my shoulder took the brunt of the punch. *Damn that girl can hit.*

We allowed some silence to enter our discussion, a welcome intrusion. Truth talks were hard on the brain and as it turns out on the body as well. I rubbed my shoulder and Nancy giggled.

"You think my pain is humorous?"

"I most certainly do."

We clinked glasses and burned another memory deep into safe storage. Our serious truth talk had shifted to a lighter moment and we enjoyed the grins it brought. We settled in for a fun evening, two old friends swapping stories and pushing each other to be better. The bar stool was feeling good since the grooves I had worn were giving back. Nancy was herself when away from the suits and laughed with me for an hour as the cold beer flowed.

And then, he walked into the bar and crashed our happy place. Stevie was quickly surrounded. Every suit in the bar gravitated toward him as Stevie held court and espoused on the day's events. The campaign manager, who hung around the fringes, happy to be with the crowd, any crowd, was now the center of attention. I turned to face my friend to make a snide remark but she was out of her stool and on the move. "I'll be right back."

She was off to join the horde that surrounded Stevie. The campaign manager was not at the top rung of the ladder, but he was close. Nancy moved swiftly into the circle of suits and gave Stevie a peck on the cheek. He attempted an awkward hug and stared at Nancy for a full second, maybe two. Nance responded with her best fake smile, the one she wore on the campaign trail. I felt somewhat better that she still saved the genuine stuff for me.

Nancy turned to leave and Stevie grabbed her arm. A flash went through my mind as I remembered the spikes she wore. I closed my eyes and prayed hard. *Please grant me this small favor*, I asked. I pictured Stevie writhing in pain on the floor while I sipped my brew. It was a sight to see, so I rewound the tapes and watched it again. It had been a while since my butt sat on a pew, ok a long while, and I was out of practice. My behind was too busy carving out that groove on the barstool. It was a priority, a trade-off I gladly made so I was not surprised my prayers went unanswered. Heck, I doubted they were even heard. *Note to self: Show up at church next month.* I closed my eyes again and prayed harder. *Come on Nance, give him a kick, right where it counts.*

Instead, Nancy moved in closer to Stevie and whispered in his ear. He turned and saw me at the bar. Neither of us waved a hand or nodded a head. First to speak loses, or in this case first to acknowledge would be the weaker man. It was a stand off. We were two dudes in a bar less than 25 feet apart with a congresswoman between them. I had the advantage. I was on my stool with a cold beer in hand. It was a home game for me and I could do this all night, or at least until the beer ran out. *Go ahead, Stevie, keep your stare on,* I said to myself.

Nancy looked at Stevie then looked at me then looked back at Stevie. She whispered again in Stevie's ear and three seconds later was back at the bar on her stool. We locked eyes and she shook her head sideways slowly left then right. I knew then to let this one go. *Note to self: the campaign manager is moving on up.*

I figured we were done for the night and reached for my wallet to pay the tab. Nancy had other ideas and signaled the bartender to pour more suds. "We can't leave yet, not until you tell me a story."

"A story, huh?

"Yes, a story. Tell me a story."

I always had a story; there were so many to choose from. A football coach sees, hears and experiences the reality of life from a wide variety of angles. The job did not pay much, yet I lived a rich life mostly because of the kids, and once in a while their parents. The thing I did not understand is why Nancy wanted to hear my stories. "Sure, I'll tell you a story. But…"

I was unsure how to ask my question. I wanted to know yet I

did not want to embarrass Nancy. *No that's not it*, I said to myself. The truth was I did not want to push her away. The truth was I enjoyed spending time with my friend.

Nancy smiled. It was the real smile again not the fake one. "QB, I love your stories. Each time you tell me a story you give a piece of yourself to me. You let me see how you are living your life and your stories help me feel a little closer to you."

Wow! This girl knew how to flatten me to the ground. Humbled again, I picked myself up off the floor. "Okay, Congresswoman, I'll tell you one story."

Nancy reached out and touched my arm. "This might sound odd, but please don't call me Congresswoman. Not when we are alone, not when you tell me a story. I need the escape from politics, from the aisles of Congress, from the suits."

Come on say it, Nance. Say it one time. You want to escape from Stevie. There was sadness in her request. It seemed she lived in a different world and they let her out once in a long while to spend a few hours with her QB. I needed to find out more, but now was not the time. Not tonight. It was time to tell a story and I wanted it to be a meaningful one.

I took a long swig of energy from my beer glass and began. "Her name is Rosalind or as she would say, 'Just call me Roz.' I met her and a lot of parents on the recruiting trail. Roz was not unique since there were many single mothers in her shoes, but she did stand out."

Nancy's back was erect and her eyes were on me not the suits, a good sign.

I continued. "Roz has one boy and two girls, and I showed up to pitch her oldest. I scheduled an afternoon meet and knew to leave before dusk woke the night crew. The house had not seen a painter in a decade or two and the doorbell would not ring. I rapped my knuckles on the front door and it swung open with a loud creak. As I entered the house, the smell of soap engulfed me. It was a tidy abode with everything in its place. The three kids sat on the only couch and Roz showed me to the chair. Lemonade and cookies were on a table that tilted hard to one side. It was a good house where manners and rules meant something. Ma'am was heard from the kids on a regular basis, but sir had not been spoken in a very long time."

Nancy sat still in her stool. She was ready for more.

"Roz served the refreshments and we settled in. I leaned forward in my chair to begin my pitch, but Roz had a different plan in mind: 'My boy is a good player. He's not a great player; he's not exceptional, but he's good enough to play for you at the U. Isn't that right Coach?' I considered my options on how to best respond and chose the easy path: "Yes, ma'am.'

"'My boy is a good player, but he's not an NFL player. He's not pro caliber. Isn't that also right, Coach?'

"I looked at Derrick and he gave me a shoulder shrug. He was accustomed to Roz taking over. His body language said to go with the flow so I did. 'Yes, ma'am.'

"'Ok then. Can we skip all the football talk and discuss things that matter? Important things. You ok with that, Coach? You can save your speech for someone else's living room.' She backed me into a corner without much choice. 'Yes, ma'am,' I said.

"I had been in the house for seven minutes and only managed to say two words, both of them three times each. I thought things were going well, but my gut told me that I was losing this guy. I began to speak: 'Mrs....'

"'Now, don't Mrs. me, Coach. No need for that. Just call me

Roz. Everybody calls me Roz and you might as well do the same.'

"'Ok, Roz.'

"'That's it, Coach. Put a strong zzz on the end. Rozzz.'

"I laughed on the outside but my gut was clenching on the inside. Who is this woman? I wondered. 'Rozzz. I do like the sound of that,' I said with some conviction or at least tried to.

"'Now Coach, let's get on with those important things.' I waited to hear more, but nothing more was said. The gap was sitting there between us waiting to be filled. I looked over at Derrick and knew he wasn't going to do a darn thing. Roz folded her arms and the only sound in the room was the clock ticking. It was time to guess what was important.

"'Should we talk about Derrick's studies Rozzz?'

"Roz nodded her head in approval. 'Now we talking, Coach, now we talking.'

"I cleared my throat. 'Well, we take great pride at State on graduation rates. Our boys do well each year and we finished in the top two or three in our conference the past three years.'

"'That got you in the door, Coach. Tell me something I don't know.' With that she wiped the pride off my face and a frown took its place. I kept going to convince this tough mother. 'We view our players as student athletes. I won't say being a student is more important than being on the football team. That would not be honest. We look at both roles as having the same importance.' I was met with silence and it was up to me to fill the gap again. 'Our players earn it on the field and in the classroom, not one or the other.

"I wasn't lighting up the room and we all knew it. Roz took us in a different direction. 'What about you, Coach? You played ball in college, ain't that right?' I confirmed that was true. 'How did you know being a coach was the right thing for you after school?'

"I struck Derrick's name off the recruiting board in my mind. Now I had a different gap to fill. Where the heck was I going to find a tailback? Roz was waiting and Derrick sank back on the couch. It was time for a new tact. I figured I might as well throw the long ball, the short game wasn't working very well. 'I didn't know, Roz. I became a coach because there was nothing else I could do and nothing else I wanted to do. I needed a little encouragement to realize coaching was the right path for me.'

"'Now that's interesting. Tell us more.' Roz finally pulled up a seat. She was peeling me back one layer at a time. I gulped and pushed ahead. 'Coach Mac, my high school football coach gave me a job. Actually, it was three jobs. I was the QB coach, the student driver teacher, the girls JV basketball coach and I filled in wherever help was needed.'

"'That Coach Mac, he's something special, Roz said.'

"My eyes went wide. Had Roz called Mac? I wondered. I concluded that she had talked to Mac and he didn't let me know. I knew coach was probably laughing somewhere on a beach right now. 'Coach Mac taught me more about life than football, Roz. He's still the best football coach I ever knew. He also showed me how to guide players forward in life after the last whistle has blown. Coach Mac held his coaches accountable to a higher standard. That's the best way I know how to explain it.'

"Roz nodded her head up and down. 'That Coach Mac, he cared about you, took care of you. Isn't that right coach?'

"'Yes ma'am, that's right.' The silence returned for a moment. 'Roz, may I ask you a question?'

"Roz debated inside her head and must have decided I finally earned the right to ask her a question. 'Sure coach, you go right ahead.'

"'What's important to you and Derrick? What really matters?'

"Roz had a twinkle in her eye. It's almost as if she was saying 'atta boy, Coach, atta boy inside her head. 'Coach, we want to play for you at State. Derrick wants that and I want that. To get our commitment you gotta make us believe Derrick will be ready when that last whistle blows. You get me coach?'

"'Yes, ma'am.'

"'We don't need much and we ain't asking for any handouts. I want my boy safe, educated and employed after football.' I nodded my head. Things were going much better now, so the less I talked the better. That was my new game plan.

"'That's it. Three simple things,' said Roz.

"'Yes, ma'am.'

"Roz leaned forward on the edge of her chair and looked into my eyes for a second or two. 'Now Coach, how are you gonna make that happen? How you gonna keep my boy safe, get him educated, and find him a job after school?' Before I could respond Roz dove in again. 'I want a plan, Coach. That's what Coach Mac called it, a plan. Show me the plan, Coach. Show me the plan.'

"I took it in. This is something I know how to do. Before I could seal the deal Roz was back up at the plate. 'There's one more thing. Derrick's sister there, Irene is one year younger and she's a star on the basketball team, a real star. Now, I'm not asking any favors, and I'm not doing a two for one deal. The only thing I ask is you put in a good word at that State school for Irene.'

"I blinked my eyes a few times and kept my mouth shut. There had to be more so I might as well wait for it.

"'You see, Coach, the same things are important to my girl as my boy. I want her safe, educated and employed. It's all about opportunity, Coach. Yeah, that's the word, opportunity. And a girl wants the same things as a boy. No more and no less.'

"I had hardly spoken in Roz's living room at all. She had gift wrapped a terrific tailback and given him to me. All I had to do was take care of him and not make empty promises. The only other thing was to find a way to treat her girl the same as her boy with no strings attached. This I can do. This is the kind of thing I want to do. Is Irene any good I wondered?"

"Hmmm," said Nancy.

I sipped some cold brew and sat back in my stool.

"Well did you get the plan done? Was Roz satisfied with the plan?"

I shook my head sideways a few times. "Nance, I worked my ass off on that plan. Or rather, Roz worked my ass off is more like it."

"How's that plan going?"

"Derrick started at tailback two years and made all conference once. He was a fine player, a very good player just as Roz predicted. And he's got a corporate job lined up right after graduation in the city."

"What about the girl, Irene right? What happened to her?"

"She's the starting center on our girls basketball team. Roz was right about her being a true star. And I review Irene's plan with Roz each and every month, the same as I did with Derrick's. I, uh, volunteered to do both."

"What about Roz? How is she doing?"

I chuckled. "Roz is the reason I'm here in town, Nance. I'm here to meet with the second daughter. Or should I say, Roz will talk and I'll say yes, ma'am and listen."

"Hmmm," said Nancy. "You went out of your way to help Irene even though it's not your job, and you're back in town to help Roz again."

Nancy got my message, loud and clear. Nancy looked over her shoulder at Stevie and the suits. Her body sighed as she turned to face me. "It's not that easy in politics."

"It's never easy."

"I can't explain it. There's a complex web we all operate in. The leadership calls the shots, the party builds the platform and the campaign managers tell us what to say and how to say it. There's just such limited room for me to maneuver, to get things done, to focus on the priorities I believe are important."

Then why are you in Congress wasting your time? I kept that thought in my head, where it belonged, and avoided another slap to some body part. If she were a player on my team, she'd be on the bench with that attitude or running stadium stairs: a brutal punishment after practices were finished.

"Wipe that sinister look off your face. I'm biding my time, that's all. I am setting things up and will be ready when it's my turn. The party promised…they promised…oh hell, QB, you'll just have to trust me on this one."

I wanted to say atta girl, Nance, but my heart wasn't in it. "I hope so Nance," was the best I could do.

I signaled the bartender for the check and boxed Nancy out of the way as she threw a credit card on the bar. We gave each other a warm hug and said our goodbyes. As I headed to the door it occurred to me Nancy used her fake voter smile as we went our separate ways. That was a first, and I prayed it would be the last time she used it with me.

Chapter 16

Stevie V2

Nancy rode out the Bush term as the Reagan train kept running under a new chief. It ground to a halt in a short four years as, "Read my lips" summed up an unfortunate tax policy and a good man was hustled out the exit door. No one quite knew what to expect from the governor who ran Arkansas, although we quickly learned we had voted in a package deal when Hillary came to town. Like her or not, she came to play.

Nancy kept getting herself re-elected. She had a difficult battle when the house turned red half way through Clinton's first term but squeaked by with a three percent margin, enough to call it a mandate, but not enough to keep from sweating. Her opponent promised he'd be back for a rematch in a short two years. I was proud of my friend; she did not go negative, although I could only imagine the back room talk with all the suits.

It had been six maybe seven years since my last meet up with Nancy. I was home to see Mom and snuck out for a couple cold ones when she went to sleep. The pub was quieter than normal, as I enjoyed the elbowroom at the bar and the comfort of my stool. It looked worn yet still welcomed me with a good groove, and I settled in for a short visit. The tunes were vintage and the beer cold, not much had changed. I sat with my back to the room and thought about the upcoming season. I took a long swig from my glass and raised my neck to soak down some suds.

The mirror behind the bar was one of those long rectangles and I scanned the place from left to right as the beer flowed. Nothing was out of place until I saw some suits in a corner, three guys at a booth built to handle four. The missing dude joined the group late and was welcomed with a few high fives. He carried some bulk and shuffled more than walked. As he readied himself for the plunge into the booth he looked over at the bar. Our eyes connected, our faces both contorted as we recognized the opposing image in the mirror. We looked at each other for a long five seconds without a blink, without a twitch, without a smile. It was Stevie in my pub, my happy place, staring at me through the mirror on the wall.

What's he going to do? I wondered. I broke the stare down and opted to look deep into my beer for some advice. *Don't look up. Don't look in the mirror. Pretend he's not here. Okay,* I thought, *good advice.* A second later I looked up into the mirror. It was reflex or just bad instinct. I couldn't help it; I had to look. Stevie's image was still there staring at me but his face looked bigger, much bigger as if he was nearer to my stool at the bar. *Uh oh.* And then I heard him talk and knew he had made the first move.

"Coach, drinking all alone again?"

Nice opener dude. Get a lot of dates with that approach? I kept my eyes locked on Stevie's face in the mirror and managed to spit out two words: "Hello, Stevie."

"Nancy isn't showing up tonight, Coach; no use waiting for her."

Was Stevie sending me a message? Was he telling me to go home, to leave the bar, my bar, my home field? Not a chance dude, I don't care if Nance is coming or not. "That will make it a short evening then."

Stevie's hand went back and forth from his chin to his left cheek. It was one of those contemplative gestures. Finally he said, "Let's start over. Can I buy you a beer?"

Now the guy was being nice, or was he? I downed my drink and faced a fork in the road: Go home and escape a bad night with Stevie or stay and have another beer. *Escape to home or beer at the pub? Did Stevie say he was buying?* "Ok Stevie, I'll have a beer."

What the heck are we going to talk about? I thought about that for a few seconds and then figured out the answer. It was so very easy. We were going to have a chat about the only thing, or rather the only person that we had in common. We were going to talk about Nancy.

"Let's sit over there in the booth. We'll be more comfortable." With that comment Stevie grabbed our drinks and headed out while I stayed put on my stool. He had not asked my opinion, he barked an order and I was not in an obliging mood. So I counted down in my head, *one one thousand, two one thousand, three one thousand* and Stevie reappeared. He needed to learn a lesson about issuing commands in another man's lair.

"The stools are good." I pushed a stool toward him and put the ball in his court. He begrudgingly took a seat at the bar where he should have stayed all along. Stevie wanted control, he needed control, and he usually got control, but not tonight, not this time.

We grabbed our beers and took a silent sip as no friendly toast was offered. "What's on your mind, Stevie?" *Might as well get the ball rolling*, I thought. *Let's see if Stevie has game.*

He played it cool. There was no sweat on his brow, no tremble in his hand and no shiver running up his spine. The man had grown a pair or found a pair somewhere, somehow and he intended to show them to me. *This could be interesting*, I thought.

"There's a good chance Nancy will lose her next election and if she does the blame will fall on you."

Boom. Stevie did not waste any time and let loose a canon shot that headed for my stool. *So I'm the bad guy huh, how the hell do you figure that?* The campaign manager wasn't afraid of a fight and began our bout with a left jab to my chin. We weren't playing tennis; the game had shifted to the ring.

"Are you putting an L on the big board? That's not going to look very good on your record."

Stevie took a long drink then said, "I'm not here to spar with you. We're on the same side. We both want Nancy to win, but only one of us is helping her."

"How do you figure?"

"Nancy can be great. She could run for Governor or Senator one day and after that, who knows?" Stevie went back to his drink to get the next words right. "Nancy has game, but she's not playing ball. She's got you stuck in her head, and you're giving bad advice."

Well this was interesting. My good friend had me somewhere inside her head and followed my advice, even though we had not spoken in years.

Stevie sat on the edge of his stool in an agitated state. He rubbed this palms back and forth on his thighs. Slime Guy was clearly frustrated. *Hmm, this is entertaining. What the heck was I telling her,* I wondered? "I don't know Stevie, sounds like I am balancing you out somewhat."

"You don't get it. Maybe you don't care about Nancy's career and how she could be blowing her big chance."

I sipped some suds and took measure of the campaign manager sitting in front of me. He was everything I did not like in a man. He was out of shape, self-centered, rude and his ego entered the room a few strides ahead of his feet. But Nancy trusted him, or at least trusted his advice, and that was something. He was waiting for me to give the signal. He knew to wait for the head nod or the okay. One more gulp and I was ready. "Okay, lay it on me. How am I so bad for Nancy?"

"You influence her to color inside the lines and follow the rules of the road. We ain't in Nebraska, Coach. We don't play a gentleman's game. It's street ball in politics these days. We play to win and we do whatever it takes." Stevie thumped the bar with his fist to emphasize his statement. "We need to be working together, helping Nancy get elected, not pissing at each other in the wind."

Stevie sat tall on the stool, his whole body taut as if he were spring loaded and ready to fire. The man was worked up.

"Whatever it takes, huh? Exactly what does that mean? Explain it to me."

"You don't need me to draw you a map or show you the plays. I'm good at my job, damn good and you're holding us back!"

"I haven't seen you or Nancy in six or seven years, and last I checked, she's doing just fine."

"She doesn't need to see you to have you inside her head. Somehow you got deep into Nancy's mind and she can't, or won't, kick you out. She's going to lose the next one if she keeps listening to you."

"You mean she'll lose unless she plays dirty, goes negative on the other candidate and slings mud everywhere, hoping some of it sticks. Let's at least talk truthfully to each other."

"Alright, Coach. If Nancy stays goody two-shoes then she loses the next election. All her work to support women's rights will go down the drain just when things are starting to change."

My temperature rose a few degrees. This guy was spewing complete crap. *To get good things done a politician had to be bad. What kind of system is that?* I wondered, "If Nancy is performing well at her job and making a difference for her constituents, why can't she run on her record?"

Stevie smiled.

Damn, I just set him up. I asked the naïve question that was expected from someone on the outside of the political circle. I braced myself for his retort.

"Human nature. It's that simple. Some people do care about the issues of the day, but it takes work and it takes time. It's a lot easier to absorb the negative ad and the slanderous sound byte. The rumor travels miles before real facts have left the starting line."

"So, essentially you're saying people vote against someone, or against the negative perception of someone, more than they vote for someone."

Stevie nodded his head up and down. "Some people do. And each election, more and more people vote against the negative than vote for the positive. Like I said, getting to truth, real truth, takes work and time."

"And who wants to spend it on politics?"

Stevie let his silent nod answer the obvious.

"How does it work? How does Congress get anything done when they attack each other viciously during the campaigns? How do they put all that bad blood behind them and work across the aisle with someone who lies, cheats and steals to get their seat?"

"They don't put it behind them, not anymore. They remember all of it every detail and they get revenge. What's that song about the back stabbers?" He was talking about the O'Jay's song, about people who smile at you but have ulterior motives. "That's Congress right there in a lyric."

"How do they get anything done? If the foundation of our government is based on getting your seat by hook or by crook then how do they ever agree on anything?"

"You see some of the sausage getting made during the campaign. The grinder keeps going after the votes are in but it's less visible to the public. The evil resides everywhere. It's in the warm handshake, the pat on the back, the friendly smile. All of those gestures are facades to the deep-rooted emotions inside the souls of those in Congress."

"What do you mean?"

"They care more about making the other guy look bad than anything else. That's how politicians score points. If you don't score you can't win." Stevie smiled.

I finally got it. "And that's good for business?"

Stevie downed his drink. "Another, Coach?"

Chapter 17

The Candidate's Wife

Nancy went negative. She won her seat by a wide margin, more than five points. The race was much closer than the final score, as Nancy trailed her opponent most of the campaign. Then Stevie flipped a switch, and Nancy shifted her message from women's rights and social programs to her opponent's bedroom habits. She wove both stories together, the sordid affair a shining example of a wife suffering under the thumb of a bad man. Slime Guy coined the sound byte and Nancy spewed forth: "If he cheats at home …how can we trust him in office?" The inference was strong: "We don't elect cheaters, do we?"

The voters knew how to answer that challenge. It did not matter the story was a lie. It was okay to send a liar to Washington but not a cheater. Everyone lies; at least a little and this was a little lie, maybe not even a lie at all. It was really a matter of perspective.

A ref would throw the yellow flag, but Nancy rationalized it some-how. When the darkness came, with her back against a wall and her seat exposed, she weighed the pros and cons and made her decision. I imagined her and Stevie sitting at a bar, hopefully not my bar and my stool, but some other bar. Stevie would say, "Nancy, it's time to make a move. You're down four with a few weeks to go. I've got the goods on this guy. We can win this thing." Then Stevie would threaten to leave. He's that kind of guy, the kind that runs when things get tough, that lies when it's more convenient than working for it, that doesn't care about earning it, only winning it.

Nancy would sit there staring at her drink, listening to the voices in her head, Stevie on the left, live and in person and me on the right a faint voice from a past quickly becoming distant. My voice would whisper something like, "It's not worth it, Nance. Don't give your soul away to Stevie." Then Stevie would slam his fist on the bar and threaten again to quit. He would not be a loser, would not chalk up an L on his resume, not when they had the goods on the opponent, not when a W was within grasp.

******

After some back and forth, Nancy would ask Stevie for a moment to think and have a pretend conversation with me:

"*QB, what should I do? I need you to tell me what to do.*" *And then silence. Even if there in person I would not tell her what to do and she knew that. We did not give away points on the court we always played to win. That was the only way to help each other be better. We expected each other to set the example for others to follow. We expected each other to be strong no matter what.*

"*QB, where are you when I need you most?*"

My voice would say, "I'm right here Nance. I've always been here with you wherever you go. I'm your best friend, the person you trust."

"Please give me some sign."

"You know what to do. You don't need a sign from me. Stay strong friend, stay strong."

"Bob, I'm going to lose."

Crap. That's not good. Come on Nance, I'm your QB. I'm right here.

"If I lose ... I ... I won't know what to do."

"It's ok. There's a lot more to life than politics."

Nancy gave me a frustrated glare, which was a bit difficult since this conversation was in her head. Nancy finished her drink. She looked resolved, hardened.

"Nance, don't do it."

"Don't do what?"

"Don't go to the dark side, stay with me."

"We were never given a chance, QB."

"Huh?"

"It's the life I chose, and it doesn't matter, the rules have changed. I must change with them. I have to adapt and call a new set of plays. Isn't that what you would do?"

I hated it when she used my own analogies against me. I was losing her. My friend was slipping away. I could feel her hand moving slowly out of mine, no matter how tight I held on.

"You're better than that. You're better than them."

"You mean I'm better than Stevie. Why can't you just be honest about it?"

"Sure, you're better than Stevie, but you already know that. He's the poster child of a corrupt industry."

"So now you're saying I'm corrupt?"

"No, I'm not saying that."

"Then what are you saying?"

I'm … I'm just saying … that … I'll miss you."

"Why will you miss me? I'll still show for our meet-ups. I know they don't happen very often, but I'll be there."

"I'm afraid you'll change and that we won't … we won't be able to talk to each other like we do now."

"That's not fair. I have a decision to make, and you should respect that no matter which path I choose."

I hesitated for a moment but knew down deep that I had to say it. There was no way out now; we had always been straight with each other, and sometimes the truth is damn painful.

"I … won't respect it Nancy."

Crap! I called her Nancy and I don't know why. I meant to say Nance but it came out Nancy as if I was angry with her or disappointed in her or…didn't…respect…her.

"Bob, we should meet soon. Let's have lunch after the campaign."

Let's have lunch? That's when I knew my friend stopped listening to my voice inside her head.

******

The media picked up the hand-off from Stevie and ran with the ball down the field. Nancy's opponent watched from a prone position, a blind-sided block had taken him to the ground. The affair happened two decades earlier when he had separated from his wife. They reunited six months later and put the past behind them, or so they thought. But they did not count on someone like

Stevie. He dug and dug and dug some more until he found her. The other woman had moved out of state but held a grudge, a willing accomplice to Slime Guy's tale. He coached her well and she lit a fuse that engulfed Nancy's opponent. My friend changed jerseys and now played for a different kind of team.

The truth was relegated to the back pages deemed uninteresting by editors who cared more about selling stories than righting a wrong. It was tough to beat headlines of a candidate's wife scorned, all part of the plan executed beautifully by the campaign manager. He held the baton and the various players acted in a coordinated fashion as Nancy sang a new tune.

The candidate's wife did her best to turn the voting tide. She opened her home, offered interviews and wrote an op-ed piece. She even begged and pleaded as her husband watched and prayed. No one cared. The entertainment value of the affair outweighed the reality of a roller coaster marriage. The only story that mattered was the other woman. Who was she? Why was she? Was she younger, prettier? Was she better in bed? It was better TV to throw some mud and see it stick in the wrong places than hear another yarn about a marriage with problems. That reality was an everyday experience for the voting public, a rerun they could watch at home.

The uninformed voters pulled their election booth levers and stuck it to Nancy's opponent just like he had done to his poor wife. She got unneeded sympathy, the voters got some revenge and Nancy kept her seat for another term. Her opponent did not promise a third bout, he slunk away from politics a beaten man. Stevie had sleighed another and put a new notch on his resume. It was a W with some bloodstain, the best kind. Slime Guy had bragging rights, as everyone knew who won the game. His dirty tricks earned high praise inside the circle and he enjoyed the head nods, fist bumps and free drinks. All were given in respect as the campaign manager established his place among those that mattered.

Nancy called a few weeks after the campaign. It had been a long while, and I was excited to hear from my old friend. She sent me a brief message suggesting a meeting sometime soon at our usual place. I stared at the invitation for a few moments and knew what I had to do. The crumpled note went high in the air toward the target, but fell short. I trudged ten steps to pick it up and dunked it into the can.

Chapter 18

Dynamic Duo

Nancy rode into the millennium with wind at her back. As a senior member of Congress who knew how to throw a punch and sling some mud, she easily renewed her seat, time and again. It was expected. It was politics. It was also the new Nancy. As the Ws piled up, Stevie climbed alongside the brand he helped make. In the circle Nancy needed no last name, it was discarded, unnecessary luggage for those on the inside.

No longer relegated to campaigns, Slime Guy practiced his craft on a new field. If dirty tricks and lies could help win elections why not apply those same tactics where it mattered most, ruling the kingdom in our nation's capitol. Stevie promoted himself to brand manager carefully and methodically crafting the image. Nancy stood for things: important things as Stevie defined the message, wrote the copy, created the ads and determined the placement. The marketing mavens in corporate America had a new colleague as Stevie developed and executed an end-to-end marketing plan that easily surpassed objectives every quarter.

The old measures were tossed aside. Passing laws had proven too difficult as Congress split far to the right and left with too few stalwarts in the middle to keep the peace, broker the deal, make the compromise. The grease that kept D.C. humming was in short supply and no one seemed to care. New objectives were needed so the nation's leaders could earn their pats on the back from a good day's work. Stevie came to the rescue with a proposal deemed brilliant by the leadership and quickly adopted by the party. The brilliance was in the simplicity of the new measurements. Rather than counting new laws passed that helped the folks, Stevie proposed the complete opposite. They would count opponent takedowns. If the Dems could not score points with new laws then, by damned, neither would the GOP. Stevie shifted the party from offense to defense, the kind that blitzed on every play. What mattered was stopping those vultures across the aisle. The policy leaders of the day accepted Stevie's proposal with a gleam in their eye. Finally, there would be a metric that would align with their preferred behavior. They could be in campaign mode all the time. They could attack the enemy at will, delay votes on important issues, lobby for an issue in the press then vote against it at roll call. Every action they took could be justified in light of the political angle. Ideology would guide them, protect them, and most importantly of all, help them keep their seats. The policy leaders would still rule and their lives would be full again.

The plan worked. In hindsight many would say it worked too well. The Dems easily shifted into attack mode and mounted Republican scalps in the halls of Congress for all to see. They were proud of the trophies that covered the nation's Capitol. Best of all, voters across the country could see the scalps and watch or hear them again and again as YouTube, Facebook and other social media platforms emerged and captured the short attention spans of the nation. Video clips and radio interviews had become the new scalps of the twenty-first century, less barbaric than olden times perhaps, but viciously taken nonetheless. The GOP got aced a few times then regrouped quickly and upped their defensive game by hiring guns of their own. Many felt the GOP was more ruthless than the Dems as they played catch-up. Sadly, there were few winners, except of course the campaign managers who raked it in as the money flowed and the airwaves got crowded on cable TV and talk radio.

The Capitol looked ever inward as the country collapsed under the weight of recession. Unemployment grew and wages shrunk as the nation slowly clawed back from the financial collapse. While the middle class and poor looked for work, scrounged for food or stood in line for their handouts, pols played the blame game as Washington got richer and the folks got poorer. Eight of the twelve wealthiest zip codes surrounded the Capitol as pols on both sides slammed each other and claimed victory. The political action committees placed big bets, often on both sides of a divided house, and the money grew too large for anyone to count. The folks watched and waited as the scalps mounted and the budget battle grounded the government to a halt. Visitors were even turned away from White House tours as the pols dined on prime rib after a hard day's work.

The worst example of the political infighting was seen on the Senate floor. Once the pride of the world as a forum for public debate and discourse, the Senate tumbled to depths never seen or imagined. Thomas Jefferson's Canon of Conduct had been discarded with the day's trash. The founding father realized every topic would be difficult and emotional, so his manual instructed Senators to not call one another by name, but rather the distinguished Senator from the state of X or Y and to address one another through the chairman and not directly. Few can recollect hearing the word 'distinguished' in the once respected chamber of the U.S. Senate.

Over the next decade, Nancy rose high in the ranks and attained the status she sought on the leadership team. As the number two Democrat in Congress, she helped set the table, prioritize the important issues of the day and most importantly of all, she appeared on Sunday morning TV. She was a takedown queen with more scalps on her belt than most. Once in a while I would watch my friend while I poured maple syrup on some cakes. Her quips were sharp, her retorts had some sting; she was always prepared and never surprised. Stevie built the image and Nancy paid it off whenever and wherever she appeared.

Nancy won a lot of battles on Sundays and on one morning in particular, she seemed pleased when the cameras zoomed in on her icy glare after another victory. I wondered if Daddy had finally given approval to his successful daughter. I wondered if Peter ever called. I paused the TV and looked closely at Nancy's face but could not see deep into her eyes. "Are you happy, Nance?" I said aloud then feared the answer, although none was given. Nancy held onto the camera lens until it cut away.

Every two years, Stevie shifted his marketing guns and aimed at the voters back home. He easily filled the pipeline with ample leads for Nancy to close at the polls. Stevie segmented his voting targets into groups, each with a unique message and an offer. His analytics team bought the best tools to gain insights from massive data collected on each segment. They knew what mattered; what to say; how to say it; where to say it, and most of all, what to promise. That's what filled the pipeline: the promise, the gift, what the corporate mavens called, "the offer." Everyone got something: young women were promised birth control; illegal immigrants were given a country; unemployed were extended benefits; the poor were given free health care; African Americans were promised equal rights—again.

It never mattered the promises were often empty and seldom delivered. Even worse, it did not matter; the promises did little to improve lives. The marketing plan was focused on other measures, those that made a real difference. The marketing plan tallied votes. It was the measure that counted most and meant everything. It's where the massive amounts of monies tossed into campaign chests were spent.

Get Out the Vote, Rock the Vote, do anything, but just get the damn vote is what mattered. It's how pols retained their seat and returned to D.C. as champion of the people for another two-year term. After each election Stevie shifted the marketing plan back to important things, like taking down the enemy: the Republicans.

They were a very good team. They were a D.C. dynamic duo. In corporate camps they were known as Chief Marketing Officer and head sales executive. In DC they were simply known as Nancy and Stevie. Or was it Stevie and Nancy? *Did it matter?* I wondered.

Chapter 19

King Maker

Nancy was an insider of the D.C. circle, highly sought by the media, political action committees, other politicians and anyone who mattered. She spent all her time with important people and seldom traveled home. She had little time for the folks, the voters who put her in office year in and out. Nancy quietly sold her house in Illinois and began calling D.C. home. She had climbed her hill and could now look down on others making the trek up the mountain. The view was better than she had hoped.

As the next election neared, Nancy got the call that would upend her life (although she did not realize it at the time). Stevie had been pulled up to the big leagues. He moved to the national scene, a larger playing field with an enormous budget, full staff, field personnel and the best tool of all: the teleprompter. Stevie had achieved his dream. He would be the one...the one and only, the campaign manager who fed the teleprompter that fed the man.

Nancy could hardly say no to Stevie. She knew there was no choice and none was given. Stevie delivered the news by phone and kept the call short. There was no time for a face to face, not for Stevie. He had bigger things to do, more important people to see and be seen with. Stevie hitched a ride on his cloud nine and left Nancy at the curb. The next day Stevie changed his cell phone number. He went unlisted as the big boys often do.

Nancy's re-election campaign got off the ground late and slow. Her speeches lacked some punch; her quips lost their sting and she sounded flat and off key. The puppet was lifeless without its master and it showed. It wasn't a close race, an eight-point stunner. Nancy lost to a newcomer who never held office. The leadership lost an insider, someone on the rise; someone with promise; someone they counted on. They grieved for a day or two then found another to take her place and moved on as they always do. Nancy packed her things and quietly left town, promising she would be back one day. No one heard her vow. The unspoken resolution would be her motivation, a constant reminder until she returned to her rightful place. She called a realtor to rent her house for two years.

Meanwhile, Stevie chalked up another W and elevated his personal status another peg or two. He tossed more mud, slung more lies and parlayed the dirty tricks he had perfected to win the big game. He joined the Sunday TV crowd and made the loop one morning, hitting three shows in the same day. Stevie was hot and he knew it. Everyone knew it. Nancy knew it. She called to extend congratulations to her former partner, her CMO, only to hear the recorded voice indicating she had been disconnected.

Stevie was a D.C. rock star, a campaign manager who got the votes for his man. He drew a crowd at the pub, in the office, on the street, wherever he went. His arm tired from high fives and his fist was sore from too many bumps. He put up with it, tolerated the pain and figured it came with the territory. He was an Oval Office regular with a reserved seat on the couch. Everyone knew which seat Stevie preferred and it remained open until he showed. It was a long climb to the top rung and now he could look down, finally bend his neck the other direction and view the world beneath. It was a damn fine view and he intended to enjoy it for a long while.

After her term expired, Nancy purchased a one-way ticket to an unfamiliar place. The rental outside the city lacked the excitement, the noise and the vibrancy of Washington. Oh how she would miss the parties, the social flow of the most powerful people in the world and all their hangers on. Her work life and social life had mixed over the years, shaken, stirred and blended into a 7x24 elixir that never turned off. She had trouble sleeping at night. The quiet of her new home did not give any peace. She awoke early the first morn out of habit and readied herself for the busy day ahead. There was no staff to greet her, no schedule of appointments, no mail to read and no calls to return. Boxes filled with memories of a life lost surrounded her. Barren walls dared her to make an impression. She searched for relief, but could not find the coffee pot.

At 9:00 a.m. a bored and frustrated ex-congresswoman sank to the floor. The tears that had been pent up for months began to flow. She would not cry in the Capitol. She was too hardened on the outside and the inside to allow that kind of scene. No one would see her cry, witness the shame or see her humiliation. She held up in public, shook their cold damp hands, smiled at the false grins and took note of those who did not call. But back in her home state, the realization hit hard. Nancy was not just alone, not just unemployed; her situation was much worse than that: Nancy did not have a plan and there was nobody to help her put one together.

Chapter 20

Father O'Malley

An ex-staffer made the call. The message said Nancy might be at the pub on Friday night. I laughed at first but soon realized the pain she must be in. My old friend needed someone and she picked me. After all these years, she reached back in time and asked for help in her own indiscreet manner. It was not hard to decipher the message, the plea she screamed or the hurt I knew she felt. It was as if the message had been written in blood. "QB darling, let's get together. Let *us* get back together. Please."

I stared at the message and knew what to do. It did not take long to pick a path. I called my assistant. Alice cleared the calendar and put the message in my pocket. A friend was in trouble, and I would be there to help pick up the pieces.

I walked into the bar and looked to my left at the empty booth where I thought she would be. I was not early or late, although I was surprised she was not already there. I heard a sound to my right, turned toward my usual place and saw my stool. It was open and invited me over. That's when I saw her sitting at the bar, saving my favorite seat. My mind repeated a phrase not used in a very long time. Memory muscle had taken over, and I had to admit to myself it felt kinda good to hear it once again. *Atta girl, Nance, atta girl.*

I stood in the middle of the bar, stuck in place, unable to move and stared at my friend. She must have gone shopping that day. She wore tight blue jeans, some high stepping boots, a red belt and a white shirt. My eyes looked up then looked down and all around. *Damn, she still looks good.*

After a few moments she saw me and smiled from ear to ear. It was the genuine smile and she flipped her hair back with a hand. She showed all the moves of the girl I used to know. It was Nance. Finally, after all these years, my friend had returned. Somehow she found her way back to me. We both took a cautious first step, keeping our eyes locked on each other as we quickened the pace. Three steps followed and we embraced in a long overdue hug.

"QB, it's you," Nancy whispered in my ear.

"It's good to see you, Nance," I whispered back. We allowed some separation after five seconds and I continued, "Good to see all of you."

I got my reward; another genuine smile and we grabbed our stools. "Red, white and blue never looked so good, not in this bar."

Nancy laughed, which was my intent. "It's a rebellious move."

"Nancy the rebel, now I do like the sound of that."

The silence lingered, both of us unsure how to proceed. We were out of practice; a couple of rusted buckets sitting idle on bar stools. It wasn't uncomfortable; it felt good to be near my friend again, but we both paused. My brain sent a message and I remembered we were in a bar and knew what to do. The drinks arrived and we quenched some thirst.

"Booth or stool?"

Nancy eyed me closely. "Let's start with the stools then switch positions for the second round." She giggled.

All tease all the time, I reminded myself. It felt good to laugh and see Nancy happy. I guessed it had been a while for her. I wanted to ask, *What's next for you, Nance?* But I knew that had to wait. She'd tell me when she was ready.

"What's a single girl do around here for fun, QB?"

"Well, I wouldn't know much about that."

"Hmmm."

"Some of them buy me drinks."

"Is that right?"

"Yep, all the ones named Nancy do."

We got another round and shifted to the booth, a setting she preferred. We needed to get some things on the table and Nancy had to make the first move. "I'm going to need a story tonight, a darn good story."

I did my best to give her the *you gotta earn it* look. Nancy stared at her glass and moved some ice around, working up the nerve to come clean. She pounded the cubes and one rimmed out of the glass onto the floor. The girl was storing up a lot inside and it would soon come out. I sat as relaxed as I could with my warmest smile, but on the inside I was a wreck. I was wound up tight and held some air, hoping she would let the steam blow. *Come on, Nance, make a move! Put something out there, anything at all, just get the darn ball rolling so we can work it out and get you back to a good place.*

She looked up. "I know. I gotta earn it first."

I nodded.

"I went negative."

The confession began. I wondered how an Irish priest would act in this moment? I had a cold beer in hand, a friend speaking some truth and I listened more than talked. *So far so good*, I thought.

"I took a good man down by playing dirty and from then on it's been a different kind of game. The sad reality of it all… is I'm good at it. I was at my best in attack mode, going after the enemy, making them look bad instead of fighting for issues I care about."

I nodded again.

"I stopped working for the voters and did everything for the damn party."

Don't say anything, not yet, I reminded myself. My silence allowed her to continue.

"Keeping my seat was more important than…being…than being…a good person." A tear ran down Nancy's cheek. "I didn't know I could be that politician, the one who would do whatever it takes." A tear ran down the other cheek.

The Irish priest in me signaled the waitress and ordered two shots of whiskey. *Good move my son*, someone said inside my head. *What?*

The drinks arrived and I held mine in the air until Nancy joined me. "We all missed you. I missed you." I downed my shot. Nance followed and two gulps later we had empties on the table.

"You're beating yourself up pretty hard."

She wiped the tears away. "It feels good to get it out."

"Just one question."

Nancy looked up, her red cheeks and puffy eyes never looked sweeter or more innocent.

"Did you go to the dark side on your own, or did someone encourage you in that direction? Maybe even pushed you?"

"It's not much of a confession if I point fingers and lay the blame elsewhere. The final decisions were all mine."

"Well said."

We sipped on our drinks and let the music roll over us as we took in some air and tried to breath normal. Confessions were hard work.

Nancy had come clean and blamed only herself. It was a show of strength, the kind of person she and I expected her to be. But it wasn't truthful, not 100%. It wasn't even close. I hesitated for a few minutes trying to get the words right. "There's just one thing."

"Only one?"

"Yes, only one thing. We both know you were influenced, and I bet heavily influenced to protect your seat, to remain in Congress, to keep all that power."

Nancy sat erect, her antenna in the air.

"My bet is you are only half to blame, the other half is your campaign manager. You didn't call the shots, create the falsehoods and come up with the dirty tricks. Someone else did all of that. You allowed it to happen, but none of that was your idea, none of it."

"It doesn't do me any good to blame Stevie."

"Don't blame him...watch out for him, beware of him, avoid the bastard. That's the only way to protect yourself the next time around."

"The next time?"

"What else are you going to do?"

Nancy grinned. She knew, I knew, we both knew she would run again. *Would she need Stevie? Would she want Stevie? Would Stevie stoop to Nancy's level and help?*

"You always knew me better than anyone."

"I did and I still might. But …

Nancy placed her hand over mine. "I got the message. Thanks for caring after all this time."

All I could do was nod. Her confession had been a good one and she had earned a story.

"How about that story?"

"Ah, a story for the young lass. First we must deal with the penance."

"The penance?"

"Yes, the penance, it usually follows a confession."

Nancy steeled herself and signaled for my serve.

"That will be three Hail Mary's, two Our Fathers, and… and…another round of drinks."

Nancy smiled. "Let's make it two rounds. We'll need it for story time."

The ball was in my court, and I readied myself to deliver a story. That's when it hit and I realized my mistake, but it was too late. The penance was wrong, or rather incomplete. I meant to include something about not going negative again, a promise of some kind to not repeat the same mistake or be damned for all eternity. In other words, *Don't listen or even associate with Slime Guy or anyone like him!* I was not very good at the Irish Priest role after all and needed to up my game.

"Ok, story time 'tis. His name is Father O'Malley, an Irish Priest from back in th' day. He was known for his jokes, many of them off color. Let's see if I can think of one…I got it.

"Two Irishmen were digging a ditch directly across from a brothel. Suddenly, they saw a rabbi walk up to the front door, glance around and duck inside, 'Ah, will you look at that?' One ditch digger said. 'What's our world comin' to when men of th' cloth are visitin' such places?'

"A short time later, a Protestant minister walked up to the door and quietly slipped inside. 'Do you believe that?' The workman exclaimed. 'Why, 'tis no wonder th' young people today are so confused, what with the example clergymen set for them.' After an hour went by, the men watched as a Catholic priest quickly entered the whorehouse. 'Ah, what a pity,' the digger said, leaning on his shovel. 'One of th' poor lasses must be ill.'"

Nancy gave me the back of her hand across my cheek; the slap was deserved, and then she let out the laugh she'd tried to hold in. *Silly girl.*

"Father O'Malley married Amy and me."

That perked Nancy up. "I didn't know Amy was Catholic."

"She's not. We had a minister and a priest. I wanted Father O'Malley there, although it would not be a Catholic service. It was a fortunate move. The morning of our wedding the minister received notice. He had been demoted and transferred to another city. He fell apart and was unable to lead the ceremony. Father O'Malley stepped in and saved the day…but he did not take over. He pulled the minister along with him and they performed the service together."

"We need more priests like your Father O'Malley."

"Yes, we surely do. He was also the coach of our eighth grade basketball team."

"Ah, a priest with many talents."

"And many lessons for those who listened." I raised my eyebrows to accentuate my meaning. "We had a kid on the team named Tommy. He was a natural athlete, best player on the team, but always in some kind of trouble. Father O'Malley had clear rules and Tommy broke them all; most more than once. He lied about being late to practice. He punched kids on the opposing team and he punched kids on our team. He loved to fight. He stole things from lockers and lunch boxes. He even stole from the church when he could. Let's just say, "Tommy did not resist temptation…" to put it in Father O'Malley's words.

Nancy started to talk…but caught herself before a word got out.

"He was also my best friend."

"Hmmm."

"When Tommy got caught, Father booted him off the team. A day or two would go by and Tommy would be back at practice. He was always allowed back on the team. This went on most of the season. The games Tommy played we won, the games he couldn't play we usually lost."

"Is that why the Father let Tommy back on the team? So you could win games?"

I laughed. "Nah, Father didn't care much about our win-loss record. Sure he wanted to win, we all did. We were a scrappy bunch, low on talent, but high on hustle and teamwork. Passing the ball to the open man and playing tough D were our calling cards. Except for Tommy. He was built different, all talent and no work ethic. He could shoot and score at will, all over the court."

Nancy shrugged her shoulders as most people do when I tell a Tommy story.

"Father O'Malley cared most about teaching us lessons we would remember all our lives. One day, I went to see him. I wanted Tommy on the team, we all did…but I was confused. Why did Father keep allowing Tommy to return? It seemed to me Father was condoning bad behavior rather than dealing with it."

Nancy nodded.

"Our conversation went something like this:

"'Father, why do you keep taking Tommy back? I…I don't understand.'

"'You want to know why I treat Tommy differently. Is that your real question, lad?'

"I nodded my head, unable to say it out loud.

"'Ah my son, 'tis a fair question a very fair question, Bobby.' He called me Bobby. 'I'm not much of a basketball coach. I think ye know that. I'm a teacher, and I'm in the forgiveness business. Some people, like your pal Tommy, need more forgiving than others. What that means lad is Tommy has more growing up to do than most. He's unlike you, Bobby. Tommy knows how to break the rules not just bend 'em. Now, if we didn't forgive Tommy and take him back on the team where would he be?'

"I hesitated, not knowing if Father wanted me to answer. He waited so I took a leap. 'Tommy…he'd probably be in jail.'

"Father smiled. He always had a warm, welcoming smile. 'That's right, laddie, our Tommy could be spending his days in a cell. Would that do him or our team any good?'

"I shook my head sideways but was still a bit confused.

"'My son, every time Tommy does a bad thing, he gets punished. When he atones for his bad deeds, we forgive him and welcome him back.'

"I nodded again.

"Father placed his hand on my shoulder, and I knew the punch line was finally coming. 'Imagine my son, what Tommy could do when he finally sees the light. When he understands right from wrong. When he stops running with a bad crowd.'

"I was speechless, but my body language gave me away. How did Father know? I wondered.

"'Yes, laddie, I know some bad people easily influence Tommy. It's not all his fault. It's one of the reasons he needs our help. Imagine the impact Tommy can have on everyone around him when he learns the right way to behave. Every time he atones for being bad and rejoins our team, we rub the edge off. We need to be patient, laddie. He'll come around, Tommy's worth the effort.'"

I looked at my friend in front of me. She stared back and didn't move. After a long five seconds she signaled the waitress. "Two more shots, please." We remained silent until the waitress returned. Nancy raised her glass and I met her. "To atonement." She downed the shot in one gulp this time, and I repeated her steps.

"Welcome back, friend," I said.

Nancy excused herself and I sat on my stool and stewed. I had omitted one part of my conversation with Father O'Malley and did not share it with Nancy. I remember to this day, keeping it to myself, thinking it went too far. In hindsight—maybe...I didn't go far enough to help her:

'I understand, Father. Tommy needs more help.'

'Yes my son, he surely does.'

I rose to take my leave and headed for the door. With my hand on the knob I turned around and asked: 'What if Tommy never learns the lesson Father? What if he doesn't change?'

'Bobby, sometimes that can happen and try as hard as we might; we can't reach everyone. We all make our own path in life, eventually.'

I inhaled that reality. 'Do you think Tommy will choose the right path?'

Father O'Malley looked at me and took measure. He must have decided I was ready for the truth. 'I don't know son, not for certain. I pray for him everyday.'

I continued to hesitate, not ready to leave. Father O'Malley knew I needed more. *'Bobby, if Tommy can't turn around and be a better man..., then we'll both visit him in jail. We'll forgive him there, but he'll be playing for a different team.'*

'Ok Father. I understand now.'"

Nancy returned and spun me around in my seat. She was feeling good, relieved and back with the human race. "You ready, QB?"

"I was born ready."

"Your serve."

"Huh?"

"That's right. I bought two round of drinks and you only told one story. You're one short."

"One short? Hmm, can you handle another story?"

"What's a girl have to do?"

I searched the memory banks but no story was found. Instead I heard Father O'Malley speak inside my head. *Keep ye focus, son. Don't let the girl move on until she has truly learned the lesson.*

"Tick. Tock." *Said Nancy.*

Now she's applying pressure. Damn, I taught this girl too well. Or was that natural instinct? Heck it didn't matter. I continued:

"Father O'Malley was a good story teller. He had three rules for us to follow. First, we had to listen when he told a yarn, no talking and no napping. Eyes open and the mind at attention was how he put it. The second rule was to take to heart the moral in each story. He asked us to wear it home and never forget."

I paused to take a sip, knowing Nancy would not appreciate rule three. "The third rule was one story a day, never two in a row."

"Hmmm, and why is that?"

"He wanted to be sure we learned each lesson."

Nancy stayed silent for a few as I downed my drink and

steeled myself for her retort. *Come on Nance; take it like a man. Reach deep inside and commit yourself to the lesson.* I always cheered for my friend inside my head, today it felt more like a prayer.

Nancy found her genuine smile and showed it to me. "Atonement it is." She signaled the barkeep as I reached for my wallet. "This one's mine, QB."

Atta girl, Nance, atta girl.

Chapter 21

Doctor Roy

Snap out of it my son. Father O'Malley brought me back to present day, and I tucked memories of Nancy back into deep storage. She kept entering my mind, taking me away from the debate back to a distant place. I could not shake her loose. I wondered if she was thinking about me. *Concentrate,* I pleaded; *concentrate!*

The game was definitely on now and the noise in the arena went up a few decibels. The fans, I mean audience, wanted some blood and they were about to get it. In the heat of the moment I had gotten a bit excited when I took off my jacket and rolled up my sleeves. Soon after, my nose felt a tingle. I used my hand to make a quick wipe and noticed a smear of blood on my finger. Without thinking about it my eyes went right to my wife and she saw the red too. I expected some reaction from Amy, an '*oh my gosh*' moment, but she remained calm and gave me strength by staring through my eyes into my soul. Then she mouthed two words that told me everything: '*It's OK.*'

I took out a handkerchief and cleaned a few drops and saw Ames give me a slow up and down head nod. She knew. Somehow Amy knew. She told me the nosebleed would be okay and so would our lives; that we could get through anything, no matter the risk, no matter what the doc says. We were that strong, together. She told me all of that with only two words and they weren't even said aloud.

I am one lucky dude, I said to myself.

Taylor grabbed Amy's arm since she also saw the blood. Ames held tightly onto Taylor's hand and gave me strength again by mouthing the same two words: '*It's okay.*'

Luckily, the nosebleed was easily solved, and I tucked the handkerchief back in my pocket but kept it close by in case it would be needed again. Then I thought of my last check up with Doctor Roy:

*****

"Doc, I'm feeling good, a million bucks good."

Doc Roy smiled, more like a grin really, at least the corners of his mouth moved a bit; no small feat with the doc. His disposition matched the sterile office and dark furniture. It was all business all the time with Doc.

"Bob, the tests confirmed our suspicions, I'm afraid it's still bad news."

He tried to say more but I did not want to drown in negativity and did not want to hear any of the details. I had heard them before. My right hand reached out instinctively to hold onto Amy.

After grabbing some air my hand returned and I felt hollow inside. It was a mistake to see Doc alone. I wanted to close down and let Amy take up the fight. She was the stronger of us and would know what to do.

Doc looked at his watch.

Come on Bob you've been knocked down before; get one leg up, then the other and...get...back...in...the...game! "Doc, let's not go through the same discussion we had last time. I'd rather get on with building a game plan to beat this thing. How do we do that?"

Doc did a two second count.

Uh oh that's not good, I thought.

"You don't beat this thing; it beats you."

I sat up straight to show Doc I was strong, I was ready, and would beat this disease no matter what it took. Once my posture was rigid I said, "I don't care how long the odds might be, we need to create a plan, some kind of plan so I know how to behave. I'm not giving up, not ceding an inch. I will fight this thing until the day I can't fight anymore."

The silence hung in the air between us. Doc had done this many times before with a lot of patients. He was used to giving bad news, patting the patient on the back, maybe holding their hand, but eventually seeing them on their way with as much kindness as he could.

What a crappy job, I thought. I braced myself and signaled to him with all my might: *Not this time Doc; I'm not going away. I'm not walking to the door until we have a plan. Come on Doc, don't give up on me, not yet. I got way too much going on in my life to start my final lap. Not yet Doc, not yet.* My insides clutched with all my might as I willed Doc to say something, say anything, so long as it was a step in some kind of plan.

Doc was an expert at the patient-doctor game and allowed ten full seconds of sheer agony to flitter away into the air as my insides struggled to keep the clutch on. "Okay, Bob," Doc said.

Take a breath, I told myself. *It's all right to breathe once again. Inhale, exhale, inhale, and then exhale again.* Doc had said okay. Usually okay meant he agreed. *He's on my side; he's going to help build a game plan. Way to go Doc, way to go! Now tell me more, I need more and I need it now, right now Doc. Lay the game plan on me, let's go!*

"The odds are indeed long, as you already know. We will build a plan, as you say, and do our best to fight it."

All right, Doc. That's perfect…just about perfect, I said to myself. *You could have been a bit more positive, maybe showed some enthusiasm perhaps moved those corners of your mouth just a tad. But I'll take it, I can work with that and you almost sounded like there was a chance. I know that's not your strong suit, what with all the bad news you deliver. But not today huh, Doc? You said okay and you said plan. You actually said the word plan.* I smiled at Doc Roy, nodded my head and said, "Thank you."

We both breathed in and let out a sigh. We were two old soldiers who both wondered how difficult the fight would be. *Could we build an effective plan? Could we beat this thing? It doesn't matter*, I reminded myself, *not now. The only thing that matters is we're going to build a plan. We can ask the harder questions later.*

"How much time? How long do I have?" Inside I was screaming, *Give me the numbers, Doc, I gotta know!*

Doc Roy hesitated. He didn't want to answer, but also knew I was not leaving until he did. He ticked off only five seconds this time.

That's it, Doc. You're getting the hang of it. You cut out a full five seconds this time, that's very good, Doc.

"In cases like yours, it can be two years or it can be eight, even ten years. We usually see around five to six years as the norm."

I gulped. It was not intentional, just a reflex taking over my body. "Five or six years, huh?" *Stop that,* I said to myself, *don't go negative, gotta remain positive or we'll lose the Doc.*

"We can do a lot in six years, Doc. We can do a lot." I was sitting forward in my chair now like an eager student in a classroom, soaking in knowledge. There was one more piece of data I needed. I simply had to have the odds. *Okay Doc, here we go, another fastball question. Bunt it back to me, Doc.* "Doc, what are the odds I beat this thing? What are the odds I make it longer than six years? Longer than 10 years?"

Doc was uncomfortable; he did not like putting numbers on the table. I gave him my best stare down so it was perfectly clear I was not leaving until the number was laid down.

"Twenty percent, maybe twenty-five."

I gulped again. "Twenty percent, huh? Well you know the old adage; the world is 80-20 so we got that going for us. I've had worse odds before, Doc, much worse. We can win with twenty. We can definitely win with twenty."

Doc remained still; he missed his chance to lay the hammer down, that moment had passed and he knew I was starting to deal with reality no matter how much I pretended not to. "Bob, think about getting your estate in good order, just to be prepared. It will be a step in our plan, okay?"

Gulp. Gulp. *Crap. Come on Do,c don't go negative on me, not after we just agreed to build a plan. We're in this together now, Doc. You and me and we will beat this thing. We're going to create a kick butt game plan and shut this sucker down. Just wait until Amy gets involved, Doc. You ain't seen nothing yet. Ames is my secret weapon, always has been and always will be. I'll hold off unleashing Amy until we need her, Doc. But, get ready, cause she's coming and I have yet to see anything, and I mean anything, that can hold her down.*

"Sure Doc, I'll get that done. Now let's work out the rest of the plan."

Doc feigned his agreement. He was not very good at remaining positive; he sunk back to the depths again and I needed to pull him back up. I stuck out my hand for a firm handshake and grabbed hold of his right forearm with my left hand. I could not think of anything brilliant to say before he hustled me out of the office. So I just said, "Thank you."

*****

That was three days ago, right before the big debate.

Chapter 22

Carla

Nancy went back to the infamous war on women. When in doubt, throw a hot coal in your opponent's lap and force him to react. "Why should a woman make less than a man? Ann Richards may have said it best: Ginger Rogers did everything Fred Astaire did on the dance floor, except backwards and in high heels."

The audience laughed and enjoyed the overused line, but my opponent delivered it well, and I even grinned myself. And then she went in for the kill and made it her own.

"Perhaps a woman should make more than a man. Pay for performance advocates would certainly agree Ginger did a lot more than Fred! Who do you believe made more money?" Now she had the audience in the palm of her hands, at least the female portion, which was way more than half the arena.

The moderator let the audience roar well after the clock time had expired. He looked over one shoulder and then the next, welcoming the thundering applause and giving my opponent every advantage he could. It wasn't hard at all to tell which way his ballot vote would be cast. But I was okay with that. My only requirement was that he be fair during the debate. I decided to step in.

"Time."

The moderator yanked his body around and faced the stage, back in the position he should have been in all along.

"Time, Mr. Jones. Shall we move on?"

My opponent was unsure how to react. She wanted to soak up more applause. She glared at the moderator and pleaded for a few more ticks, just a couple seconds longer. The TV cameras were rolling after all.

"Mr. Newton, I am running this debate, not you."

"By all means. Glad to have you back in charge."

It was never a good idea to challenge the referee, but he had it coming and I was tired of his bias. *Might as well get in a good jab while I could*, I thought.

"Ok Mr. Newton, you have 90 seconds to respond. The clock is ticking."

There he goes again. I know the clock is ticking. I most assuredly know how much time remains on the clock. Ok, forget about the clock, I told myself. *Relax. Breathe. Launch.*

I inhaled deep, thought about Carla and wondered if I should tell the audience her story. Maybe, just maybe, the voters would warm up to a candidate who spun a good yarn rather than lob grenades across the stage. It wasn't just any story; it was a true story about real people and real events.

Where do I begin to tell Carla's story? There were a lot of chapters to select from. *Might as well use the first*, I decided. "Football is a man's game. It's where young boys learn about life from dedicated, stern men. Coaches teach and players gain knowledge and insight about character, discipline and teamwork, among many other important lessons. It's an environment to help young boys create a path in life to something meaningful after their playing days are over. It's a game where boys become men and only males are allowed in the club."

I paused to look at the moderator and his priceless snicker, wondering how far off the mark I would let this go. Or so I thought.

"Then one day Carla busted into my office and demanded an interview. I was head coach at the U and wanted to hire someone to manage our communications with the media and Carla wanted the job. She was all fired up and said I was a sexist if I did not give her a chance. Carla stood there in my office hands on hips, sixty-five inches tall; all of it toned muscle, and waited for my reply. Her face wore a determined look; her eyes met mine and she did not blink, not even once. I'll never forget my assistant Alice looking on and nodding her head in agreement—with Carla. Usually Alice blocked for me. She was my gatekeeper and never cowered, no matter how large some of those intruders might be. Most men feared Alice while I did my best to meet her on the same level. In Carla's case I am fairly certain Alice helped kick the door open. The gatekeeper let Carla through the door and her stare made it very clear I was to sit my butt down and have a chat.

"So I took the easy way out, sat down in my chair and agreed to an interview. What the heck? I thought, Carla would surely back off when she learns part of the job requires some locker room time."

The audience laughed, a good sign.

"I was naïve. Carla did not care one bit about locker room time, saying she had seen it all before and besides, most of the time the sights were not that impressive."

A few of the blue hairs opened their mouths and pulled some breath in deep then covered their smiles with their hands so no one could see or hear the giggle.

I continued the story. "She had a way about her that warmed you up with charm, then slow boiled you with her wit, and finished you off with her smarts. The girl had the goods and for some reason wanted to use them as part of the football team. That evening at home around the dinner table with Amy and Taylor, I talked about Carla busting down my door with Alice by her side. I portrayed the episode as humorous, just another day at the office. That was a mistake, a tactical error on my part and I paid dearly for it. Amy and Taylor had other thoughts, as you might imagine, and made sure I knew where they stood.

"'Bob if you interview Carla then you better be prepared to offer her a job...if she is the better man, Amy opined.'

"'Of course, of course, I'll be totally fair about it,' I said. The better man, uh oh, I wondered where this conversation was going.

"Taylor set her fork down and eyed me carefully. 'Pops, do you mean it when you tell me I can do anything I want in life?'

"'I most certainly do. You have no limits. You can dream big dreams and go after them,' I said.

"Something was not right, I felt like a fish and Taylor just hooked me. I tasted the steel in my mouth and knew she would reel me into the boat next. Damn, I hate the taste of steel.

"'Pops, do you think Carla's dad said the same thing to his daughter?'

"The steel fishhook yanked me toward the boat. 'Huh, what do you mean, Tay?' I asked. My tongue moved around my mouth looking for the steel hook.

"'Well, maybe working on a football team is Carla's dream. And maybe her father encouraged her like you do me.' Taylor picked up her knife, possibly to emphasize a point. She was signaling her next move after reeling me in. A sharp knife to the gut was in my future.

"'And maybe, Carla's dad is telling her to…just go for it….' Taylor paused to let that sink in, a trick she had learned from me. 'Like you always tell me. Isn't that right, Pops?'

"The knife moved slowly up and down and my eyes moved with it. 'What's right, Tay?' I spit out.

"'Wouldn't you agree that Carla should go after this job on the football team if that's her dream?' Taylor gently tapped the knife on her plate. The sharp edges had my full attention. She had me out of the water now, flapping around on the boat. I feared the next step in her game plan. 'Well sure honey, if that's her real dream?'

"'Why don't you ask her?'

"'Ask her what?'

"'If working for you on the football team is her dream job? Then you can get those prelims out of the way, focus on the interview and see if Mom's right.'

"I shook my head to clear some cobwebs. 'See if Mom's right about what?'

"Taylor angled her head and gave me the *you idiot* look. 'Pops, you need to find out if Carla is the better man. That's the only thing that matters, right?'

"Now I was in the frying pan over the open fire. Dinner was

being cooked and I had been fileted. I had seen the whole thing coming, but I was being cooked anyway.

"Without thinking about it I said, 'Uh, right. That's right Taylor, you should chase your dream.' I shook my head again as Taylor kept her eyes locked on mine. 'And Carla should be allowed to chase hers too,' I confessed.

"Amy and Taylor went back to their meal. They slowly peeled back thin layers of meat from their entrees with a sharp knife, looked at each other and smiled. It was Wednesday and we always had fish on Wednesdays.

"I met with Carla the next day. One of us showed up to play some ball and the other, well let's just say Carla was ready for the interview and nailed it. I was fairly certain Alice was listening through the door. She had a broad, *I told you so*, grin when we were done. Carla aced the exam and scored higher than the eight other candidates, all men. She was Taylor times two in the sly wit department with a bit of Amy and Alice mixed in for sheer delight, or terror if you were on her bad side.

"I took a week to complete the interviews, tally the results and make my decision. That night at dinner Taylor asked for a status. 'Well Pops, is Carla the better man?'

"Even though she was hitting me in the gut, the kid knew how to light up the room, and her father, with her eyes and smile. 'Carla? The better man?' I wondered aloud.

"'Come on Bob, give it up, she waited a week to ask,' said Amy.

"I didn't have much of a play here. The only card available was to let some tension into the room by allowing the silence to hang in the air as long as possible. I took a big bite and chewed and chewed some more. Ames and Taylor watched my every bite, knowing I was out of delaying tactics and needed to come clean after the swallow. I went to the napkin instead and wiped my mouth to add two more seconds of pain. And then it was over. 'Carla was indeed the better man. She nailed the interview with me and with Big Willy. Her resume sparkles, she has the experience and top notch recommendations.'

"Ames' eyebrow shot in the air and she asked, 'You got Tom involved?'

"Ames never called Tom Willy or Big Willy. She liked the man too much and gave him respect even when it wasn't earned. It's a college thing I guess, once they became friends at school it stuck for life. Plus he was my boss, so she was polite, but that never stopped me.

"'Heck yeah, I got Tom, I mean Willy involved. It's a big job and it helps to have Willy in our corner. Plus, Alice suggested it.'

"'Good girl, Alice, she's got your back…again. Must be some office chit chat going on about hiring the best person for the job, huh?' Amy wondered.

"'You know Alice, she sniffs these things out and makes sure I get all the right people on the same page, even when I have no idea why they are all involved.

"Taylor pitched in, 'I think Alice wants some female companionship at the office.'

"Ames and I both turned to face Taylor, our mouths both open and ready to speak, but nothing came out from either parent. She was probably right.

"'Are you giving Carla the job tomorrow pops?'

"'It will be offered tomorrow. There will be one happy lady named Carla tomorrow and a bunch of guys wondering what's going on at the U.'

"Taylor beamed. I put my serious dad look on and reached out to hold my daughter's hand. 'Tay, I want you to know that you helped open my eyes a bit. You threw my own words back at me to find out if I truly followed what I preached and that was so helpful. I might have allowed a bias to prevent me from considering a female for the role.'

"Ames and Taylor perked up at the word female.

"'Er, I mean, I nearly lost out on hiring the better man.'

"We all had a good laugh and once again I was proud of my kid. That was one bias I would quietly allow.

"I've told you this long story about Carla getting hired, but I haven't told you much about her. I guess the best way to sum up Carla is to tell you an example of her doing the job without worrying about taking credit."

The moderator was about to signal time had expired. Before he could make the call I interjected, "I'll use some of the time I ceded earlier."

He frowned as expected but acquiesced. I suspected he wanted to hear more about Carla, most everyone usually did.

"One of her main responsibilities was to help the coaches and players with the press, ensuring we did not fumble our quotes. If I could get away with it, we'd be ensconced in a bubble all year and only come out for games but that was against the rules. We had to give the media something, and we needed an enforcer to get us through the landmines. Bottom line, the role required brains and balls, and some creativity to boot."

A few people in the audience cringed at my slang use of the word balls. I am fairly certain some of the cringers had blue hair, but some didn't. *If they cant take a joke…*

"I asked Carla to work with Vince, our star QB to get him media trained and ready for the press. They had come after him with half facts and shady innuendos, which resulted in a suspension at the end of his junior season. It was a long three months before he was cleared of all charges. We held a press conference to begin the next season and Vince took full advantage of Carla's instincts and creativity. As I began the press conference in a crowded room full of local and national reporters eager to witness Vince's return from shame, V (as we called him) took over and called an audible. V reached out and grabbed the microphones that were pointed at Willy, V and me and turned them around to face the vultures instead. Then he got us rolling with a question: 'I believe the press has something to say before we begin.'

"It was perhaps the most enjoyable moment I ever had with a room full of media, as none of them knew what to do. They had been thrown a curve and whiffed at the ball. Finally, a brave soul stood and took the fall on behalf of the press. It took him a long while to work up to a full apology and it took three attempts before Vince was satisfied.

"It was all part of Carla's training and Vince executed the play with precision. That was Carla. She protected our blind side and then some. Carla never took credit for Vince's performance with the press, and I did not know she called the play until the end of the season at our annual awards banquet.

"I was on stage as host of the evening. I told them, 'Before we begin the formal awards part of our program, the coaches and I got together and created a new category. Our first award of the night is titled: The Media Mogul Award and is given to the student-athlete who best handles the press. And the award this year goes to V for his daring audible last spring, which resulted in the first ever press apology.'

"The audience roared with laughter and yelled out 'V, V, V.' Vince glided up to the podium and accepted the award. He knew we were poking fun at his expense, but he also knew we treasured that moment and how he handled it.

"Vince also laughed and gave me a quick hug as he accepted the award. I had not intended for him to speak, but Vince had other plans in mind. 'Thanks Coach. I humbly accept this award and am honored to be the Media Mogul of the year.'

"More whoops from the crowd.

"'Coach, there's just one thing. I may have executed the play that day, but I did not call the play. I did not design the play. I did not think we could run that kind of play with the media.'

"The audience had quieted as Vince turned a humorous moment into something more serious. 'Coach, the person who deserves this award, who earned this award, who taught me how to behave as a leader in front of the press, the person who gave everything of herself so others could look good is Carla. She is the one who deserves the Media Mogul Award.'

"On that note, all the players leapt out of their chairs to give a standing ovation. Five of the guys nearest Carla's table walked over and hoisted her onto their shoulders and paraded her up onto the stage. Vince extended his hand and gently helped her to the ground as if she were a princess. Carla and V embraced, a long and meaningful hug. Vince handed her the award and bowed low then showed Carla to the microphone.

"Carla looked out at the audience and the ovation that had not died down. She wiped a tear with the back of her hand and asked for calm. Finally, the room quieted and necks leaned forward to hear from the true award winner. Carla looked downward and soaked up a few more seconds of the silence, treasuring the moment. Then she moved closer to the microphone, peered over the audience and said, 'Thank you.'

"Carla looked over at Vince who caught the signal and arrived to escort her away to a cheering crowd. I heard Carla's voice in my head as she exited stage left. *Why use a lot of words when only a few are needed in some moments. A lot of words can trip you up when a few seconds of silence and a well-chosen sentence can leave a lasting impression.*

"That was Carla. She taught a bunch of young players and a few aging coaches about dignity, about poise and how to effectively communicate a clear message. I hope I am following her lessons today."

I turned to face my opponent and said, "Nancy, in my experience, a woman is often the better man for the job." I looked over at Carla, my co-campaign manager, sitting next to Amy and Taylor and mouthed two words: 'thank you.'

The mostly female crowd cheered their approval. That was the only sound I needed to amplify my message.

Chapter 23

The Mayor

Nancy gave me another scowl, looked at the moderator and said, "Time." She was stealing a play from my playbook but did not know how to execute it well.

The moderator shrugged his shoulders and put out his hands palm side facing up. He was being smacked around by a teammate and was confused. The tag team duo was befuddled and it showed, much to my delight.

I shook my head and wondered to myself, *What happened to you Nancy? You were one of the good guys, why have you gone so bad?*

"Enough," the moderator mumbled under his breath just loud enough for me to hear. "Enough."

He realized his mistake, looked at me and just moved on. I stared back, all the while thinking, *The audience will cheer again, dude, get used to it.*

"Our next question goes to Congresswoman Smith. What or who inspired you to run for the United States Senate? You have two minutes."

We took a time out from the real debate so the candidates could get on their soapboxes. Nancy stood a bit taller and readied herself to deliver a speech. "Thank you for that question. I first got into politics…"

I stopped listening. There was nothing to learn and I was bored again. *What was I going to say next? How would I answer this softball question? Should I take the easy out and dish some gibberish that makes me sound like a distinguished Senator? Or, should I tell the truth? Can I tell the truth? Am I able to spit out the story without falling completely apart?*

"Candidate Newton, what or who inspired you to be a Senator?"

My hesitancy was becoming very apparent as the audience rustled around in their seats. Each tick of the clock pounded away in my head, trying to jar loose the memory banks where the story lay buried. I had only told this story once and that was to a room of five buddies from school that forced me to get it out. I cried a river that night and didn't care how it looked.

I thought about passing on the question and then I saw her. She rose from her seat and stood in the back of the room, tall and beautiful and strong. Janelle was one of the women in my life who I adored and respected as much as Mom and Amy. Janelle had anticipated this moment, this question, and knew her presence might help me through the challenge. It must have been so very difficult for her to relive the memory, to hear me tell the story of her only son.

I scanned the audience and saw them, looking at Janelle and

then back at me. I took a very deep breath and exhaled. *Okay,* I said to myself, *if Janelle can do this so can I.*

I stood erect with my shoulders back and said, "The Mayor is the reason; he was always the reason, my inspiration, and my friend. That's the nickname I called him, Mayor. His real name was Jerrod and he was the finest person I have ever known."

Amy saw Janelle, got up out of her seat and walked over to greet her. They embraced. They had known each other a long time and the emotions spilled from their hug to everyone around them. Amy took Janelle's hand and escorted her to the front row to an empty seat next to my family. Carla realized what was going on and had exited stage right, making way for Jerrod's mom.

I let out another large breath, gave one last look at Janelle and began to tell the story of Mayor Jerrod:

"Jerrod was a great athlete, a student scholar and a dreamer. He played quarterback on the high school team I coached and then for me at the U. Each day after practice, we would sit in the bleachers and talk. Sometimes we'd talk for hours, other times just a few minutes. You'd think our conversation was all about football, but it seldom was. We mostly talked about life and how we saw our futures unfold.

"When he died, near the end of his senior year, I gave him a nickname and called Jerrod the Mayor, partly because it was difficult for me to say his name, but mostly to remind myself about one of his dreams."

I looked at Janelle and said, "Jerrod called it the small town turn around play. His plan was brilliant, creative and bold. If nothing else in life, Jerrod was always bold. We worked on the small town turn around play every day for nearly four years as we soaked in the sun or sat in the rain on those bleacher seats. Jerrod's plan was to help a small beaten town become a great town again. Jerrod would provide the funds from his own money, from his endorsers in the NFL, and as many athlete buddies as he could persuade to make the investment. Jerrod would also provide the leadership. He would bring money and jobs to a town that needed it most. Then he would invest in homes, schools, roads and bridges. He would recruit shops, restaurants and businesses. Jerrod would put the town on his back because he could. He knew if people had jobs and money, then they would then have respect. And if they had self-respect, they would pitch in and the 'small town turn around play' would accelerate. People that used to ignore each other on the streets or worse, steal from each other, would say hello, shake hands and wish each other well.

"Jerrod would have been a fine mayor in that small town. He would have ridden on the fire truck during parades and toss candy to the kids, knowing it wasn't just the candy bringing smiles around town. Jerrod was someone who cared more about others than he cared for himself. He's the type of role model, the type of leader and the type of politician I aspire to be.

"Helping poor, down and out street kids get a leg up, motivated Jerrod. He saw them on the football team in high school and again in college. He knew his life had been privileged compared to his mates and he took it upon himself to do something about it, something real, something that made a difference. The small town turn around play was his plan, our plan, and now…it's my plan."

I paused to collect myself as not any of the 2,500 had moved. "Jerrod was…no, is my inspiration. He knew how to restore nobility to politics through his beliefs, through his behavior and through an unselfish approach to solving problems for others to benefit."

I looked at the audience from left to right and top to bottom.

"When is the last time, maybe the first time you thought of politicians as noble, unselfish?"

The 2,500 strong stared back.

"When is the last time you had trust in your congresswoman or senator to do the right thing? To do their job even if it meant losing the next election and ceding their power? The cornerstone of Jerrod's small town turn around play was just that. Restore nobility to those who govern and re-establish trust between the people and their elected representatives."

I was out on a ledge, my story told and needed some way to get back on safe ground. That's when Janelle rose out of her seat as if on cue and looked at me as she wiped the tears away. Then she blew me a kiss, walked slowly to the aisle and out of the arena. The audience had remained quiet during my short speech, yet each row stood as Janelle walked by. They clapped and cried with her, and for her, as I reflected on my most recent visit with Jerrod two days ago.

*****

"Hey buddy. How are you?"

The tombstone gave me it's customary stare, a stoic look that seldom changed.

"I know it's been a while, friend." I reached out and placed my hand on the corner of the stone. "No excuses pal, it's good to talk with you."

The stone felt cold and hard. Jerrod was making me earn it today so I upped my game. "You ready for some news buddy, some big news? It might give you a stir, you'll be so shocked."

The autumn wind whipped up a few leaves and threw them

against Jerrod's stone. They hit with a thud then fell to the ground. For an old QB, Jerrod had learned how to play some tough D.

"I entered the Senate race last fall and the big debate with Nancy is in a couple of days. Yeah, can you believe it, Nancy of all people? I'm running against an old fling that I should be running away from. The circles of our lives are indeed full of irony aren't they?"

The sun peeked out from behind the clouds and it seemed as if Jerrod teased me with a smile. It didn't last long as the clouds took back the sky. "You'll have to call me Candidate Bob now. What do you think of that huh? Bob Newton for U.S. Senate! How's that one grab ya?"

Jerrod took it in quietly. He had become an excellent poker player over the years. I could never tell if he had an ace in the hole. "Yeah I know. I skipped right over the mayor role we had planned. I wanted to run for governor, but that race was last year. The clock was ticking. I had to do something because the senate race was right around the corner. So, I took the leap."

There was more silence from my friend. I kicked at the ground, paced back and forth and thought back to one of our bleacher chats when Jerrod played college ball and I was the QB coach.

*****

Practice had just ended and we took our usual spots in the bleachers alongside the football field. A cute girl walked by and seemed to wiggle a tad more than normal. She stopped in front of us, looked up at Jerrod and said 'call me,' and then slinked off the field and joined two friends. The three of them giggled loudly and walked through the goal posts out of our sight. It was just another day for the QB; one more admirer showed him how to score.

Jerrod looked at me, shrugged his shoulders and didn't say a word. We both knew he was in for a beat down if he uttered a syllable, any sound at all would bring some wrath. Since he behaved I moved us along.

"Jerrod, there's something troubling me about the small town turn around play." Jerrod snapped out of a trance and replied, "What's that coach?"

"To put the plan in motion you have to go into politics. You have to become the Mayor."

"Uh huh, that's part of the game plan. But you know that, what's your real concern?"

"I just don't see you transitioning from being the hero on the gridiron to being the mayor of a small town. Politicians aren't very popular these days. They may have displaced used car salesman at the low end of the totem pole."

Jerrod just laughed and laughed some more. "Coach, that's the whole point. Who is the last politician you would name as a hero? You'd have to go back a few decades, maybe more. We need our politicians to be respected again to be seen as hero's and the only way to do that is get into politics for the right reasons."

"Huh. So, the small town turn around play is your vehicle to become a political hero? Is that the ultimate plan, Jerrod?"

"Coach, I want to be Mayor so I can make a difference in people's lives."

Jerrod let the silence surround us then grabbed his helmet, slapped me on the back and ran off the field. I sat there and watched his fluid strides move him gracefully down the field through the end zone and toward the locker room. The skies darkened and a few drops of rain fell as I remembered where I heard Jerrod's words before. *Jerrod and Nance, who would have thought the two of them, once had the same motivation?*

******

I had stopped pacing as the memory faded and the sun came out from behind the clouds and shined a light on Jerrod's name. "It should have been you, buddy. I'm just running the play we put together during those bleacher talks, the play you designed."

My feet started moving and I was pacing again. I needed to confess something to my friend, come clean with the other piece of news. I found some resolve and knelt on the ground.

"Ok, I'm going to give it my all. There's one thing you should know, and I meant to tell you before." The sun faded and the clouds brought the dark. *Figures, just as I was about to confess my innermost fear the skies let me know there could be some hell to pay.*

"Jerrod, I could be joining you before too long. The doc says about five, maybe six years is all I got left. That's one way to force term limits, huh? I'm not ready to see you yet, but I know you are keeping a bleacher seat warm for me. I'll be there soon enough and we can pick up where we left off."

The wind howled as I rose and gave one last nod to my best friend. "See you, buddy, see you soon."

Chapter 24

The Guv Part 1

There was another reason I was running for Senate and he called himself 'The Guv', not Governor and not his first and last name. He was precise when he said, "Just call me The Guv." He even emphasized the word THE to increase it's importance. I should have known right then he was all ego, all the time. The mirrors in the State Capitol worked overtime as The Guv took a peek on a regular basis.

I did not know 'The Guv' until Big Willy arranged a meet that I felt obligated to accept.

We were playing poker at Willy's. It was an off-season treat away from the football grind, which I had left behind. Our usual poker crew included Willy; Mike, a defense attorney and high school buddy; Tom, the special teams coach; and Tony, a former defensive end who played for me in high school and was now VP of Sports Operations. We had a few other players who rotated in and out. Tom and Tony worked for Willy, and I used to, although at the poker table none of that mattered. We hurled insults at each other as if we were still kids and attempted every trick to increase our pile of chips.

We usually played on the back porch, which was screened in and had a fan in the ceiling—important features for the cigar smoke that always joined our fun. The table was made of dark wood and green felt, the kind that grabbed hold of a chip thrown on the table and did not allow it to bounce very high. The table fit six people comfortably though we squeezed in seven or eight on occasion.

Willy shuffled some cards and called the first game, "Ante up, boys. We're playing seven card stud, low spade in the hole splits the pot." Willy did not raise his head from the deck of cards, though his eyebrows inched up to await the response he knew was coming.

"What kinda girlie game is that?" asked Mike. "Low spade splits, come on call a real poker game. A man's game."

Willy's head popped up. "Just watch me take all your money, big guy. Put your ante in or take your griping down the road." Willy tried to keep a straight face as he pressed Mike to toss a few chips in the center of the table.

"I'll take your money, Willy, no matter what kinda silly game you call," said Mike with a wink to the table.

The rest of us followed suit and tossed our chips into the fray. Entertainment hour had begun as Mike and Willy put on a show. I often wished the seats at the table had belts to strap me in for the bumpy ride ahead. I knew my cheeks would be hurting soon and looked forward to the pain. Willy finished his shuffle and set the cards on the table to his right. "Cut right and deal left, here we go gents."

I sat on Willy's right and played along just like we were back in high school. "Cut 'em thin to win," I chimed in and cut the cards.

Willy dealt two cards down and one card up to all the players, starting with Tom on his left and circling around the table. Mike had an ace of diamonds; I got a jack of hearts; Tom, an eight of clubs; Tony, a three of clubs; and Willy got a duck: the two of spades. We called twos ducks and I never remember the reason.

"Gawd darnit," said Willy.

The rest of us cracked up as Mike just sat there staring at Willy. Finally he spoke, "Is that the two of spades across the table? Damn shame it's not in the hole, Willy, damn shame."

"Ace bets," retorted Willy.

We were playing a friendly game—most would call it nickel and dime. A good-sized bet was a buck and a two-dollar raise got everyone's attention. Mike toyed with his pile of chips, threw out five blues and the room went quiet. It was a five-dollar bet to get the evening started.

Note to self: drink slower, a lot slower.

Tony sat to Mike's left and the bet was to him. "That'll be five big ones to you, Tony," said Willy. Tony looked at his hole cards, set them down then looked again. After some hesitation he threw them to the side. "I'm out," said Tony.

No one made fun at Tony's quick exit; we knew he'd stick around and up his courage after Mike had his fun on the first hand. The bet was to me and I looked at Mike then Willy. My hole cards remained face down, no need to check 'em again. "Count me in boys, let's see where this one goes."

Mike often threw down big bets to flush out players with weak constitutions, although he usually waited for a few hands. No need to run from Mike, though caution was needed when he was tossing poker chips. Willy was a bluffer with a face built for the game. His lawyering skills worked over time in his basement as his contorted expressions never gave others a clue. Willy kicked in quickly even with the duck on top. Now it was to Tom Norman, a terror on the gridiron who took more risk with special teams play than any coach in the conference. Tom folded; the five-dollar bet was too steep for his liking. He had more fun watching than playing.

Willy dealt more cards, a king of the same suit to Mike, a second jack to me and a seven to himself. "Pair of jacks bets," said Willy.

Time to size up the competition, I thought. *Looks like Mike was playing for best hand and Willy must have had a low spade in the hole.* My plan was straightforward, beat 'em both and take the whole pot. I had the five of spades down and a pair on the board. *Note to self: don't get greedy.*

"Jacks bet a buck," I said.

Willy threw in his blue chip and Mike did the same. There was no blood on the second round of betting. Willy dealt three more cards, a ten of the same suit to Mike, a five of hearts to me and another duck to himself.

"Jacks still bets," said Willy.

This was getting interesting. Mike was filling out a royal straight, Willy had a low pair on top and I paired up my five for two pair, a good hand with a potential low spade in the hole.

"Jacks are in for two dollars," I said.

Willy picked up his hole cards, rested his chin on a hand and grimaced then tossed two chips onto the growing pile. "I'm in."

Mike played it cool and did not show any emotion as he said, "Raise," and tossed in four chips.

"Another two bucks to you Coach," said Willy. I looked at Mike, then back at Willy, then to Mike again. "I'm not going any- where." I tossed two blue chips into the pot and Willy did the same.

Another round of cards and more bets and another raise from Mike followed. No one got any help from the cards this time and I breathed a bit easier when I saw the four of spades dealt to Mike. The two and four of spades were face up on the table so my five in the hole was looking darn good. I could still lose to the three, but the odds were in my favor.

"Last cards coming face down," said Willy.

"Wait a minute there, Willy. What do you mean face down? Last card is up, just like all the other times we played this girlie game," said Mike.

Willy wore a Cheshire smile and quickly adapted. "Just making sure you're paying attention gents, good to see you boys came to play."

Interesting, I thought to myself, *very interesting.* Mike caught Willy's playful act a bit too quickly. The roles in this game were actually reversed from my initial view. *Mike must have had a low spade and Willy was going for the high hand.* I laughed to myself that Mike was betting to win half the girlie pot with low spade down. He was playing to win some chips, girlie game be damned.

Willy dealt the final round of cards face up, a queen of dia- monds to Mike, another five to me, and another duck to himself. Mike had a pair of tens up top with a potential flush and straight flush; I had two pair showing and Willy had three ducks on top. I had a damn fine hand, full house fives over jacks. Willy looked a close second with the three ducks and I wondered if Mike had the straight flush and low spade in the hole. There were only a few cards that could beat me: the three of spades in the hole to split the pot, the last duck for Willy to give him four of a kind, and the jack of diamonds to Mike.

What are the odds, I wondered? My pile of chips had been severely depleted, same for Mike and Willy. One or two of us would be digging into their wallet after the first hand, an embarrassing way to start a full night of poker. The money lost at our poker game hardly mattered, especially to me. I pulled down a few million per year my last five years of coaching and would feel no pain, but that wasn't the point. I wanted to win just as much as the next guy, the money never mattered. Beating your buddy and having a good laugh at his expense made for a great evening and I intended to have one.

"Trips ducks, hmmm looks like it's my bet boys," said Willy. The three of us eyed each other closely, looking right, then left, then right again. We played a serious game when we could hold back the grins.

Willy took one last look at his hole cards then pushed the rest of his chips into the pot. "All in."

Crap, he has four ducks, I thought.

Now it was to Mike. He never picked up his hole cards, didn't need the confidence boost. "All in," said Mike as he shoved the rest of his chips into the large pile.

Crap, he's got the three of spades, I thought. The son of a gun had laughed at the girlie game, but he was going to walk away with half the pot just because he got the three of spades in the hole. *Damn.* I played with the few remaining chips left in my stack. Of course I was going to stay in the game, I came this far and would not bow out, but it would be torture, pure torture to lose half the pot to Willy and his four ducks and half the pot to Mike and his girlie three of spades. *Damn.*

It was time to make my move, "That makes three of us, I call."

We all paused for a moment, clutching onto our cards each of us enjoying the tension in the room. Although Tom and Tony exited early, their eyes were glued to the table and the remaining players. After a few moments of silence had passed, Willy flipped over his hole cards first. They were both red and no ducks. He was betting the three ducks on top were good enough to win and hoping no one had a spade underneath. Mike was next. He filled in a straight, but it wasn't flush so it did not matter. However, he did have a low spade. It was the six, not the three as I feared.

Holy crap! It took a moment to register then a wide smile hit my face and I couldn't hold it back. "Full house with the five of spades. Read 'em and weep boys, read 'em and weep." I stretched out both arms and reeled in a big pile of chips.

Mike and Willy both reached for their wallets like it was a gunfight at the OK Corral. They did not hesitate one bit and Mike said, "Where's the beer."

Willy chimed in, "Over in the corner in the cooler, grab two." We all did a double take, as Willy didn't drink a lot of beer. After losing that first hand I would have drunk two beers, one right after the other. As usual when I won, it was more about luck and balls than skill. I had built a large pile of chips that would last the rest of the evening no matter how unlucky I might get. *Damn fine game*, I thought, *damn fine game*. The entertainment would be free for me the rest of the night.

It was Tom's turn to deal, and he shuffled the cards then placed them on the table next to Willy for a cut. "Baseball is the name of the game, nines and threes are wild and fours get another card."

"Oh my god, does anyone wanna play some real poker around here?" Mike wailed. "Are you kidding me, baseball with wild cards and freebies for fours? It's gonna be a long evening."

We all cracked up. We managed through the baseball game, not my favorite either as Willy won a small pile of chips. Now it was Mike's deal and I listened carefully to hear the name of his game.

"Five card draw, let's play some poker," said Mike.

As Mike dealt some cards for a real man's game, Willy looked over at me. "Bob, can you take my place at a function next week. I'm double booked and the governor asked if you would be a good sub."

Willy seldom asked for favors. I had a lot of his money in my chip pile, so I said yes without asking any questions. I never made that mistake again, not when The Guv was involved. Besides, I was having way too much fun counting my stacks of chips. I did notice Mike raise an eyebrow when he heard Willy say governor and wondered what that meant. Mike was a connected guy in the city. What did he know?

It was risky to mix politics with our poker game, as the views around the table never came close to a consensus. Mike got the ball rolling. "How long will this governor be around? I put the over/under at 15 months until he takes the stroll."

The Governor Stroll had become an inside joke across the state, meaning the walk of shame to the pen. Mike didn't care one way or the other about this governor; he just liked placing a bet and agitating the boys around the table.

Willy chimed in, "This Guv is too smart, and he's not taking a stroll anytime soon. He's not going to improve our state's batting average, we're headed to 500."

Willy was referring to the four out of seven governors who had taken the stroll the past few decades. If the current governor kept his hand out of the cookie jar for the rest of his term, then we would be four out of eight. While a step backwards from our market-leading ratio, we would still lead the country by a wide margin. A 500 batting average still gave our state bragging rights and that's what mattered.

Mike blew some cigar smoke across the table at Willy. "Check the Guv's finger nails lately? He's got crumbs buried beneath his nails."

Tony did not get the innuendo. "Crumbs?" He asked.

Mike explained, "Cookie crumbs Tony, the Guv has been in the cookie jar a number of times."

"Yeah, but he's too smart to get caught," said Willy.

"And you want me to have dinner with this guy Willy?" I asked.

"Just calm down. It's a function for education and a good cause. The Guv is the host, that's all. Eat a good meal, support the event and have some fun," said Willy.

"And watch your wallet," Tom chirped in.

Well that's just terrific, I said to myself. *Wait until Ames finds out about The Guv and his crumbs.*

Chapter 25

The Guv Part Two

"Hi Coach, I'm Larry, Chief of Staff for The Guv."

"Good to meet you Larry." *The Guv? Seriously is that what he calls the governor? Sounds a bit strange, but what the heck, I've heard worse...a lot worse.*

"He's been looking forward to meeting you, Coach."

I nodded to Larry. I wasn't necessarily looking forward to meeting the governor and reaffirmed that feeling when Larry called him, The Guv. Politics wasn't my thing and I had no idea what I was doing at the State Capitol for a fancy dinner. *Oh yeah, the boss asked me to be his sub.*

"And this must be Amy," said Larry.

"Larry, please meet my wife, the better half, much better half."

Amy gave Larry a polite smile and swatted me in the butt when he let go of her hand and glanced over his shoulder at an assistant. She wasn't much for fake conversation and the better half introduction did not take much thought on my part. So the swat was well deserved, and I took it like a man. *Come on Ames; hit me again.* I grinned.

I swear that girl could read my mind as she glowered at me for a quick second then put on her best smile for Larry who turned back around to face us. The girl knew how to multitask. Lucky for me she never dated two guys at the same time back in college or high school—where we first met. *Heck, maybe she did and I just never knew. Crap.* I shook the thought out of my head and tried to recover.

"Larry, good of you to meet us before the dinner. We are both excited about the event tonight and appreciate the invitation from…The Guv."

I sold out and went with The Guv. I was trying to impress my wife and show her I could get with the program. She gave me a slight nod and warm smile, my reward that I gladly accepted. We had been married 30 years now, and I never stopped trying to impress her. She was well worth the effort.

Larry's assistant escorted us into The Guv's office that had a large desk with nothing on top and walls adorned with pictures… of The Guv of course. The Guv with Coach Ditka, The Guv with Bill Murray, The Guv with Ernie Banks, The Guv with Michael Jordan, and The Guv with Mayor Dailey, naturally. There was not a single square inch of space on the walls—The Guv had it covered—all of it. I looked back at the big desk again just to make sure there was indeed nothing there. *Do guys who have immaculate desks do any real work? Who spends more time in this office, the Guv or the maid?* I wondered.

Standing next to The Guv was a beautiful woman who must have been ten years younger, maybe fifteen. *Uh oh,* I thought, *Ames isn't going to like her, not one bit.* Trophy wives were not very high on her list and this one had first place all wrapped up.

Larry handled the intros. "Guv, I'd like to introduce Coach Bob and his wife Amy."

The Guv stood about six five and must have weighed 250, maybe 260. He removed an unlit cigar from his mouth, stuck out his paw and grinned from ear to ear. His suit was pressed, not a wrinkle showed; his white shirt stood at attention and his cuff links shined a light into my eyes. "Howdy there Coach, good to meet ya, damn good to meet ya."

I lost my hand in that paw for a few seconds as The Guv held on with a tight clasp. He was one of those who valued a firm shake and sent a message with each squeeze. *I'm bigger and badder than you and will crush your hand until you say uncle, little boy.*

I let the Guv have his fun for a brief moment then gave a firm tug of my own. We locked eyes, gave each other a respectful grin and pulled our hands away. I felt some cookie crumbs in my hand when we unhooked and looked at my palm to see the evidence that wasn't there. The poker game was still fresh in my mind and playing some tricks. I shook my hand to rid the imagined crumbs and The Guv smiled as if he had won a match. *Crap.*

Larry did not miss a beat and moved us forward; clearly he had seen this act before. "Guv, I'd like to introduce Amy, Coach's wife."

The Guv did not extend a paw this time; instead he did a half bow. *Smart man,* Amy would not put up with his crap and I'm guessing he knew it. The Guv took over from there and introduced his wife as Mrs. Guv. I went for a gentle shake and Amy stepped in and said, "Please call me Amy, pleasure to meet you." I roared with laughter inside my head as Amy avoided being called Mrs. Coach by anyone in the room. *Nice move, Ames, well done.*

We did the small talk routine for a bit until Larry ushered us out of the room and down the hall to the circular steps. The Guv stopped at two mirrors on the way, once to check his hair and the other time to straighten his tie. I scanned the walls leading down the staircase and did not see another mirror and thanked the lord for small favors.

As we walked, I started thinking about seating arrangements for the upcoming fete and began to sweat. One of us would be next to The Guv, trapped in his sights for an entire meal. The other would sit next to the shapely Mrs. Guv. It was no contest; I knew where I wanted to sit. Some sacrifice would be required to make it through the meal. That's what marriage is all about, sacrifice for your mate. "Thanks Ames, good of you to take on the Guv," I whispered softly.

Amy took my hand in hers and gave a squeeze. "Don't you dare strand me with mirror dude," she whispered back.

So much for the sacrifice plan, which in the end did not matter as The Guv sat between us. We were both hosed for the night. Amy had Mrs. Guv on her left while I had a Chicago Alderman on my right, a tall man named Gus. I was sitting between Guv and Gus for a formal, sit-down meal and had Big Willy to thank. He'd get my thanks all right, though I would keep his money, every cent.

Gus had been an Alderman, "just about forever," is how he described it. He grew up on the south side of the city in a tough neighborhood famous these days for drugs and murders. It was tough being number one at something and even tougher to retain that distinction, but Chicago held on as our nation's murder capital year in and out. Gus wore a black suit, black shirt and black tie with a silver clasp. I didn't look, but would have bet a million on the color of his shoes and socks. I saw a black hat on the table and put two and two together. He had a gentle shake and a warm smile, and we had a nice chat until it was time to be seated.

As soon as my butt hit the chair Gus went to work. "Coach, when will the NCAA start paying our players? It's time to pay these boys and spread the money around to the kids who play on your team and get you the big bucks."

Our players? Interesting way to phrase his question, I thought. "Well Gus, I've been a proponent of providing a stipend to scholarship players, both men and women, for a long time."

"Yeah coach, but nothing is happening and our boys are done being slaves to the NCAA masters."

Did he just say slaves? I looked at Gus and was not quite sure what to say. He took advantage of the gap and kept on plugging away.

"You work the system, Coach. You know what's going on. Every year you and your coaches come up to the city, to the south side schools and lay your big pitch on our boys. You promise them rewards, scholarships, playing time, dates with girls...and what happens? You keep getting yours and our boys get injured, drop out of school and too few get a real education."

I looked to my left and saw The Guv chatting up Amy and Mrs. Guv. *Should I interrupt them and save myself from Gus?* I debated the options in my head. *The Guv or Gus?* Now that was some choice. I looked left at Guv then right at Gus then left again. I could not pick a winner; the lesser evil was more like it. *The Guv or Gus?* I gave up and decided it was time to go to the men's room. I didn't have to go, but I had to go.

Just before I made my move, The Guv must have noticed my dilemma and shifted into our conversation as if he had been listening all along. "Gus are you being friendly to our Coach here?"

"I'm giving your boy an education about the real world."

"Now which world is that?" asked The Guv.

"The black and white world Guv, what other world is there? Coach here lives in his clean white house with his white picket fence and his pretty wife while our boys are paying for it. It's time to fix things, make 'em right and you know it."

"That's right Gus, I do know it, but you're not going to help matters by making it a racial thing now are you?"

"It's black and white, Guv. I call 'em as I see 'em and you know that too."

This conversation was going nowhere fast, so I shifted gears and moved us to safer ground—or so I thought. "Gus, how do you solve difficult issues like this one on the city council?"

That was the Guv's cue to shift back to Amy and Mrs. Guv. *Crap. Could this evening get any worse?* I actually missed having The Guv in this conversation. When I first met The Guv I didn't think I would ever miss him.

"Now that's a fine idea Coach, a fine idea. Your school and the other big schools in the state should give money to the city council and we'll take care of our boys. We know our boys and what they need. You and your school use them like cattle, then throw them into the grinder when you're done with 'em. Just give us the money and we'll spread it around where it's needed."

I thought to myself, *Gus, you're good at this game, twisting and shaping my words into your plan. So that's how politics are played in the big city, huh? Give you the money and let you decide who gets what. Yeah, I understand your motivation, Gus; I understand it all too well.*

"I do spend a lot of time recruiting kids from the city. There's a lot of talent there, most of it raw, immature and unaware of the opportunities in front of them. Opportunities that come from work, from earning it on the field, in the classroom and by changing behaviors learned on the street. Why do so many kids from the city grow up in an environment filled with bad influences?"

Gus glared at me. He smacked his lips, rolled his tongue around inside his mouth and smacked one last time before he replied, "What would a rich white dude know about our streets? You just skate across the surface and cherry pick our best boys so the man can get paid. And so we are not confused here, you da man. You and that Athletic Director are both the man and we're tired of you taking, always taking and never giving back."

Well this was going well, I thought. *What did Willy say, eat a good meal and have a fun evening? Did he really have a conflict or was he avoiding this hot seat he put me in? Damn Willy.* It did not matter if he was my boss, payback was coming—at least I hoped it would.

It was time to put Gus in his place. I dropped my napkin and reached down to pick it up so I could turn to face Gus and avoid the long reach of The Guv's ears that seemed to hear everything. "Does the black and white shtick work for you on the city council? Do you ever get tired of playing that race card or is that the only play you got going?

I locked on Gus and he locked back on me.

"You know Gus, there's two kinds of people I see in the city when I go into their living rooms and give them my recruiting pitch. There's one kind that expects something, a handout of some kind, some money on the side, some special treatment. I can see it in their faces, it's etched deep in their eyes and they wear the stink on their skin. Their shit eating grins give them away before we even begin our conversation. The other kinds of people are those who want to earn it, that don't expect freebies and would be insulted at shady deals. They might be struggling financially, might not have the best clothes or cars, but they have a clean house and their kids have good manners and show up to their classes. These parents are invested in their kids and they pass down morals and teach behaviors that matter."

I paused for a moment to see if any of this was sinking in, but Gus had a great poker face and I didn't have a clue what he was thinking.

"I see both kinds on your streets, in your neighborhoods, in your ward. So tell me, Gus, why are you so focused on getting money for the good kids, the ones that have a chance to make it? Why aren't you focused on the other kids who need your help? Why do you allow so many of them to get murdered each and every day on your streets?"

Gus was pissed. People did not speak to Alderman with that much truth, especially to the Alderman who had, "been there forever."

I wasn't done yet and went in for the zinger. "What's your plan, Gus? How will you stop the murders and drugs and turn around the city? Is your racial shtick making any impact on your streets? You've probably been playing that card, "just about forever," huh, Gus? How's that working out for you?"

Gus was fuming. His hands were clenched; his body rigid, and I half expected a punch to be thrown my way. *Come on, Gus; bring it.* I balled both hands into fists and readied my arms to block the first punch. The odds were low he would throw anything at me, but you just never knew. Fortunately, for both of us, he was interrupted at just the right moment. Gus was needed back home urgently. A double murder had occurred in his ward and a riot had broken out on his streets.

Chapter 26

The Guv Part Three

The empty chair offered much needed elbow room as dinner was served. I went into silent mode, began to eat and hoped conversation was done for the evening. I was one bite into my salad when the big paw slapped me on the back and I choked down some greens.

"Coach don't let Gus get to ya. He's a talented Alderman, knows all the tricks and probably invented half of them. The NCAA money is stuck in his craw and all he can see is white men getting rich on the backs of black boys. I know it's not that simple, but to Gus there's always a straight line."

I gave The Guv a head nod, went back to my meal and hoped he would do the same. *The salad's not half bad*, I thought, and wondered how Ames was doing with Mrs. Guv. I looked her way and she rolled her eyes. *Crap*. This meal might have been free but it was going to cost me.

The Guv slid his chair closer to mine and leaned forward.

I cringed, *So much for elbow space,* I thought to myself.

"There's not many like the two of us here in this large room."

The Guv waited for me to reply, to utter some kind of response to whatever the heck he meant with that comment. I did the best I could and said, "Huh?"

"Only a few people are meant to be rulers of the earth. You led the football team on the field and I take care of the rest of the state. Everyone else follows. They heed our call, sate our desires, and honor our wishes. It's our world Coach, everyone else is here for our pleasure."

My fork stopped in mid air, I thought about turning it into a weapon and ridding the earth of one of its rulers. *Tempting, very tempting.* Instead, I turned and looked at The Guv. He laughed, swatted me on the back with that paw again and said, "Gottcha!"

I faked a laugh and turned my fork back around. It was poised to jab The Guv and I reeled it back in, regretfully.

"Looks like you and Gus are going to be close friends. Good thing you aren't recruiting in his city any longer."

Guv wanted a laugh from me, but I wasn't in the mood. I went back to the salad and hoped the waiter was bringing entrees soon. The Guv was waiting for my reply so I gave him one. "How do you get anything done in this state when the city is such a financial drag?"

"I can see you feel my pain. It's not easy not with Gus and his cronies. They think they run the city and by extension the entire state."

I was letting The Guv off the hook too easily by allowing him to lay all the blame on the city. "Tell me something. How do you feel about being in last place? I read recently we now trail

California as the lowest rated state financially."

"Are you paying attention to the issues in our state?"

He was waiting for me again, that was his trick, *Just wait 'em out and let the other guy make the mistake.* "I'll answer your question when I get an answer to mine."

The Guv smiled. He may have not liked my parry but he did respect it. "It honks me off and every citizen in this state should be angry. Not about being in last place, that's bad enough. We should be mad that we have run this state into financial ruin over decades." He waited for my response.

"I'm paying a lot more attention to local and national politics than ever before. From the outside the system looks like a mess at the national and state levels. I won't even get started on the city up north. A lot of us are damn angry at the lack of action, the constant bickering, pols who prioritize politics over policy and only show up when its time to count the votes."

The Guv had a serious look. He leaned forward and asked, "Have you considered doing something about it?"

I looked at Guv and sized him up again. The man wore a determined look as if something important was happening at this very moment, here at our table between the two of us. It made me nervous, suspicious and surprisingly a bit excited. "I would like to do something but I don't know what would be effective. I usually get mad, toss the paper and drink a beer or two. That's the extent of my political activity these days."

The Guv laughed and edged even closer, removing the last two-inch gap between us. "Have you considered running for political office?"

I had no reply to that stunner, but I could feel my brain kicking into gear. Something was moving in my head that had not moved in a long time. Sure I played this game in my mind, usually after a few beers. The announcer would say, *Coach Bob, the next Illinois Governor,* and the crowd would roar. Then the announcer would introduce Amy the next first lady of Illinois and the crowd roared even louder as my wife smiled and waved.

The Guv brought me back to reality. "I asked Tom to send you to this dinner. I wanted to meet you and see how you would handle ole Gus."

"So Gus was some sort of test?"

"Yeah, Gus is always a test, mostly a test of my will these days. The party is looking for new blood. We need a strong candidate to run next year and a lot of us believe you can win. The people are fed up and want to follow someone who will tell the truth, build back some trust and get things done."

"I'm lost. What are we talking about?"

"Coach, the party wants you to run for the Senate."

There it was out in the open. The Guv just asked me to run for the Illinois Senate. *What would Jerrod think of that?* I returned serve and made sure Guv could hit another one back at me.

"I don't know if I can spend that much time in Springfield, but thanks for the thought."

The Guv did not waver. He kept the determined look and smacked the ball back on my side of the net, "Not Springfield."

"Huh, not Springfield?"

"No Coach. You would not be spending time in Springfield."

I whiffed at the ball and had no idea where this was going. Ok Guv, I'll state the obvious. "That seems a requirement for the job."

"You and Amy would be spending time in D.C., Washington D.C., our Nation's Capitol."

Holy crap, I thought and took a quick note to self: *Don't play poker with Guv or Gus. I don't know how to read these two politicians.*

Did he really say Washington D.C.? I did a quick check. My pulse was racing and trying to keep up with my heartbeat, which pounded against my chest. My head finally recovered and sent a signal. *Say something ... now!* "I appreciate the gesture, but I'm not a Democrat."

The Guv did not hesitate one bit; he was expecting this small issue. "You're not a Republican either. The party will take care of everything. Think about it, Coach; I'll be in touch."

The big paw patted me on the shoulder one last time and then he was gone. The Guv was smart when it came to politics and allowed me to eat the rest of my dinner in peace. He left the table on a high note to attend to more important matters. He delivered his main message for the night and went to find some better grub.

Ames slid over and kissed me on the cheek. "Did you make some new friends tonight, dear?"

Chapter 27

Poker Game

I was back at Willy's a few weeks after my evening with The Guv and Gus. I tried to stop saying that in my head, *The Guv and Gus.* It sounded like some bad Country & Western duo or an old TV show, black and white of course.

Kevin was in town so we were a table of six. After college, Kevin did well as a business executive and was currently with a private equity firm. Kevin brought an A game to political conversations. He crafted strong arguments backed by facts and he listened to the other side. He might not agree, but he always listened and then he probed and queried until his opponent cried uncle.

Willy shuffled the cards and we all settled in for a few hours away from the world. I enjoyed this escape from reality where men could make fools of themselves and each other and laugh about it. Willy's poker game had become my office. I didn't make much money but enjoyed the camaraderie. We checked our cell phones at the door to minimize interruptions. The only way to reach us was the old landline or in person if you dared. While we kept most of the world out of our game, politics seemed to be on everyone's mind these days. It intruded early and often in conversation, reflecting how people tended to vote in Chicago.

Willy completed his shuffle and set the cards down on his right. "The game's seven card stud, low heart splits the pot."

Mike heard his cue and said, "Come on man, let's play some real poker, not another girlie game."

We all laughed at the routine that never got old for any of us.

I cut the cards and said, "Cut 'em deep for a heap." I never knew what heap meant when it came to cards but we'd been saying it for so long, it was one of those natural things.

After the cut, Willy yelled, "Ante up boys. Let's play some poker." As Willy dealt the cards he asked me how dinner went with The Guv.

"Willy, I meant to thank you for that wonderful evening. I sat between the Guv and Gus and learned a lot about the men running our city and state."

Kevin joined in, "The Guv? He's taking the stroll soon, I give him less than a year."

Tom Norman pounced, "Not this Guv, he's not strolling anywhere. He just fixed the pensions and put the city unions in their place. It was a Republican move Kevin, you should give him a standing O."

Kevin glared at Tom and shook his head slowly left then right then left again and said, "Tom, they put a Band-Aid on a gun shot wound to the gut. We got a deep bleeder gushing out and we're dying. And all the Governor and the politicians could do is slap on a bandage that will do no good in the long run. Now they're giving high fives to each other as the cameras roll."

The lines were drawn and we knew the polar ends, Kevin on the right and Tom the left. Willy leaned right and Mike leaned left. The wild card was Tony, the only minority in our group. I felt fairly certain he straddled the line with me and knew we would find out soon enough. There's nothing like a poker game to draw out truths and emotions often kept bottled up. I had learned a lot about life from playing cards with my buddies and expected there would be more lessons taught and maybe some learned.

"Alright boys, keep your yapping going about politics and don't focus on those cards so I can take all your money," Willy said.

Nice try Willy, I thought. *Once Kevin and Tom get going there's no turning back, we might as well enjoy the show. They might need some encouragement. Now how can I stoke the flames?* I wondered.

"You know, gents, I think we should all pick up and move to Texas. There's a good thing going on down there and we're missing the party." *That should get things started*, I thought.

"Oh my god, Texas! Are you kidding me? Their schools are terrible, their prisons full and everyone is packing a gun. Not the life for me," said Tom Norman with a grin.

Tony surprised with a retort. "Well, that's where the jobs are going, companies are moving there, the weather is good and the taxes are low. And that state sure loves its football! It's not a bad idea."

"There's probably more hand guns in Chicago than all of Texas," said Mike.

"Good luck selling your house in Illinois unless you're willing to take a huge loss. That's a big check to write on your way down south," said Kevin.

I chirped in again, "Let's compare the important things, the things that really matter." Everyone looked up, paused for half a second then we all said at the same time: "Sports!"

Tom quickly said, "Da Bears." Heads nodded around the table as if Tom laid down a trump card, and I had to admit it was fine play. There are few fans more loyal than Bear fans. This first compare would not be easy for Texas but I dove in and tried.

"Texas has two pro football teams, and Dallas has that new stadium, nothing like it. The Cowboys have won four Super Bowls and the Texans are hard to beat.

The boys looked at me and all shook their heads.

"Alright, gotta give this one to Illinois. Next."

Tom threw another one down. "Da Bulls." Heads nodded in unison again and a few high fives were given, as memories of Jordan and six titles were still strong. Da Bulls were a gritty team, more hustle than talent and drew a strong following.

But Texas could compete, I thought, *and compete well.* "Texas has three pro teams boys. Dallas won it all a couple years back and San Antonio is a repeat champion, perhaps the best managed team in all sports. Throw in Houston and I think Texas wins this one."

The boys were silent and their heads did not move. They had to give this one to Texas, although it hurt. "Texas takes this one," I concluded.

We all looked at Tom. "Da Cubs."

Smart man, I thought, he was saving the best for last. "You're kidding, right? Da Losers is more like it. I love Wrigley Field, but I only see a couple games each year. You can do that when you visit Chicago in the summer while living in Texas the rest of the year. The Rangers and Astros have new stadiums and both are better than the Cubbies."

Tom was getting desperate. "Da Sox." All heads turned toward me. "Let's call this one a draw." The boys agreed and we looked at Tom to throw his last card down.

Tom beat the table like a drum. The roll grew louder and everyone else joined in with a two-finger tap. They knew what was coming. The ringer was about to be tossed. I braced myself for it. *Let's get this over quickly*, I prayed. Tom allowed a few more taps...then a few more...then he let loose with a loud roar. "Da Hawks!!!"

The boys joined in, the chorus roared again and again and again as everyone repeated in unison. "Da Hawks. Da Hawks. Da Hawks." Hockey was indeed the trump card in Chicago and across the state. People went to hockey games or went to the neighborhood bar to watch games with their pals. It was a communal thing, the game and this Blackhawk team drew you in and made you part of it.

"Alright," I finally said. "Da Hawks take it."

The boys all grinned as they took home a W for their state, but I wasn't ready to take the loss, not yet.

"What are you boys willing to pay to chalk up that W?" I asked.

"Huh?" A few of them said.

"When's the last time you looked at your paychecks? How much income tax are you shelling over to the state? It's 5% right? You do realize it's zero in Texas, don't you? I had the floor and pounded on. "You boys enjoy shoveling those driveways? Trudging to work through the snow and ice? You like that grey color that hangs around the city for months on end during winters?" The boys acted as if I were hitting below the belt but inside they knew the truth brought the pain. "Texas has the sun, the weather, the rivers and the ocean. All of that trumps Lake Michigan—so don't even go there."

It was time for a low blow. "You boys enjoy living in the murder capital of the country? The world? We're way ahead of New York, Detroit and even Saul Paulo." These guys didn't like the murder stats anymore than me and ceded the point. Now it was time to play my trump card. "You probably don't know the Texas State Government only meets every two years for 140 days. That's it, 140 days out of 730." I paused here for the obvious question.

"And that's a good thing?" Tom asked.

"Yes, it's a good thing, a very good thing."

"Why is that, Coach?" Tony asked.

"It limits the trouble the government can cause and forces them to focus and get stuff done in a short amount of time. The state has a budget surplus, low taxes, less regulation, jobs are plentiful, crime is low and people friendly."

The boys were quiet.

"And of course there's Austin. The State Capitol where live music is king, restaurants and bars plentiful, and tequila drinks and brew pubs all around. It's also a place where liberals mix with conservatives and somehow it all comes together and works."

"Yeah, but aren't all those jobs in Texas on some oil rig or in a burger chain?" Tom asked.

"Well I thought much the same until I read more. The state is very diversified with jobs in high tech, healthcare, energy and even manufacturing. Something is working in the Cowboy State, just not the pro football teams," I said.

Kevin smiled and said, "Texas is doing to California and the rest of the country what Michigan, Wisconsin and Indiana will do to Illinois."

"What's that Kevin?" I asked.

"They're going to slap us silly then take our lunch money. Just like the bully on the playground."

"How so?" I asked.

"Illinois raised tax rates on businesses and consumers to fund pension holes for unions, which causes negative job growth as firms leave the state. It's a death spiral for Illinois and a boon to other Midwest states."

Tony chimed in, "It's entertaining to watch the states compete with each other, stealing each other's businesses and jobs. They play with real fire."

"What a waste," said Tom Norman. The states should share best practices with each other, not go on raiding parties."

"Tom, why so afraid of competition? Kevin asked. "It makes everyone improve, except of course our state. We are now worse than California without any of their natural resources. Our ship is sinking but the rats are still here. Bob's new friend Gus is the Rat King."

Tom smiled. He had an ace up his sleeve, and it showed in his face. Not a good thing when playing poker. "Ok Tom, throw it out there. What you got?"

"Pizza!" Tom wailed.

"TexMex!" I yelled back.

We all laughed and the conversation lagged as Willy directed the betting. Mike raised, Tom Norman and Tony folded and our first game was underway as usual.

I decided to spur on the boys again, this time on a national level. "Okay gents, a new survey is out and our Prez is not faring well with the people. What's going on in D.C.?

"Someone has a lot of time on their hands, you reading the *Washington Post* again?" Mike asked with a grin.

Kevin jumped in to answer my question. "The Prez is unengaged. He has no idea how to govern and keeps using the same excuse, 'I didn't know,' to answer any question or crisis. They just keep piling up."

Tom Norman joined in. "You watching Bill O'Reilly again, Kevin? You have his talking points down pat."

"I just go where the facts tell me. O'Reilly isn't biased toward the Republicans no matter how much the mainstream press wants you to believe it."

"How about you, Tony? What do you think of the job our President is doing?" I asked.

The table went silent, as everyone wanted to know Tony's view. Being the only black man at our game gave him an edge and an audience.

"I was proud to vote for him back in 2008. I bought in to his message of change—all the way in. The man can sure give a speech and paint a vision. I give him props for running a terrific campaign."

I could tell there was more coming from Tony but was uncertain which direction he would be going. Tony took a sip of suds and said, "But not in 2012. The Campaigner in Chief is all talk and no action. The man has game no doubt, just not on the basketball court or the links or on Capitol Hill. His game is playing people and he's damn good at shading the truth to get what he wants."

"Shading the truth? Are you saying our President lies Tony?" Mike asked.

"They all lie, the Prez is just better at it than anyone else. He's had lots of practice," said Tony.

"So you voted for the other guy?" I asked.

"Nope. I wasn't comfortable with him either, he threw 47% of us away and that was just stupid. I don't like taking sides with stupid."

Tom Norman was crestfallen. His main ally at the table had soured on the President. "Come on, Tony, the Republicans keep stifling the President from getting anything done. Don't give up on the man yet."

Kevin replied, "Maybe it's high time the Prez took a stroll. That's our best practice in Illinois, Tom. We can show him how to take the long walk all the way to Joliet...with some style."

Everyone at the table had a good laugh except Tom Norman who went to get another cold beer or two.

"The President Stroll, now that would be entertaining. That's a ticker tape worth seeing," I said.

Mike opined, "The Prez wouldn't pound any rocks at the pen. He'd get the EPA to rule limestone is an endangered species."

The table laughed again, even Tom Norman this time around.

I needed to shift the dialog one level deeper, a tad more serious to get real learning from my friends. "The Guv mentioned the Senate race would be heating up soon. What would you boys do if you were a U.S. Senator?"

Willy eyed me carefully. *Did he know about the Guv's offer?* I asked myself. *He must know.* I shook my head sideways carefully and slowly so only Willy would see. He got the message and went back to his cards. *Phew.*

"I wouldn't move to D.C. That's where all the traps lay. I'd stay at home and work remotely and put in a new voting system over the internet. That way I can avoid all those politicians," said Kevin. A few of us chuckled at Kevin's idea, and then we realized he might be serious.

Willy chimed in for the first time. "Bob, I'd focus on tax reform, individual and corporate. It's time to close the loopholes, remove the complexity, and allow corporations to bring money home earned overseas without the additional U.S. tax. The accountants have had their fun for way too long. If we reform our tax model so it's more competitive with other major countries and less complex it should help revitalize growth here at home."

"Wait a minute there, Willy," said Tom. "You think it's fair that Apple worked a deal with Ireland to avoid paying their fair share tax?"

"The Irish have a sweetheart deal for a lot of U.S. firms that establish hubs on the isle, book orders for all of Europe and avoid taxes on the mainland. It's a bit of a game, but the same rates and rules apply to all," said Willy.

"So the big firms just keep their money in Europe. That's not good for U.S. citizens. Not good at all," said Tom.

Kevin saw an opening, "Large corporations won't bring money home to the U.S. because they will pay more taxes. If Ireland is 15 percent and the U.S. is 35% they would owe the difference, a full 20 points. We are the only country that taxes profits earned outside our borders. Our tax code is incenting U.S.-based firms to invest abroad instead of home."

Kevin has a very good point, I thought to myself. Willy dealt more cards to the four remaining players. "Pair of aces bets," he said to Mike. "Where Ireland gets in trouble is they allow companies to transfer revenue to Bermuda and avoid paying any taxes. That's the same thing as the Guv getting caught in the cookie jar."

Mike laughed and said, "Pair of aces bets two bucks." He tossed two blue chips into the pile as I looked at my hole cards, thumbed the two of hearts to make sure it was real and tossed two chips onto the growing pile, "I'm in."

Willy looked at me, then Mike's pair and tossed his cards. "Count me out of this one." *Damn, he must have seen me thumbing the low heart.*

Kevin had a pair of eights on top. "Raise a buck."

Mike remained calm and did not reveal a thing. He tossed another chip in the pile.

I put a blue chip on the table and saved my big raise for the next round. "Deal 'em."

I could see Tom swirling the tax reform topic around in his head. "Then tax reform should be an easy lay-up for Congress and the Prez. They're arguing about the 10% they don't agree on rather than fixing the 90 and tackling the 10 later."

Kevin nodded in agreement. "Sad but true, our Congress in action: sticking it to the U.S. tax payer."

If Kevin and Tom could agree on tax reform at our poker table why couldn't Congress get something done? I wondered.

Tom decided to move on. "I'd build and repair roads and bridges and establish an efficient, high speed cross country train system. Our infrastructure is falling apart and it's sad how much we lag parts of Europe and Asia with our aging transportation grid. Plus that would put people to work, which makes Kevin happy."

The ball had been tossed to Kevin. "Some infrastructure spending is warranted, I have no problem with that. The key thing I'd focus on is re-establishing trust between the people and government. I know that's a softball from someone like me, but the trust has been severed and it's killing our country."

Willy dealt the next round of cards, a ten to Mike, a three

of spades to me that did not matter, and a Jack to Kevin. "Aces bets," said Willy.

"Check," said Mike.

The bet was to me. I had nothing on top, a three, a nine and a queen all different suits. "Let's keep this game interesting, two bucks to see another card."

Everyone knew I had the low heart and was playing to split the pot. "He's got the duck," said Tony.

The bet was to Kevin. "Raise it two bucks." He kept his gaze on Mike.

Mike had a stone face, a look many players would kill to make their own. "Another two bucks, huh? Alright, I'm in."

"That's four big ones to you Bob," said Willy.

I tried to mirror Mike's stone look but my smile took over, as everyone knew half the pot was headed my way. "Everyone's raising, I might as well join 'em. Make it another two bucks."

"That's four bucks to me," said Kevin. "I'm in."

"Two bucks to you, Mike," said Willy.

Mike quickly tossed two blue chips into the pile and Willy dealt another round. "Here we go boys, a three of diamonds to Kevin for two pair on top, an ace to Mike, he's got trips aces and a four of hearts to Coach, no help to the man that needs none."

"Trips aces bets," said Willy.

Mike played with his chips. "Trips aces bets three bucks, one for each ace."

I tossed in three blue chips and wondered if Kevin would fold or stick. He too had a stone look that kept pace with Mike.

"Raise two bucks," said Kevin and he tossed his last two chips onto the pile.

"We're gonna need more chips, Willy," said Tom Norman.

Before Willy could respond, Mike pulled out his wallet and threw a five-dollar bill on the table along with his last two blue chips. The game had turned green, my favorite color so long as the two of hearts was in my hand. I looked at my hole cards again just to be sure.

"Raise five bucks," said Mike.

"That's seven bucks to you Coach," said Willy.

I reached for my wallet and pulled out a sawbuck. "Let's make it an even ten," I said.

Kevin and Mike called. We had another round of betting to go as Willy dealt the last cards face up. "Another three to Kevin, full house on top, a five of spades to Mike no help, and a ten of hearts to Coach."

"Full house bets," said Willy to Kevin.

Kevin threw more green on the table. "Let's start with five bucks." No one said a thing as Mike contemplated his move. "Make it ten," said Mike.

I thought about making it twenty but opted to keep the betting calm until it moved back to Kevin. "Call."

Kevin did not hold back. "Raise ten."

"Call," said Mike.

"Call," I said.

Kevin picked up his hole cards and threw another eight on the table. "Four eights." It was a damn fine hand.

Mike picked up his cards and play acted defeat for a slight moment then tossed a card out in the air, which hovered a second, then fell on top of his trips aces. "Four aces."

"Wow," said Tom Norman and Tony simultaneously. The table then looked to me for the reveal of the low heart. I put the two on the table and Mike and I split the large pot. *What a great game,* I thought to myself, *great game*. I didn't have to do a darn thing, just keep tossing more chips onto the pile, knowing all along at least half was headed my way.

Kevin took the defeat well and went outside to drown his sorrows. That moved the next deal over to Mike. He shuffled the cards, and I was waiting for him to say five-card draw, a real man's poker game. Instead, he said, "Five card stud, one down and four up. Let's see some antes on the table."

The silence lingered as we watched Mike deal some cards, one down and one up to each player before the first bet. Kevin came back to the table and watched the game in progress. I figured he needed a distraction and I needed more learning.

"Kevin, what would you do to fix the broken trust? What are the top two or three things on your list?" I asked.

Kevin hesitated. He didn't have a list but I wanted his brain to spit out something. "Top of mind, what are the first few things on the top of your mind," I encouraged him.

Kevin reflected for a moment then spoke. "You guys know I lean conservative and there are ten things I could cite right now that would not surprise any of you. None of them would fix the trust issue, they would be good policies that one side would like and the other would not. To fix the trust issue, I think the most important action is to somehow change the culture of the U.S. Senate back to its origin as a place to debate, to hear argument, to have smart dialog. That's just not happening any longer. It does not matter which side wins and which loses. What matters is the public discourse. Citizens want to know their views and opinions are being shared and argued in an open environment. And they want to know Congress is making deals, giving and taking, compromising to keep things moving forward. That's not happening either."

No one disagreed. We all stared at our cards and nodded our heads, even Tom. Mike broke the trance, looked at Willy and said, "King bets."

Willy did not pick up his one hole card; instead he picked up two blue chips and said, "King bets a couple bucks." Willy's bet brought us back to the poker game and we locked out politics for a few minutes.

My mind was not on the cards, and I lost a few dollars as Mike's game was on that evening. He and I were the big winners; everyone else gave at the office. On my way out, Willy gave me a knowing look and whispered, "Should we get together soon?"

I replied, "Not yet. I got some thinking to do, but after that would be good. Thanks."

I walked home from Willy's; it was only a half-mile. I thought about trust, or rather the lack of trust Kevin talked about. Trust was something we worked on very hard on the football team. Without trust in your teammate, we could not run a play or defend one either. Trust enabled teamwork and that enabled efficiency and good performance. Without trust on the field we would have lost every game and spiraled out of control. I could not imagine going to work everyday to such an honored and respected place as the U.S. Senate, knowing there was a complete lack of trust among the 100 Senators who worked there. The Senate had become a place for back room games and in your face put downs as the cameras documented the slurs and insults and the papers scribbled the rhetoric.

"One hundred senators," I mumbled. That's about the same number of players we had on our football roster. *Coincidence?* Our players were a very diverse group from all walks of life. We had rich, poor, black, brown, white and every combination in between. The Senate seemed mostly a fraternity of rich white males with a few minorities and females thrown in for good measure.

I kicked a stone in the road as the white picket fences and expensive houses passed by. Maybe our players on the football team were diverse, but my neighborhood was as white-bred as you could get. Gus was right about that part. My neighborhood was much like the Senate itself.

What a shame, I thought. *How could we have more trust in the locker room of a college football team than the U.S. Senate?* Trust was everything on the football team but nowhere to be found in the Senate. You did not have to like your teammate, but you did have to trust him to make the block, defend the edge, and catch a poorly thrown ball. *Is this where I could apply my passion and maybe a little spit? Perhaps my knowledge and experience from football could be used for greater good after all.*

I walked up my driveway with one last thought. *How could I help restore trust in the U.S. Senate?* This was Jerrod's original plan, and now it was mine to get done though on a larger scale than we had envisioned.

Chapter 28

The Plan

Willy called another game two weeks later and everyone quickly responded they would attend. The political discussion at our last game had not turned anyone off, which was initially surprising to me. After some reflection, I realized no one was happy with our government and they wanted a forum to spout off, to share their views, and even debate with a buddy whose opinion might be counter to their own. Willy's poker table had become our place to decide the fate of a nation. *Why not?* I thought. A poker table is just as good as any other place and maybe even better. We hurled fewer insults at each other than Congress, we were honest and we held each other accountable.

Prior to the game Willy and I met at his office to discuss my potential run for US Senate.

"Senator Bob," said Willy.

"Huh, don't get started with that just yet."

"Just trying it out loud to hear the sound. How about Senator Coach?"

I let Willy have his fun. It was a bit foreign to hear him say Bob. I was more accustomed to being called Coach. *Senator Coach? Nah...not sure that will ring with the voters.*

"Well, what did you think of the Guv and his suggestion to run for Senate?"

"The Guv? He's a piece of work. Give that man a mirror, no make it two and he'll be happy all day long."

"Quit stalling and answer my question."

I hesitated to respond and Willy filled the gap.

"Tell me what's in your gut, Coach. How did you say it the other night at poker? Top of mind, what's on the top of your mind?"

Smart man, I thought. He went back to calling me Coach to set me at ease. "My gut says to run but my feet are stuck in cement."

Willy shook his head up and down and hummed a few times. He was waiting for me to say more.

"And I don't want to run as a Democrat."

"Do you want to run as a Republican?"

I didn't hesitate this time. "No, if I run it will be as an Independent. We need to break the gridlock in Washington and picking one side over the other when my views run the gamut is not going to help. I want to change the system not become part of it."

Willy hummed some more. I didn't know what to say so I hummed along with him. We were two school buddies humming at each other, both off tune.

After a few bars we laughed and Willy broke the ice, "What about your family? Are they in for the grueling ride? You know how bad these races can get."

"Amy is up for anything that comes her way, you know how tough she is. I'm more worried about hearing her opinion on some of the thorny topics. If she arm wrestles me I'm dead meat."

Willy hummed and nodded then the image of Amy kicking my butt in arm wrestling must have reached his brain because a wide beaming grin was displayed.

"And I'm worried about Taylor and how she will handle the inspection of our lives. I don't believe the press will keep their hands off my only child."

"Nah, they won't, anything to get the inside scoop. She's a tough kid. I bet she gets into the campaign and helps you with the social media side of things."

I grinned, "Yeah that's probably true; she could teach us all a thing or two on how to communicate to the younger generation."

"Have you thought about your message? What are the issues important to you? Your platform?"

"Slow it down, Willy, which one of those questions should I answer first?"

We looked at each other and shook our heads, knowing how much work lay ahead.

"I do have an idea and you just might like it. I need a place, a forum of some kind to debate the issues that people care about and hear different opinions from all sides. Ideally a small group to begin with, perhaps a round table of buddies where trust is earned and measured. Where pals hold each other accountable, where brutal honesty is required behavior."

Willy raised one eyebrow and then the other.

"I know just the place."

We schemed for an hour and agreed he had the place, the forum, and the round table where we could test ideas and receive raw feedback. What place better than a poker table to kick around important world events, perhaps even solve a problem or two and possibly define a game plan for a football coach to get elected?

"Do we need to tell 'em?"

Willy donned his serious look and rubbed his chin with his right hand. After two rubs his decision was made. "Yeah, if you want their vote you better tell them."

I nodded my head, although inwardly I kicked the curb.

"We don't have to tell them right away. We have to tell them before they figure things out for themselves. It won't take them long so we need to be ready."

"Do you think it strange to use a poker game to gather input from...potential voters?"

"It's not odd. It might be a bit unique; it's not much different than a book club or a bowling team. These are all natural forums for every day Americans to spout off about what's important to them or bothering them."

"There's one more thing and you might not like it very much."

"What's that?"

"We need a little diversity in our poker group, perhaps a female voice would help keep the boys honest."

I waited for Willy's scream instead he laughed and laughed some more. "I love it. Can you see a lady sitting between Kevin and Tom Norman? Who do you have in mind?"

"There's one person who would be a perfect match. She would give more than take and she just might walk away with our money too."

Willy waited for the name.

"Carla. She's not afraid of anyone or anything."

"Hmmm, bring her to the game, but have her show up an hour late. We already got six players, maybe seven, so we'll need to get a rotation going."

"A rotation?"

"Mike can't play his real man's poker game with more than six people. Do the math on five card draw."

"Should we get two tables going instead of the rotation?"

"Let's try the rotation. That way we can have one forum for the political stuff."

"Ok, Carla can take my seat when she shows, great idea."

Willy hesitated for a moment. "What's up?" I asked.

"Does she have any game? Can she play?"

I laughed so hard I had to bend over. "Does Carla have game? Hmm, you worried about losing some coin…to a girl?"

Willy smiled.

"In my experience Carla always has game. We'll find out Friday night if that includes poker. I don't believe she'll be smoking any cigars."

We shook hands and made our pact. Friday night would come soon and I was anxious and excited at the same time.

"Why not a poker game? Why the heck not? What's the worst thing that can happen?" asked Willy as I exited his office.

Chapter 29

Carla's Game

Seven showed for a six-man game and an eighth would be on her way in an hour. Willy turned down a few others but did not tell me until the next day. *There could be some highs and some lows,* I thought as we gathered around Willy's table.

Harry was in town for a business meeting. He was a good buddy from school, a voracious ladies' man back in the day. He was now a grandfather times two, another reminder how fast our circles close.

"Gather around, boys, everyone gets a card, low man sits out the first round then we rotate."

Willy dealt a card to each potential player. "Ten to Coach, jack to Tom Norman, nine to Harry and three to Kevin."

"Crap," said Kevin. He spun on his heel and went to the beer fridge.

Willy continued, "Jack to Mike, king to Tony, five to Coach Bob and a three to the dealer."

"Three? Did I hear another three?" asked Kevin.

"Pipe down, pipe down. Three's go again, everyone else is safe," said Willy.

Kevin popped the top off his beer and took a swallow. "Alright, Willy, I got you this time."

Willy eye balled Kevin and dealt some cards, "Queen to Kevin."

"Yeah! I'll take that queen to the bank," said Kevin.

Willy flipped over the next card and set it down softly in front of himself. "Ace to the dealer. Kevin you sit out a round."

"How long is a round?" asked Kevin.

"A round is one game by each dealer. After one round the person with the fewest chips rotates out and Kevin rotates in."

Willy looked for acknowledgement from the group and received six shrugs. "Ok boys, let's play some cards. Ante one of those blue chips and let the games begin. The first game—is five card stud, one down five up, low spade splits the pot."

Six heads shifted to look at Mike. We awaited his criticism to get our poker night started, but Mike played it cool and went in a different direction. "What's an ace Willy, high or low?" asked Mike.

"Ace is high and if you get the duck be sure to let us know," said Willy with a grin.

"Oh, I'm getting that duck alright, it's the only way to win at this damn girlie game," said Mike.

Laughs went around the table as Mike came through with the delayed criticism we all expected. Now our game could finally begin, it was time to play some poker.

"All you winners tonight be sure to report your winnings to

the IRS. You never know who's watching," said Willy as he dealt one card down to each player.

"The IRS, what are you smoking?" asked Mike.

"You need not worry yourself, I was only talking to the potential winners."

Mike grinned, as did everyone else at the insult between buddies.

"First card up, ten of hearts to Tom Norman, jack of spades to Harry." Willy paused to catch himself as he dealt a card face up to Mike. "And the duck of spades to big Mike." The table let out a roar as Mike indeed got the duck, but it was face up not down where it would have done some good. Willy continued his deal, "Ace of diamonds to Tony, seven of hearts to Coach and the dealer gets a king of spades. Ace bets."

Tony threw in a blue chip. "Ace bets a buck."

Our game was underway but my mind was somewhere else. I glanced at my watch for the third time in five minutes. Carla was due in an hour. I could not concentrate on the game and played conservatively so I would lose my chips slowly. I did not care about winning coin this evening, there were bigger things at stake.

I was down to a few chips when Carla finally showed. Willy raised a hand, indicating he would handle the intros. "Gents, we're adding some spice to our game tonight."

The boys looked stunned. I could almost hear their inner thoughts and it wasn't pretty. They had no idea how to behave with a lady at the table. They did not want to lose money to a girl. *This might be very entertaining indeed*, I thought to myself.

I ceded my chair to Carla and Tony gave his to Kevin. *Smart man*, I thought. Tony was down and Kevin had sat out long enough. He was wearing down the carpet in Willy's basement with his pacing and we needed to end it. Tom Norman called the next game and the fireworks started early. "Ok boys…and lady…the game is baseball, nines and threes wild and fours get another card." All heads looked to Carla to see if she understood what Tom had said.

Carla did not miss a beat. "What kinda girlie games do you boys play? Hopefully someone at this table will call a real poker game."

Most jaws hit the felt with a thud, except for Mike. Carla had stolen his best line, and I wondered how he would handle the poke. Mike held firm, then spoke out. "Welcome Carla, glad to have ya." The boys picked up their jaws and faked some grins as everyone settled in to play cards. Carla delivered the line we rehearsed as if it were her own. *Well played, Carla, well played*, I thought to myself. She required no further instruction on the finer rules of the game. Her daddy schooled her when she was young as they moved from one army base to the next.

There was a shark swimming in shallow waters at Willy's place and she looked hungry. Carla hardly smiled and did not count her chips. She knew the unwritten rules and gave losers respect, although their games hardly earned it. The boys had quieted as the game wore on and the chips piled up in front of Carla. After an hour, the winner had been clearly separated from the pack and we all knew a rout was in the cards. Carla broke the peace and asked, "What do you boys talk about at the poker table?"

Willy heard his cue and steered the discussion where we wanted it to go. "Lately we've been discussing politics and how to fix all our problems. Isn't that right, boys?"

Mike gave Willy a quick look, he knew the fix was in and decided to play along. "We're betting on the Guv to take a well deserved stroll."

"A stroll?" asked Carla.

"That's right, a stroll. It's an expression. Some of us are betting he'll stroll out of the capitol and into a jail cell within the year. Just like most of those before him," explained Mike.

"Well, it doesn't seem the governor is the solution to all those problems. Which ones have you already solved…at the poker table?" asked Carla.

"We haven't solved anything but we did have a lively discussion around tax reform, war in the Middle East and the debt," I offered.

"Why am I not surprised? Money and guns, why is it always money and guns when the boys are in charge?"

Everything stopped. A gauntlet had been tossed on the green felt and no one wanted to pick it up. Carla was outnumbered but not outgunned so to speak. My money was on her to wipe the floor.

"Ante up boys and lady," said Willy, not missing a beat. He dealt some cards to a quiet table. "How would things be different with the girls in charge?"

"You might think all we care about is the false war on women."

"False war?" asked Kevin.

"You might actually believe the top issues for females are abortion, free contraception and equal pay."

The table remained quiet. These were much easier topics to pick apart when no females were present.

"If those aren't the top issues for women, then what are they?" asked Tom.

Carla laid her cards down face up a clear signal the conversation had become more important than the card game. "First, I reject the premise of your question."

"Huh, the premise?"

"Yes, the premise. Females are not a single group, not a unified voting block, not a segment that can be carved off from the rest of the country. There are many different types of women with different viewpoints on what matters. You can't put females into a bucket just like you can't put males into a bucket."

"Then why do we hear so much about the war on women?" asked Tony.

"Because that's what the media reports. At the margin women do have a greater interest in healthcare, family and equal rights than men. And women are generally less inclined to support a war and prefer greater controls on guns than men. Elections are won at the margin; a few points in either direction can swing the outcome."

"So…now you're saying these are the important issues to women? asked Willy.

"No. I am saying politicians tune their message around these issues to get votes, but that doesn't mean they are focused on the most important things to women."

"Ok, I give. What's the most important thing to women?" asked Mike.

"Again, you can't bucket all women into a single group. If I had to pick one issue that most women would support the answer is very clear."

We all waited for Carla to lay it down. She looked at each of us, one then the other as her head went around the table. Finally she said a single word. "Opportunity."

"Opportunity?" the table asked.

"Yes. Opportunity. Women want a choice in the lives they lead, the careers they work, the religion they practice, the family they manage, in everything they do just like a man has always had."

"Say more Carla, explain it a bit further," I encouraged.

"I'll give you a recent example in the news. The High Tech Industry is a key driver of our economy, right? That's where a lot of innovation and creativity come together to make new things possible." She paused to gain acknowledgement from our heads shaking up and down.

"How many women work in high tech, in Silicon Valley?"

We all shrugged, not knowing the answer.

"The answer is very discouraging. The big firms like Apple, Facebook, Google and many others are significantly skewed to men, white men. Women only represent 15% of the work force on average, yet we are more than 50% of the population."

"Why is that?" asked Tom.

"I saw an interview with Sheryl Sandberg the other day and she gave the best answer. Girls are not encouraged to study science and math so they don't become engineers and computer programmers like the boys do. Until the front part of the pipeline is filled with girls, the back end will not have as many females employed."

There was not much reaction to Carla's statement.

"How many of you have daughters?" asked Carla.

Most everyone put a hand in the air.

"Are any of you encouraging them to study science and math? Are any of you encouraging them to play sports? If your daughter wanted to put on the pads and be a hockey goalie, would you let her?"

There was dead silence at a poker table of all places.

"I've been lucky. My father encouraged me to follow my dreams and make my own choices. That's why I fell in love with football. I chose a boys' game and Coach Bob allowed me to make a career out of it."

"Da Coach!" A few boys yelled out.

"There's one other thing my father did for me and I'll never forget it. My fiancé took my dad to dinner to ask permission to marry me. He was so nervous. My father had a single question for my fiancé, just one question. My fiancé braced for the question and had his answer ready. He had prepared and knew what it would be."

The boys with daughters all nodded. They knew the question, everyone knew.

"My father said, 'I'm not going to ask if you will take care of Carla. I expect you will and I expect she will take care of you as well.'"

The boys' smiles turned to frowns. The expected question had been tossed aside by Carla's dad.

"Instead, my father asked a much better question, a question that showed he knew me, understood me and supported me. He asked my fiancé if he would enable me to be anything I wanted, not hold me back, not hold on to old traditions that no longer mattered."

The boys nodded their heads again, this time in full recognition and acceptance of the lesson Carla was teaching.

"You can't legislate the behavior of fathers and coaches or business owners and CEOs. I was lucky to have two great mentors that made a difference in my life. But, I believe politicians can influence how quickly our culture changes so that girls have the same opportunity, the same choices as boys."

I heard a new voice inside my head that night. The words were familiar and had been used many times before, but there was also something new, a different tone. *Atta girl, Carla, atta girl.*

My platform was shaped on the green felt of Willy's poker table. Willy set the cards aside as too many showed in the weeks and months ahead for a six-man game. He served brats and beer, two important staples in any campaign. Most added mustard and a few chips, the potato kind, then gathered around for a lively discussion. We refused to call it a debate, believing that was a fighting word. Instead, we wanted a forum for ideas, suggestions, raw input, some give and take and we surely got it.

Chapter 30

Thunder Dome

The Guv invited me back to the State Capitol. He wanted a reply I was ill prepared to give. I drove to the Capitol not knowing my answer, or rather, not knowing how to say it. "Yes, Guv, I want to run for U.S. Senate. No, Guv, I won't run as a Democrat, but thanks for giving me the idea. Can I use you as a reference?" *Argh!*

An assistant escorted me to The Guv's office. The walls were still covered and the desk bare, no folder, computer or speck of dust. I wondered again if any real work happened here. The Guv entered through a different door, followed by a female I could not see. His large frame blocked my view until his paw was upon me. "Coach, good to see you."

I braced myself for the shake and reached out my taut hand. I was ready, for his grasp...this time. His large hand connected to mine and we began the ritual. A second later, I saw her. Nancy gave a weak wave along with a semi-grin and I lost my balance as The Guv squeezed some life out. *Damn that hurt.* The Guv gave a victor's smile, knowing he trounced me again, then we parted and I refused to shake it out. He would not get that satisfaction from me, not this time.

"Good...good to see you...Guv." I pivoted to my right to get a full view of Nancy clinging to the wall. "Hello, Nancy."

"Hi, Bob."

The Guv beamed. He was a proud peacock, strutting his stuff, knowing he had pulled a surprise. *Well done, Guv, well done. But what's the play? Why is Nancy here?* I wondered.

"Coach, Nancy, I understand the two of you...have some history together. I hope that's not inconvenient." The Guv wore another sinister grin. *What's going on? What the heck is going on?*

"Let's have ourselves a drink and sit over there on the comfy chairs." The Guv picked up the phone and barked an order.

Then I got it. Nancy did not know I would be here. We were both surprised. It was entertainment hour for The Guv, and we were the actors in his play. We took our seats and settled in for...I had no idea what we were settling in for, none at all. I came here to deliver bad news and get the heck out of dodge. For now, I held my news until I could figure out what was happening.

The Guv sat in a big chair as Nancy and I shared a couch. We eyed each other for a second, maybe two, then The Guv let out a big chortle and slapped himself on his right thigh. He laughed at his own joke, his prank, whatever this was.

Why would The Guv put Nancy and me in the same room? Think Bob, think!

A burst of light hit my eyes and lit up the gears in my brain. *Damn, he has some brass ones,* I thought. He invited Nancy and me to the same meeting, or rather the same pretext of a meeting. *Say it simpler,* I yelled to myself! *Nancy is contemplating a run for Senate. That's it. A Senate seat is her way back to D.C., back in politics, back with some style. She could be one of a hundred rather than 435. I bet The Guv asked her himself. That's why we are both here; he's playing power broker.* I could see Nancy looking for the same light bulb, trying to figure out the ruse, the set-up. She would have no idea about me running for Senate, the thought would not even cross her mind. And worst of all, she would expect a call letting her know. *Could this damage our friendship?* I wondered.

The drinks arrived, providing needed sustenance to get through the next few minutes. The Guv took a swig and said, "Ahh."

Nancy gave me a shoulder shrug, asking figuratively if I knew what was going on. I returned serve with a deep sigh and nodded my head, *Yes, Nance I know what's up and you're not gonna like it, not one bit.* Nancy strained her neck forward pleading for me to fill in the gap but it was not mine to fill.

The Guv, tired of watching our body language, kicked off the meeting.

"Opening bids begin in five."

What the heck did that mean? I remembered a movie: *Thunder Dome.* Two go into the ring and one comes out. *Is The Guv crazed, whacked out, a devil in a tailored suit? Is the Guv for sale? This must be a sick joke, right? He's one of the rulers of the earth, isn't that how he put it at dinner?*

Neither Nancy nor I replied to the opening bid, forcing The Guv to fill the void. "Gottcha! A lot of former governors would take your offers, not this Guv. Nope, I'm not taking the stroll." He laughed again at his own joke.

This guy is a real piece of work. Ok Guv, you got me. What's your next move? I looked at The Guv, downed my drink in one gulp and said, "Guv what kind of game are you playing?"

The Guv sat straight up and wiped the grin off his face. "The game is politics, welcome to the big leagues."

"Hmmm. The big leagues, huh? I'm not here to play any games and I'm sure Nancy isn't either." I looked over at Nancy sitting rigid on the couch beside me. She figured it out. *Crap. I need to end this meet now!*

"I came here to deliver some news." I arose from the couch and turned to face Nancy. The Guv could only see my backside, more than he deserved. "Not interested." I set my empty down and kept my eyes on Nancy. She watched me the whole time and did not say a word. I could only guess what was going on inside her head. *Maybe we could meet up later and hash it out. Share a good laugh. Maybe.*

I pivoted and met The Guv who was now standing. We were eyeballs to chin once again. "Excuse me, I'll see myself out."

Nancy did not follow, did not move a muscle or say a word. I guess she stayed to finish the game. The Guv was serving, and she looked ready to return the ball.

Chapter 31

Endorsement

Nancy did not call the next day. I was unsure what to expect, yet I hoped for a call, a message, a bat signal from Gotham would have worked for me. It was her move to make. She stayed with The Guv and played a game with unwritten rules. I knew she was intent on getting back to D.C., even if she had to crawl. *What was she willing to do? What was she willing to give?* My friend was strong but she was also desperate. The craving inside would compel her to act, to cheat, to lie and to play dirty again. It saddened me that Nancy and The Guv were in the same league. One wore pants; the other a skirt and both had starring roles in a game I did not understand. My Father O'Malley story had not worked. Nancy's atonement would be short lived.

Nancy sent the campaign manager in her stead. Stevie left a message with Alice that said, "Regular place tonight 9:00 p.m." It was a command performance from the campaign manager. The candidate must have been too busy.

Alice sneered when I returned to the office. "Someone named Stevie rang your bell."

Uh oh. Alice and Stevie go into a cage...where does the mind come up with these crazy ideas? Gotta finish this one later, I reminded myself. "Stevie, huh?"

"A very persistent man. He expects to see you tonight."

"Hmm."

"Coach, I don't like him. Best avoid the meeting if you can."

"If only I could."

My mind made the calculation much faster than I anticipated. Of course I would meet with Stevie. I owed Nancy and she sent her collector. A pound of flesh was due, and I was carrying some extra.

"Tell Stevie I'll be there."

Alice turned back to her desk to hide the disappointment in her face.

*****

I walked into the pub ten minutes early to carve out my space. If I had to meet Slime Guy at least it would be on my turf and on my stool. I looked left and saw Stevie in the booth. A waitress hustled over with my usual and Stevie gave me a wave. His body language said, "come hither." *Crap.* Outfoxed by the campaign manager, I slithered over to the booth, grabbed a seat and sipped on some suds. It seemed a silly game, first to speak and all that, so I broke the silence. "Hello, Stevie."

"Coach."

I went back to my beer and readied for the serve. Stevie was host and had the ball. *Send me your best shot, Slime Guy. Let 'er rip,* I thought to myself.

"Nancy is announcing tomorrow and she wants your endorsement."

Boom. Stevie sent a fastball over the net past my racket. *My endorsement? Or, does she really want to box me out from running? Hmmm, smart play* I mused, *smart play.*

"The voters like you, Coach. More importantly, they trust you, and we believe many will follow your lead in the Senate race. That's what our polls say."

Stevie had some trouble spitting out the compliment and served a ball into the net. He had been sent here with marching orders to get me on board. *Who sent him? Was it really Nancy or someone else? Hmmm. The Guv? Yep, this was his kind of play, had his fingerprints and big paws all over it.* The Guv was calling the shots, he wanted to balance Nancy's political career with my football fame. I had to give him some props for a good move. The folks were weary of sending a lifelong pol back to D.C. but they might pull the lever if someone they trusted greased the skids. Stevie wanted to close the deal and get out of the bar unscathed.

Polls? Did he say polls? If he had polling data on me that means it was run weeks or months ago. Hmmm. "What else does your poll data say?"

Stevie sighed. He had hoped for acquiescence, a quick agreement to my endorsement.

Not yet big boy, you gotta earn it. I sat back in the booth and got comfortable. It was not going to be a short evening after all.

"Nancy will win if she gets help, the right kind of help."

I waited for more.

"The Guv helps Nancy cement her base, the liberal left. Your endorsement rallies the middle and pulls females fed up with both sides."

"Females?"

"You're a big hit with the ladies."

"Luck over skill I guess."

We sat there both unsure of the next move. My beer gave me courage, at least that's what I told myself and moved us along. "How will you beat the Republican candidate?"

Stevie sipped his drink and delayed a response as he calculated the angles. The question was not difficult, not at all. The calculation was whether to speak truth or give the standard reply. I wore my serious face, the one that said, *Don't mess with me, dude, not tonight*, I hoped.

"We'll destroy the man and his family." Stevie chose truth and let one fly over the net.

"Why would I want to be part of that?"

"Because you owe Nancy."

"Is that you or her talking?"

Stevie shrugged his shoulders and his crumpled pin stripes went along for the ride. "Coach, I'm not the bad guy. I know you think I'm the bad guy; but I'm not."

"Then who is the bad guy?"

"Think of me as the drug, the opium that the politician can't do without. They want that drug, they need the drug, and they can't live without it."

"Hmmm, explain that to me."

"Politicians are motivated by fear. They are deathly afraid of losing their seat, their power, their place at the table. Most cannot imagine their lives without being in the circle."

"The circle?"

"DC. It's the epicenter, the heart, the only place that matters. When Nancy is in D.C. she feels alive. When she is back home… she's dead."

"Are you saying Nancy is the bad guy?"

Stevie broke eye contact and looked down at his drink. The flash hit my brain. Slime Guy cared about Nancy. Maybe he loved her or thought he did. *Can Slime Guy love anyone?* I wondered.

"Nancy's an addict. She's not bad on purpose, she's…forced to be."

"By who?"

"You'll figure it out."

Our drinks were done and the easy move was clear. Give the nod and lend my name to an old friend. Then get out of harms way and never see Nancy again. All I had to do was agree to a small favor, one last gift to a friend I no longer knew…maybe never knew. My head was pounding and that never happened, not in this bar, my happy place. It was time to vote. My head chose the safe path and my gut reluctantly agreed. My heart was torn and could go either way. Mr. Ego was uncertain, perhaps for the first time and asked for a recount. *Damn, why can't this be easier?* I asked and answered my own question. *Life decisions aren't meant to be easy. The re-vote changed everything.*

I went in a new direction. "How would you beat me if I ran against Nancy?"

Stevie did not need to answer but I knew he would. We had achieved a level of honesty that had escaped us previously, and he would enjoy taking the coach down. We both knew that.

"You're an easy target. I'd attack your program at the U and peel it back one layer at a time. All the sordid details would come out, some of them true, some half true, and some made up. You have a lot of players from questionable backgrounds and your self-imposed suspension is a gift from the gods. Then I'd go after Vince, the street kid who embarrassed the school."

"Is that it?"

"I'm just getting started. Money, you made a ton of it and voters don't like rich guys."

"My family?"

"Them too, there are no limits."

I had three choices. Endorse Nancy and save a friendship that was slipping away. Do nothing and ignore politics all together. Or, enter the race myself and run a clean campaign focused on things that matter. I debated my choices for a few minutes all the while wondering, *Who's the bad guy? How did Stevie say it, the bad guy this time?*

Who's the bad guy? Who's the bad guy? You idiot! It was so damn easy. There was only one possibility: The Guv.

"Is the bad guy pulling all the strings or is he taking direction from someone else?"

Stevie realized the endorsement was not coming, not tonight. He delivered the message and asked me to join the team. Stevie, Nancy and The Guv wanted a fourth to play ball. Once I put that picture in my head the decision was not hard at all.

"Rookies don't do well in this game. By the time they figure out the rules and who's on their side, the game is over and the rookie is sitting at home wondering what and who beat him bloody." Stevie stood to leave and reached for his wallet to pay the tab.

"My bar, I got it."

Stevie did not argue, did not utter a single word. He nodded to me on his way out then turned and said, "Nancy will be disappointed, but she'll get over it." Stevie spun on his heel and walked away.

Chapter 32

The Campaign Part One

Stevie's game plan was predictable. He kicked off the campaign with The Guv and Nancy together on stage. They stroked each other's ego as if they had been doing it for years. The announcement went off without a hitch and the media lined up to meet the royalty, get a smart quip and play their part in Stevie's grand plan. The campaign manager took great pride in the beauty of it all, the orchestration of all the pawns under his command.

He did not take long to launch a strike at the heart of the GOP. Three candidates vying for the Republican nod all whiffed at the ball as the Dems rallied around Nancy. The infamous war on women was the first grenade tossed into a crowded room of befuddled campaign teams. One candidate wanted to close abortion clinics, another railed against contraception, and the third said something stupid about rape. None of the candidates had the skill or smarts to return the ball and change the discussion to things that mattered. Women might not vote for a candidate that championed abortion and free contraception, but they would definitely vote against someone that did not understand these topics. The Republicans showed their ignorance and Stevie had the first point of the game.

Nancy soared in the polls, as no other choice seemed relevant. Her quips were sharp, once again, as Stevie breathed life back into the veteran pol. She basked in the camera glow, held court around the state and looked good doing it. Nancy was back in the place she belonged. It saddened and heartened me at the same time. I felt good for my old friend, yet there was emptiness in her return to the ring. I knew too much this time around and did not look forward to the ugliness ahead. The second part of Stevie's plan blamed the Republicans for all the failures in Congress. It did not matter his candidate had 30 years at the helm, not one bit. It was another opportunity to rally voters against Republicans with a little help from a friend.

One evening, I yelled at the reporter on TV, "Ask if she owns a home in Illinois!" But the reporter tossed another softball to Nancy and she crushed it back over the net. I tried again, "Ask if she owns a home in D.C." The female reporter pretended not to hear me and gave Nancy more free time on the tube.

I could envision Stevie giving high fives and fist bumps as the strings he controlled obeyed his every command. *Was the reporter on Stevie's team, in his web? Did it matter?* I threw a pillow at the TV when the next lob went high in the air. "Why is the Congress so inept at getting anything done?" Nancy turned to face the camera rather than the reporter. "The Republicans take great pride at stopping our president. They would rather make our president look bad than make our country better."

Stevie blamed the Republicans and drew voters tighter to Nancy by cleverly using the word "our." Much to my chagrin, the campaign manager was indeed a master at his chosen craft. Two-zip, Stevie zoomed ahead. *What's his next play?* I wondered. It wasn't hard to figure out. It was time to go negative just as the GOP was narrowing the field and one man stood out among three. Poor guy had no idea how to play the game that lay ahead. I thought to myself, *Another good man is going down.*

Nancy took great delight calling out the Republican candidate as a privileged business owner who failed to pay some taxes. She called him "Dollar Dan," the man with no plan, and waged class war against his ill-gotten gains.

Dan fought back and painted Nancy as a liberal loon who wanted to take from those who made it and give to those that didn't. The slugfest over the airwaves played out for months with each candidate drawing equal quarts of blood. They were on opposite spectrums, two partisan voices that knew what was best for the country and for each other. He built a private business and saved his gold. She served the public, spent hers and then some. Many looked forward to a heated debate, including those who seldom paid attention. Then Stevie played his trump card, an ace he patiently held until it was needed.

She charged $500 an hour for a client's pleasure. Her rules were flexible if you tipped well and she only worked weekends. She favored repeats and Dollar Dan was a premium customer. She always kept Friday 10:00 p.m. open, knowing he would take an hour and usually two. Then she would call it a night and get her rest for the long day ahead. When Dollar Dan tossed his hat into the ring, he cut the chord and she had time on her hands, the kind of time that burned a hole in her wallet. Slots were not as easy to fill as in her younger days, although the mirror still showed a body that worked. When Stevie came calling it was difficult to resist his offer. Thankfully, he didn't ask for a freebie in return, although she would have made that deal too.

Dollar Dan was a single man, a widower times two. He clicked with both brides, the first bore two children the second had none. The first marriage ended suddenly when her car skidded on ice and down a ravine. The kids were young and he raised them with a firm hand and gentle heart, earning silent praise from people that mattered. It took ten years before Dan was ready for love again. She was younger but not too young. That's what the society ladies said in public, although everyone knew she looked much like Dan's first wife about ten years ago. They were a happy couple, avid tennis players at the club, solid fundraisers for the right causes and she adored his kids. He flew in the corporate jet for business and she for pleasure. They flew together often and occasionally alone. He declined the Colorado ski trip to focus on another business deal but agreed to join in three days. The jet got caught in a storm and missed the landing on a small strip. Two pilots and three passengers went missing and Dan lost more than a wife the second time around.

Dan's sad story did not matter to Stevie or the voters when they learned of the $500 call girl. She said escort service, but everyone heard hooker and even the friendly society ladies could not sell this one to the community. Dan thought he found his passion, a new cause, one last fight where he could apply himself. The campaign manager thought differently and showed Dan the exit door.

Chapter 33

Cookie Jar

Stevie put a W on the board at campaign headquarters and the celebration began. Nancy stood tallest in an empty field, a sure lock for the Senate seat and a glorious return to D.C. She called her realtor and demanded an early eviction for the tenants she never met. It would cost some coin, but she didn't care. A move back where she belonged was worth some pain, besides there were plenty of funds to cover these kinds of things she argued to herself. Nancy dipped into the cookie jar and bought her way back home.

She did not fit in Illinois, not anymore. The state wore like an old coat that hung the wrong way and looked out of date. Even the big city was void of her kind of people. The language, the vibe, the parties were just not the same. One night, alone with her thoughts, she came to a stark realization. Nancy missed D.C. Republicans as much as D.C. Democrats. She wanted; no, she needed the endless fights with the enemy across the aisle. She did not agree with them, but she understood their argument, their angle and their motivation. She thrived on playing the game in the big leagues, the national level, the only arena that mattered.

She realized the air was different in D.C. It wasn't cleaner or fresher, just different, the kind of air she could breathe, inhale deep and let out slowly. She had not realized how much she needed the Capitol until it was out of her grasp. She could live again if she made it back to D.C. She had to get back. It became her internal theme song: *Get back to D.C. Get back to D.C. Just get back.*

Stevie had the ship on cruise control and pulled the attack ads since there was no one standing to take a punch. He packed up shop, left a skeleton crew behind and booked a first class seat. He had performed the requested favor and could now get back to important things on the international scene. His Oval seat was still on reserve, although he knew it was made conditional on Nancy's win. It never hurt to do a solid for the Oval. He went to sleep dreaming about his reward, the sleek black Mercedes he would drive around the circle. He could buy more than one with the huge checks they sent. It almost seemed criminal to charge such exorbitant fees, almost. He had earned it. As the plane took off, he left the Midwest behind and looked forward to getting back home and his next campaign. He didn't like The Guv, no one he knew did, but that didn't matter. The Guv was next in line and Stevie wanted to keep his Oval seat. He went to sleep with a smile knowing he would soon be back in D.C.

The Guv made some rounds and claimed his share of the credit. Most thought it sounded like Nancy and Stevie worked for The Guv and more than a few heads shook as he droned on. It was

The Guv's turn to bathe in the limelight, move up another rung and position for bigger things. The Guv had Oval plans of his own and the party owed him, Nancy owed him, Stevie owed him, they all owed The Guv.

He straightened his tie before the next interview and asked the mirror to confirm the obvious. His smile gave the validation he expected. The Guv deserved a bonus, yes indeed. It did not take much persuasion as he dug his big paw deep into the cookie jar. He was very familiar with the jar, having visited it often. Might as well seed his next campaign and get the wife something pretty. After all, he had earned it. The Guv slept well that night and wondered how it would feel to live in the nation's capitol. He had never lived outside his state, never knew the feeling of walking amongst his own. He had taken a big step toward his dream, helped out when asked and brought home a big win. It was his turn next. He had to get to D.C.

The GOP had their own campaign manager from D.C., just not any candidates that could compete in a deep blue state like Illinois. There was plenty of time to run another yet no one credible could be found. Dollar Dan took a hike and left his cell phone behind, so they hatched a new plan—a defensive maneuver learned in the congressional aisles. If the GOP could not win, they had to ensure the Dems didn't win either. They had money and big donors willing to keep the campaign chest full, all they needed was an Independent to run, someone the voters could trust, and the GOP could hope to control. Instead of playing to win, they opted not to lose. Whatever it took to keep the Dems from a Senate seat in D.C.

Willy got the call. The GOP knew about the poker games that had turned into a political forum. Neither party had paid much attention. It was harmless, a few folks from a Midwest state played some cards and talked about things they did not understand. Sure poker had an edge, more intrigue than a bowling league or farmers market, but it received no respect, none at all from the boys in D.C. Yet the GOP needed some help, they needed a play and were desperate so they gave the poker host a call. Willy listened and the GOP talked and talked some more. They were selling and Willy wasn't buying, so he made it a short call and hoped the GOP campaign manager would realize his friend Coach Bob was not for sale, not if Willy was in charge.

He called again the next day and the day after that. Willy still wasn't buying, not until the conversation changed. On day five the GOP campaign manager began to ask some questions, important questions about the coach and what he believed in, what he stood for and what would convince him to run. Now Willy was interested. And then he got excited when the campaign manager explained the two-step Democratic game plan. Nancy was only step one and The Guv was using the cookie jar and a promise from the Oval to fund step two. If I ran, I would be up against the entire system, not just an old fling. Now that was a fight worth fighting. Willy thought it might just work and invited the GOP campaign manager from D.C. for a visit.

Chapter 34

The Campaign Part Two

Nancy settled in and felt at ease. She breathed in deep and exhaled slow just like old times. She was back in her place with her people in her city, the nation's capitol. She was home. It was a tad early, perhaps very early to make the move, but she didn't care. She couldn't wait to get back and start her life again. The polls had spoken and they were seldom wrong. Her lead was insurmountable and the only question was the margin. Would she win by ten, twenty, more? She stopped thinking about the campaign to focus on more important matters; there was a party tonight in the circle and she had to prepare.

The S Class AMG slithered around the curve at twenty miles faster than allowed. Limits did not mean much to the campaign manager. He who broke all the rules didn't pay much attention to road signs built for the masses. Tickets did not deter him;

they piled high then got brushed aside when he made the call. Campaign managers didn't have time for small matters or things settled in court. Forgiveness was easily obtained in the circle as long as the Ws kept coming.

The private jet felt small, his large frame could have used a bit more room. He took a mental note to lodge a complaint before the next trip. His wife looked happy, her shapely legs stretched out on the carpet, heels tossed aside. He glanced around the cabin to find the right place and planned his move. He had never been to the mile high club. The server returned and was quickly dismissed with a wave of his big paw and a terse statement. "That will be all…for a while." He grinned at his young wife and gave her the nod. She had hoped he would wait until they landed and checked in. The D.C. hotel would be more comfortable; it was the most lavish in the circle.

They met the next day in the Oval. She was tingling and ready to celebrate with the man she adored. The Guv was surprised at being nervous, his big paw off its game. Stevie felt triumphant and reclaimed his seat lest anyone think it was no longer on reserve. They were an odd team, a trio strung together by a force not in their control. They waited together in silence, unaware they were being played.

The hidden door in the round wall opened and each of them braced for his entrance. They were eager to please him with a gift-wrapped election win ahead of schedule. They could almost feel the slaps on the back and hear the praise from on high. Their lungs inhaled a deep gust of air, as their bodies stood at attention and held steady for his reveal. Nancy realized it wasn't him before the others and plopped onto the couch. The Guv and Stevie stole a quick glance at Nancy, then back at the door. The hand on the knob gave it away as the Chief of Staff strode into the Oval. He was all business all the time and called the meet to order.

"You shouldn't be here."

"You invited us," The Guv replied.

"You did not meet the condition."

Each of them shrugged. "What condition? Stevie asked.

"It's customary to win the election before coming to the Oval."

Stevie held back a rant. He knew how to behave when the Oval was not pleased. Let someone else take the hit was how he usually played it. She watched Stevie for a signal and knew it was time to duck as she slunk further back in the couch. The Guv lacked D.C. experience and didn't know how to keep his mouth shut, not after the reprimand from a staffer.

"The election is a done deal. We did our part, now let's get on with the commitments your boss made."

Stevie's eyes went wide. The Guv showed his ignorance every time he said a word. He would up his fees for the next campaign. Remedial training took time, patience and a lot of money.

The Chief of Staff stared down The Guv as the clock ticked past five seconds. "You got work to do."

The three of them shrugged again, not understanding the work required. Then the Chief looked at his watch, picked up the remote and turned on the TV.

Chapter 35

Press Conference

It was a larger crowd than expected. Willy called his contacts, Carla managed the press and Taylor had the social media engines revved and ready. I was accustomed to all the microphones from my old job, but I did not recognize the faces. News reporters looked and acted differently than the old sports crowd, many more were female and most were younger and a lot better dressed. There were suits and ties and dresses along with serious faces. *Hmm, it's going to be difficult to warm up to this crowd,* I thought.

I was nervous and excited at the same time, much like a football game just prior to kick-off. After the first big hit, the nerves are gone and the game is on. I hoped it worked the same way in politics but I wondered about that first hit. *Where would it come from? How would it feel? Would it release all the tension?*

Willy walked up the short flight of stairs to the microphones with grace and confidence. The man was good in a crowd. "Thank you all for coming today. We have some important news for citizens across Illinois." Willy paused a few beats to let that settle in. "I have the distinct honor and pleasure to introduce a dear friend. You all know him around the state as a winner, a leader and a mentor to young men…and women, someone who built more than a football program at the U. He gave us something we lacked, something we needed. He showed us how to win the right way. He taught us about teamwork and how to bring diverse groups together for a common goal. He built a legacy of excellence on and off the field. He built a winning tradition that continues long after he moved on."

Willy looked over at me and smiled. "When I reflect back on his accomplishments and what he taught all of us, I can't help but wonder what he could do in the political arena. Our country is not in a good place, we are divided and polarized more so than ever before. We need someone who can help bring us together, someone who is not tied to ideology, someone willing to listen, willing to roll up his sleeves and get the job done. We need someone in Washington D.C. who cares more about helping the people than themselves; someone who will do the right thing without hesitation, without calculating the political angles whenever a tough decision needs to be made."

Willy looked out at the large crowd. "Citizens of Illinois, I urge you to elect a new type of leader, a leader who cares more about governing than campaigning. It is my honor to introduce to you our next United States Senator…Coach Bob."

Short and sweet, that was Willy. *Here we go. Don't trip on the way up to the podium,* I reminded myself. Don't trip and be sure to smile, a big grin. Willy stuck out his hand as my foot hit the front edge of the first stair. He felt my body jerk and held on tight as I righted myself and got back on plan. *Geez that was close! Way to make a grand entrance,* I chided myself. Then I realized it was the first hit. I took the blow and with Willy's help made it up the stairs. My nerves had been rattled and were now gone. *Ah, I'm ready!*

I stared out at the audience and had one last thought before the show began. *Is Nancy watching? Is she watching me tell the state and the country that I would be her opponent, that I wanted to take her rightful place and deny her throne?*

******

Nancy's jaw dropped to the floor and stayed there. Inside her head pounded and her voice screamed at a loud pitch, *You bastard!* Willy's short speech felt like a skewer piercing her vital organs, each word carefully chosen to create distance from the typical politician, show the gap between Coach Bob…and Nancy.

The Guv chortled and shook his head sideways. "The Republicans are making some kind of play. This rookie gets the idea from me and must be making a dirty deal with the GOP. We're gonna kick his coach butt all over the field."

Stevie did not move nor say a word. He looked for the signs and didn't like what he saw. The press conference was well attended, organized, scripted and had all the media on hand. It was a very professional debut for a football coach.

"What's your assessment, Stevie?" asked the Chief.

Stevie looked away from the TV at the six eyes focused on him. "Let's see what the coach says first."

******

I looked out at the throng of people and the signs. *Where did they get all those signs?* I wondered. *Okay, here goes, just talk don't preach,* I reminded myself. *Just talk.*

"Tom, thank you for the kind introduction." Willy jerked his head and looked at me. I don't believe he had heard me say his real name in a very long time.

Talk don't preach. "Hi folks, thank you for coming today."

What the heck am I doing up here on this stage? Relax, take it easy, take a deep breath and get on with it. "Have you ever thrown a pillow at the TV when your team was losing a big game?"

The large audience laughed, most of them had done something like that.

"I find myself doing that a lot lately. I threw a pillow at the TV once because my team, our team, was losing again and it just didn't make any sense." *Get to the punch line, Coach. Don't make them wonder about this analogy too long.*

"The thing is, I wasn't watching football…or basketball… or baseball, hockey or any sport. I was watching the news. One of our congressmen had been arrested for taking bribes, a senator was disparaging his enemy across the aisle, and tours had been cancelled at the White House due to a budget impasse."

The audience had quieted.

"So I tossed that pillow and lucky for me, it missed the television, by a wide margin."

The audience laughed.

"I had my usual aim that day, friends would say I hit a hook or was it a slice? Either way, it was not a straight shot and my television lived another day." *Take advantage of the humor, use that Mark Twain quote and shift to serious mode and play on their emotions....* "'Mark Twain once said: 'Patriotism is supporting your country all the time and your government when it deserves it.'

"Folks, when was the last time you were proud of the representatives we elected to run our country? When is the last time you saw congressmen and congresswomen from both parties work together to improve the lives of the citizens who voted them into office? When did the senator across the aisle become the enemy?"

Heads were nodding.

"Do you believe the Democrats and Republicans in Washington, District of Columbia can work together? Can they have a spirited debate about the important issues of our day and compromise to get a good result decided? Do they even try?"

More heads were nodding and a few were yelling their approvals.

"Folks, do you trust the United States Government to create and pass laws that solve problems or enable new opportunities?"

Just about every head was moving sideways, as I expected.

"There are a few smart analysts in our nation's capitol with deep insights into why our political system is in gridlock. Charles Krauthammer wrote the following: 'Every two years the American politics industry fills the airwaves with the most virulent, scurrilous, wall-to-wall character assassination of nearly every political practitioner in the country—and then declares itself puzzled that America has lost trust in its politicians.'

"Folks, I'm not confused why our government is failing today, and I don't believe you are confused either."

The audience was biased, most knew me and maybe even liked me but they seemed to enjoy the speech so far. It was time to feed the media. They needed a sound byte for their news clips that shortened everything to the time allotted.

"Fellow voters do you believe the United States Congress has your back? Do the representatives from our state, Democrat or Republican, that we send to Washington, have our back?"

Loud cheering from the crowd urged me forward. I heard a few shouts of "No!"

"When I threw that pillow I was frustrated, I was angry and I still am. We have a losing team in Washington. I don't like losing anymore than you, and it's time we built a new team, a winning team that gets the job done. To do that we need to make some changes." I peered out at the throng. *How many people are here?* I wondered.

"I am running as an Independent candidate for United States Senator, and I am asking for your vote."

Loud applause erupted from the audience.

"I am asking you to work harder, to think deeper, to pay more attention than usual. Not only am I asking you to vote for me and the policies and values I believe in, I am also asking you to vote for an Independent candidate, not one of the two parties. This means some of you need to spend a few more minutes in the voting booth. You can't just pull the red or blue lever in November if you want to elect an Independent to shake things up in Washington D. C."

There was light laughter from the crowd. That encouraged me to keep going.

"I invite you to my website 'Voteforcoach.com' which went live this morning to understand my views on important topics or to send in your questions, opinions and feedback. For today, let me summarize my views with the following:

"I favor an inclusive approach to government regardless of race, gender, ethnicity, religion, sexual orientation or any other measure. Our diversity is a great strength of our country, not a weakness.

"I believe the cornerstone of our country is the family unit and we should do whatever it takes to support a strong family culture. Sadly, today about 25% of American children live in single-parent homes, twice the level in Europe. More than 20% of these children live in poverty. There is ample research that tells us what we know in our gut. Single parent children are more prone to abuse, behavioral problems and psychological issues than kids who grow up with two parents. And the statistic most people won't talk about for fear of being called racist is only 30% of African American children and 50% Hispanic children are born to two parent homes. We have a long-term societal problem on our hands and need to face this issue directly, not hide from it."

"I favor a government whose primary role is to enable citizens to have a better life. Government should not intrude needlessly, not try to manage large sections of our economy, and not dictate how we live. Government establishes the rules and ensures a level playing field. If you'll forgive my crude analogy, government wears black and white stripes. It is the referee, not the player, not the coach, not the fan…not the star. A good government exists in the background, much of the time, providing help where needed and throwing the yellow flag when required. At times the government is in the foreground helping ensure we are safe, secure, free and setting the right example for other countries to follow.

"We need people in the U. S. Congress who understand the right balance. Our elected officials need to recognize they are not the stars. They are role players that support the real stars in our country. The real stars are the small business owners that wrestle with endless regulations, the family struggling to make ends meet, the farmer working his crops, the secretary at the office, the artist who entertains a crowd, even the corporate executive can sometimes be a star. Our senators and representative act as if they are rock stars. They bathe in the limelight rather than representing the people who put them in office."

Time to wrap this one up. Remember, it's the economy stupid. Nothing matters if you forget the economy.

"Perhaps the most important role for government is to help ensure we have a strong economy where jobs are plentiful, growth and investment are encouraged, taxes are fair...and easy to determine...and there is ample opportunity for those willing to earn it, willing to work for it, willing to take risk and put themselves out there. Our government should help those that need it, but the sweet spot should be for those willing to earn it. And, that includes the government itself. To that end I support zero-based budgeting for all federal spending. Since when did a slower rate of increase equal a budget cut?

I shook my head sideways and said, "Do they think we don't get it?"

Use the Thomas Jefferson quote, I reminded myself. *What was it? I need the memory flash now, right now! One one thousand, two one thousand ... Bam!* "Thomas Jefferson was right when he said, 'The democracy will cease to exist when you take away from those who are willing to work and give to those who would not.'

I steadied my self; *Go back to trust, that's the closer...trust.*

"It does not take much to realize our federal government is a mess. Pick your favorite topic: taxes, budgets, debt, immigration, energy, entitlements, foreign policy...there is an endless list of important challenges that go unsolved. I used to believe partisanship was the sole reason for lack of progress in D.C., but I fear there is also something worse than ideology causing the gears of government to grind to a halt."

The audience had stilled.

"Our federal officials have no incentive to solve these problems. Complexity is the best friend of elected officials who want to retain their power. Large budgets and greater regulations allow our federal government to control their destiny and keep their seats. The federal government in Washington is too big, too powerful and too far removed from the people."

The audience remained still. I could tell they were ready to rally and only needed a spark.

"Do you have confidence in our federal politicians to get the job done?"

A loud roar of, "No! No! No!" erupted.

"Do you have trust in our federal officials to do the right thing?"

"No! No! No!"

"Folks, will you help me restore trust in our government? Will you help me restore nobility in our elected officials? Will you help me change our federal government into a winning team?"

*****

The Chief of Staff grabbed the remote and turned off the television. The six eyes moved from the TV back to Stevie. He saw the anger in Nancy's eyes, the disappointment from the Chief, and jealousy from The Guv. The six eyes gave themselves away, they always did.

Coach was a godsend, a surprise certainly, but a godsend nonetheless. The coach was good on TV, maybe better than average and certainly better than expected. He was running against the system, against D.C. and what it had become over the past decade. Coach was running against everything Stevie had helped create. The circle was under attack by a football coach who threw pigskins for a living. All Stevie had to do was point the circle at the coach, the full weight and wrath of the circle upon him. It would take a lot of coin to unite the circle, get everyone together on the same page and unleash its ire to clear the field of the unwanted threat. The coach and his family would get crushed.

Stevie felt the eyes penetrating him. They wanted his opinion, they needed his view, and most of all they dared him to come up with the plan. Stevie laughed inside at the hilarity of it all. A man he hated more than anything in the world had become public enemy number one. Da Coach was going to make Stevie rich.

Stevie held back his grin and said. "We're going to need more money, a lot more money."

*****

"There's one last thing I'd like to say today. I make a promise to you, the voters of Illinois, that my campaign will focus on the positive change I hope to bring to Washington. We will not spend a nickel on negative advertising of any kind. We will not spew the usual vitriol and hatred you have grown accustomed to seeing in political campaigns."

The crowd applauded.

"A D.C. insider once told me voters have a much easier time voting against the negative than for the positive. He said something like 'the lie goes around the block before the truth gets out of bed.' And then it dawned on me the only choice we have been given lately is two sides of the same coin attacking each other viciously, one negative against the other. I believe we are better than that. I believe more people are paying attention to the issues facing our country than ever before. Perhaps it took us a while to realize how poorly our country has been managed. Perhaps it took us too long to realize our politicians are not governing because they spend all their time running, all their time and their money in campaign mode. It's time to put a stop to that.

There was loud applause from the crowd. They were getting my message, and it was resonating. I was way over time but had the momentum. *When you got the mo... keep going!* I called an audible and spoke from the gut. My scripted speech had long ago ended.

"I view the campaign period as a pre-season. It's the time to get things right, to tighten the game plan, to ensure my positive message resonates with you the voters and the policies you care about. My campaign will close at the end of pre-season not continue into the aisles of congress. We will not go negative no matter what the other candidates and their campaign managers throw at us!"

That was for you, Stevie. Bring it campaign manager. I'm ready.

"Thank you, Illinois! Vote for Coach!"

The crowd was thundering our simple tagline, over and over.

"Vote for Coach! Vote for Coach! Vote for Coach!"

Chapter 36

Low Blow #2

The first low blow missed its mark and did not take me down, but Stevie had an arsenal built up and surely planned to use them. Nancy lost the last couple of rounds and failed to score. Based on the audience reaction, her low blow had backfired and allowed me to put some points on the board. Knowing Nancy as I did the initial punch was only the preliminaries; she would save her best shot for last.

"Can Congress truly learn something useful from a coach?"

Nancy was ready to launch again. *Let's see where she goes now.*

"Making $15 million is one thing. Making that amount of money on the backs of college kids, many of whom are street thugs, at least in your program, Bob, is a different animal."

Hmm, Nancy sounded a lot like Gus. I wonder who connected the two of them together? Thanks Guv, I owe you one, too. Stevie was predictable so very predictable. There's no need to discuss real change when it's so much easier to get votes by making the other guy look bad. As Nancy started her rant, I thought about Vince, the greatest quarterback I had ever known and the player most responsible for the championship ring I was wearing. He was the thug she was talking about, the street criminal who saved me.

I saw Vince just the other night, a Thursday evening performance on ESPN. He threw four touchdowns and more than 300 yards against one pick to win the game. Amy and Taylor watched with me, as usual, whenever Vince was on. We thought of V, the nickname we called him, as part of our family. We had taken a risk on a down and out kid who lost his mother to drugs, his father to indifference, and his sister to shame. All three had abandoned V by age sixteen. He was left alone on the street corner in the big city. He spent three years on the south side and built a fearsome rep. No one messed with V, the thug who beat a larger man with a baseball bat. He was defending Serena the sister in shame who hurried away before Vince could see her belly grow. He turned to drugs and dealt more than he consumed. It was a good life on a relative basis, the only comparison he knew. He got caught more than once and felt the bars closing in. He realized life would be short on the south side streets and somehow found a path to Mike who worked a deal with the judge to release Vince to me. It was a set-up for the new coach who desperately needed a QB at the U.

"Why would we send someone to the U.S. Senate who built his fame by taking advantage of young African American teens? That's right, the $15 million Coach Bob took home was on the backs of poor black kids who seldom graduated college. Shame on you, Bob, and shame on the system you helped put in place."

I looked over at Nancy with sadness in my eyes. She refused

to face me; instead she kept the attack going. I guess she was on a roll and felt she had the momentum.

"Why would we reward a coach who brought shame to his program and had to suspend his star player and himself for the mess they created, for the embarrassment they brought to our state school? I remember the headlines. How could any of us forget? 'Street Thug Brings His Game to the U.'" Nancy shook her head back and forth and said tsk, tsk a few times.

I looked over at Willy and saw him seething. Normally a cool cat, Willy was one pissed administrator. He took as much pride as I did in the program we installed at the U. It's one thing to go after me; it's a whole different ballgame to attack my friends and family. I looked past Nancy and saw Stevie grinning and pumping his fist. Our eyes connected and he raised his right hand and pointed a finger at me. His face contorted, and I could read his lips as intended. "You're going down."

I shrugged my shoulders and wondered again: *Why have we allowed politics to steep this low in our country?*

"Time," said the moderator. "Mr. Newton, do you have a response?"

I had prepared for this attack; it wasn't difficult to guess Stevie's game plan. He drew out the plays for me last time we were together. Still, I did not want to trudge through this muck. I looked out at the audience and saw their taut bodies awaiting my retort, my counter attack. *Sorry folks that's just not going to happen.* "We have reached another low point in this campaign. My opponent and her campaign manager have thrown another fastball in the dirt and they hope I swing at it."

I breathed in deep and let out some air slowly. *What were all these people in the audience thinking? They have to see through these false facts, innuendos, and outright un-truths, right? They have to realize Stevie will attack anyone and everyone, don't they? No one is safe not my friends, my family and certainly not me. Does the audience expect me to defend myself here, on stage and in public, against the lies Stevie rolled out for their entertainment? His game plan is obvious, so very obvious at least to me. The folks have to realize I'm not swinging in the dirt. I'm not going to play hardball with political professionals.*

I looked at Nancy, my former friend. "Nancy..." I waited for her to look at me and slowly she shifted in my direction. "Nancy, I won't reply to your false attacks. I will not give them any credence." I turned to face the audience. "Instead, I will let others speak on my behalf and allow the facts to set the voters straight on my record and performance as coach at the U. Folks, I invite you to my website, Voteforcoach.com. You can watch videos of the press conference where I announced the suspension of Vince and myself and also the press conference five months later where reporters apologized to us. It's all on tape, the truth preserved for you to view."

Nancy could not let this one go. "We all had our fun in college, didn't we, Bob?" Nancy eyed me with a knowing smirk and those beady eyes. "The difference is the fun for you never ended."

Did she just say that? Don't look at Amy. Don't look at Amy. Please don't look at Amy, I chided myself. I looked at Amy. Fortunately she wasn't looking at me, instead she stared bullets at Nancy. If two women get into a cage...geez, wipe that idea from your brain and fast I told myself.

I faced the moderator and said, "Next topic."

Chapter 37

Good Enough

The moderator scowled at me again. I should have counted the number of glares, stares, and smug looks he sent in my direction. Not sure what I would do with that tidbit but for some strange reason I wanted to know.

"Ok, Mr. Newton, what is your view on the role of government? In your ideal world, what should our federal government do? You have ninety seconds."

I repeated the moderator's question in my head. There was something that struck a nerve. Ideal world. There is no ideal world, that's the whole point.

"I believe it's helpful to listen to criticism from people outside our country. A world leader once had the following observation:

The United States brags about its political system, but the President says one thing during the election, something else when he takes office, something else at midterm and something else when he leaves.

Does that observation ring true to you, the voters from Illinois?" A lot of heads were nodding in the audience. "It does to me, too. The source of that quote might surprise you, it was Deng Xiaoping, leader of China from 1978-1992."

"I read in the *Wall Street Journal* recently that China continues to learn from the West and they visit the U.S. often to gain firsthand knowledge. Their travel itinerary includes stops in Silicon Valley and Wall Street in New York so they can learn about capitalism. They don't bother stopping in Washington D.C."

I paused for a moment. "Why do you believe the Chinese skip D.C.?"

The audience knew, but I had to tell them anyway. "They have seen the data. Government spending in the U.S. has increased from 7.5% of GDP in 1913 to 42% in 2011. Voters keep demanding more stuff and politicians are all too willing to oblige them. The left spends money on social services, the right on security and defense. Meanwhile, our country is going broke, regulations are strangling growth and voter ratings for Congress is at an all time low, near 10%."

I let the audience chew on that one.

"I am struck by a quote from Mark Twain, 'When I think of the primary responsibility of the U.S. Congress. Laws control the lesser man…right conduct controls the greater one.'

"Folks, my view is we have the right model of government just not the right leadership and not a good way to measure success. Today we measure government through voter approval ratings on the President, Congress, and the Senate. Our politicians read and respond to these polls with a sense of urgency. Their usual actions are to appear on cable news, talk radio, and maybe hold a press conference so they can spit out new talking points to sway voters. It's all that really matters: the vote.

"Then come the analysts that pour through all the data to rationalize the rating trends on topics such as unemployment, jobs created, wage levels, number of people in poverty on food stamps, etc. etc. etc." I shook my head sideways. "The left and the right both have political analysts that back them through various interpretations of the data, the same data. Every political opinion has some factoid to back it up and we the voters are stuck watching the tennis ball bounce back and forth over the net."

I shook my head again. "So why is our federal government broken? I believe we are trying to be too perfect. Each side, left and right, would rather allow the folks to suffer than bend or give on their ideology. Each side wants their own idealistic view of the world to come true. Their heels are dug in, their pride is on the line, and they refuse to budge. They refuse to give up on their slanted state of perfection, their Garden of Eden. It's perfection or bust in Washington, and folks, that's not good enough. The conduct of our government is flawed, and as a result, the common man and woman are stuck with the mess. And the Chinese fly over Washington D.C. to visit more important places."

I paused to let that sink in. This was an important topic to me, and I needed everyone to understand it.

"Henry Kissinger once said, 'Ninety percent of the politicians give the other ten percent a bad reputation.'

"Henry understood and that was back in the 1970s. Today it's probably ninety five percent and the reason is this false sense of perfection. The left and the right keep chasing their ideals regardless of what happens to our country, to the middle class, to the countless number of people who could climb a rung on the opportunity ladder if only our government could do its job rather than chasing some false dream…a dream that has become a nightmare for too many in our country.

"Let's stop chasing perfection, stop insisting on the ideal and instead focus on being good enough…on most things. I bet our elected officials would find more common ground, approve more laws, and make a positive impact in more lives if they got it 80% right rather than fighting tooth and nail for the full hundred. It's often that last twenty that polarizes politicians against each other when in many cases, perhaps even most cases, they can agree on eighty.

"So what stops them from agreeing on eighty? Pols are more interested in getting credit for the win than helping the folks. If they can't claim credit then they don't look good to the voters and that's all that matters. The vote that puts them back in office, on their well deserved thrones. Folks, our politicians have become rock stars. They crave the limelight, the attention, and most of all the power. They have forgotten their role to represent the people."

Heads were nodding in agreement and the audience looked alert.

"Let's take an example. I think most people agree our tax laws are too complex, the tax rates too high and uncompetitive with other countries, and there are too many loopholes. Yet nothing gets done and nothing will get done because each side is determined to claim victory. They are more focused on positioning tax reform through their ideological lens so the voters will give them credit."

Heads were nodding. "While Congress keeps fumbling the ball, some large U.S. firms borrow money to pay dividends rather than repatriate funds from abroad. Then others merge with European companies to avoid our heavy burden. If we had a fair tax system these moves would be unnecessary. So, how does our government respond? Does Congress get jolted into action to stop the madness? Does Congress change the system to influence investment back into our country? You know the answer folks. Our government calls our best companies un-loyal and penalizes them rather than fixing a broken tax system.

"I believe most people want immigration reform to finally deal with a decades' old problem. What comes first, closing the border or granting the 13 million a legal status? Do they get full amnesty or get in line with everyone else? Don't these issues seem like they could be resolved? Our political leaders would rather let immigration reform collect more dust on some shelf because they will not take any risk that voters will throw them out.

"Folks I only cite these examples to illustrate a larger point. Our federal government no longer works because we have allowed our country to be run by zealots who are more concerned with self-preservation and protecting their power in the nation's capitol than solving problems and improving lives. To stop the madness we should stop electing the usual slate of democrats and republicans. Instead we need independent thinking and action.

I was preaching but couldn't help it. *Maybe I should lighten things up a bit.*

"If we were on the football practice field and two players were fighting and not getting along there was always a solution. We called it the nutcracker drill. The entire team would circle two combatants who lined up against each other between two practice dummies. The whistle blows and a collision follows. The first man blocks for a runner and the second man tackles. If this were a cockfight it would be illegal. In football parlance it's how we separated men from boys."

I paused for a moment to ensure they got the right picture in their mind.

"I have often thought the nutcracker drill could be put to good use in the U.S. Congress. Can you imagine the Senate Majority Leader and the Senate Minority Leader in a nutcracker drill? What about the Speaker of the House and the Minority Whip?"

The audience laughed.

"You know, folks, I'm only kidding about the nutcracker drill, but I'd settle for our political leaders getting in the same ring together and just talking to each other. I'd settle to see them roll up their sleeves and work on important issues rather than spending all their time with campaign managers getting their sound bytes and factoids ready for the press. I'd love to see our political leaders shake hands once in a while, across that aisle, and view each other as teammates rather enemies."

"Folks, when is the last time you saw a Democratic Senator and Republican Senator shake hands?"

Chapter 38

Foreign Policy

My weakest topic had not been addressed, and I feared it was coming soon. The campaign team had given me all the facts, figures, and talking points and encouraged me to memorize my positions. I could not win on foreign policy, but they felt I could surely lose. *Memorize my positions?* Heck, I didn't have any position on foreign policy. I had not earned the right to have a position since I had not studied the world enough. It was very clear I would not be on any Foreign Policy Committee in the U.S. Senate if I happened to win the seat.

"Congresswoman Smith, what is your view on U.S. foreign policy? Where are we at war in the world? What relationship should we have with other countries?"

Thank God she's going first, I thought. I had more time to come up with a response. It could take hours for us to answer those questions to truly give reasoned opinion, yet we were going to squeeze it all into a few minutes because that's the TV time allotted. Nancy reeled off a memorized set of answers, yet she sounded strong, educated and in the know, so to speak. *Crap, I would definitely cede a few points on this one.*

Nancy began to wrap it up as the seconds wound down. I needed a pep talk. *Get your game face on Coach. So what if you're not an expert in this area? Just be honest about it and speak from the heart. That's all you can do. All right,* I said to myself, *here goes nothing.*

"Candidate Newton, please answer the same question. Your turn."

He means my turn in the barrel. Cut it out, Coach, the glass isn't half full. That's right it's empty. The heart, Coach...just speak from the heart. Be honest.

"When I coached at the U we published a report prior to each game listing injured players, suspensions, and starting line-ups. We told the press and our opponent the truth about our capabilities before each game. It was the rules."

The moderator had his red pen out and was slashing at the paper on his desk. No surprise there.

"Folks, I am no expert at foreign policy. I'm not in the starting line-up and probably not on the practice squad. I have a lot to learn to contribute to the team." *Ok, that wasn't so bad, Coach, you told the truth.* I thought to myself, *The press accepted your answer as if it was red meat, but don't worry about them. They would skewer you anyway.*

"That said, there are a few guidelines I am using to help define my views on this important topic. First, we should have extreme clarity on which countries are friends in the world and those we count as our enemies. It looks to me that we are sometimes unsure and that should never happen. For example, in the Middle East, Israel is our trusted friend. They face enemies every day and depend on the United States to have their back. In that same part of the world, we must prevent Iran from adding nuclear capability to wage war. We also must understand whom we can trust in the world and those we cannot."

I paused for a moment. "Would you make backroom deals with President Putin?"

The audience laughed and shrugged.

"Me neither. The second guideline is regarding war. If we bomb someone we are at war. If a country declares war on the United States, we are at war with them. If a group kills innocent citizens from our country and recruits and trains militants to hate the United States, we are at war with them, too. And when we are at war we must play to win. If we play to not lose or if we just show up to get credit, then innocent people will die and we will waste time, money, and confuse our friends and ourselves."

I was not wowing anyone with my great oratory and even saw a few yawns from the crowd.

"Now let's turn the page. Too often we view the world through a negative lens and that limits us and it limits others around the globe. I see so much positive opportunity out in the world, so much room for collaboration, cooperation, increased trade, more sharing of ideas, and resources than ever before. We don't have to come up with all the best ideas, here in the United States, just most of them."

The audience was back to laughing at my silly jokes again.

"Folks, the United States should lead but we should also listen and learn from others. I advocate more cooperation in finding energy sources, protecting the earth and open markets without heavy regulations and taxes. I favor a tax structure that most countries practice, tax revenues in the country where earned and not again at home."

Fortunately, the clock had wound down to zero. I had given ground to Nancy in this round and had some work to do.

Chapter 39

Final Question

I was exhausted. Debates were hard work, and I was suddenly glad we only had one. Standing on stage for two hours in the hot, bright lights had shaken my bones. Trying to phrase my responses with some wit or sharp retort, yet remaining friendly and honest had completely wiped me out. Wearing a smile like a sorority sister the entire time had squashed my cheek muscles to dirt. Nancy looked great, but I knew she had been through the ringer, same as me.

We had reached the final question of the evening. It would be a softball each of us could whack for a home run. The moderator looked at the two warriors in front of him and smiled. It was more a sneer than a smile; he could afford that risk since the cameras were on Nancy and me.

"Congresswoman Smith, please summarize your message

for the voters of Illinois. You have sixty seconds."

While Nancy spewed away I thought about my own reply. I wanted to say throw her out, kick her butt back to Illinois where she belongs. She represents everything that is bad about Washington D.C.—her and that sidekick Slime Guy. *He's got to go too.* I felt betrayed by Nancy when she chose the dark side over me. Most of all, I was disappointed in my friend, my former friend. We had been good for each other. We held ourselves to the highest of standards, set the bar for others to leap over. We were the examples to follow. We were the good guys until the day Nancy lost her soul. She placed greater value on protecting her turf than doing her job and something had to be done. Someone had to put an end to her career. I shrugged as I usually do when Nancy enters my mind. I did not want to be the dragon slayer but there was no one else.

"We need experienced leadership in Washington, someone who understands how the system works, how to get things done. I will continue to fight against Tea Party Conservatives who only want to repress the middle class and preserve a capital system that works for the 1%."

"Time."

"Thank you citizens of Illinois for the trust you have placed in me the past 30 years. I will never let you down."

"Time. Candidate Newton, it's your turn. You have 60 seconds."

It had been a long two hours and the end was near. There was time for one last citation, one last sound byte for the press or a heartfelt comment for the people. Which would it be?

Tick Tock.

The faces in the audience encouraged me. I saw Mark and thought of his mom and how much she was missed. There was Toby who survived Coach Bubba with my help, and Jesse was there and tipped his cap for me to see. Janelle had returned and stood in the back of the room, her strength shined through. Carla sat in the front row with my family, a perfect mentor for Taylor. I saw a large black man on the far left and looked a bit closer. It was Vince in person to support his old coach. Willy sat tall in his chair, a friend I was so lucky to know. The last person I saw and the one who inspired me most was of course Amy. She blew me a kiss and said her usual, "Love you, babe."

I set the exhaustion aside and ripped out one last short speech.

"Folks, we've talked about a lot of important issues tonight and many of you have already made up your mind. Nancy is the safe choice, she's a known entity and it's not hard to predict how she would represent our great state in the nation's capitol. If you fear taking risk, if you are worried about shaking things up, if you are against change, then you should vote for Nancy. I voted for her in the past…more than once."

"On the other hand…when I cast my vote for senator next week, I will not go with the safe choice. I will not support the status quo. I will not send someone back to Washington D.C. who calls the Capitol her home rather than the state she represents."

I could feel Nancy's daggers on my back. I simply told the truth and she felt I was tossing some mud.

"Folks, I will not repeat what you have heard from me tonight and the past few months. You know my stance on the important issues and how I would work for you and represent you. Instead, I'd like to share one more piece of news."

The audience had been a bit restless but quieted at the pending news.

"I will only be your Senator for a single term. I will not seek another six years. I will not become a fixture in Washington,

District of Columbia. My home, our home, will remain here in Illinois."

I thought to myself, *Six years is all I got. You will get the best of what I have left to give.*

I had five seconds remaining and wanted to beat the moderator one time this evening. I looked out at the 2,500 strong and made my last comment. "Vote for Coach."

One one thousand, two one thousand. The clock expired. The moderator nodded his head and said, "Thank you Congresswoman Smith and Candidate Newton."

The awkward moment was upon us. I looked left and saw Nancy on the move. She was determined to meet me more than half way. It was a race to see which candidate was the most gracious. Whichever one crossed the imaginary half way point on stage would get a leg up with the voters, especially those with blue hair. At this point I was too tired to care about that nonsense. Rather, I was more concerned what to do with my hands. *Do I give Nancy a good shake, a warm hug, a kiss? Crap,* I had no idea what to do. It was Nancy…but she was no longer the person I once knew.

Nancy crossed midfield and broke into a smile. The small victory was hers and she felt good. Geez, the things our politicians believe are important never amaze me. I trudged a few steps toward her and instinct took over. My right hand reached outward for a strong shake. It was the safe move to make. Nancy put her hand out and we closed the space between us. Just another few inches to go when I saw her hand reach up and wrap around my shoulder as Nancy leaned in, lips near my left ear. "My turf, my house. You lose, QB."

Instinct took over and my mind sent a recorded message to my mouth. "You look good, Nance." Fortunately I stopped the tape right there and did not play another quip. I had called her Nance even though every bone in my body wanted to pummel her to the ground. The realization hit me hard. I missed my friend but doubt she missed me.

Chapter 40

The Trail

The campaign trail was more fun than I expected, more tiring than my body wanted and more exhilarating than any of us imagined. Carla and Paul set the schedule, while Taylor worked the social media engines, Amy greeted the throngs of people and I tuned our message. We toured the state by plane, train, automobile, and boat and also rode a bicycle or two. We had no idea if people would show for our events and were bowled over by the many who came to listen, speak, and debate issues they felt strongly about. The voters were coming out for this election, which was more than fine with me.

My favorite part of the campaign trail was the smaller venues, when we had time for conversation with a few people, usually at breakfast or lunch. The large gatherings, when I had to deliver a speech, seemed like a bad movie we had to watch again and again and again.

We met and talked with so many interesting people who taught us more than we taught them. Thankfully our ears were open and we willingly adapted our own thinking more than once. As always, there were a few standouts I remember more than the rest.

*****

Charlie

Charlie is 72 years young and in terrific shape, both his mind and body have a lot of tread left. He's an avid biker, the kind that requires some pedaling and a retired radiologist who once dated his bride to be via airplane. He has not used a pilot's license in some time but he remembers flying through the clouds with a daredevil look in his eye. We all fell in love with Charlie and his outlook on life. We met him at a breakfast and shared some eggs. He had not planned to show for our meet-up. Nope not Charlie, he didn't care that much about politics, and he did not attend political events. Charlie happened to be in the right place at the right time for our needs, and hopefully his too.

Charlie held court as we took notes about the health system he worked in all his life.

"The game is rigged," said Charlie.

"How so?" I asked.

"It's supposed to be about quality of care but that's not what matters, not to enough doctors."

"What matters?"

"Volume."

"Huh, say more, Charlie. What do you mean by volume?"

"Doctors make their money by the ton, not by the outcome."

We let that sink in as Charlie intended then urged him forward.

"The ton?"

Charlie knew he had our attention and gave us a warm smile. I learned later that was his poker tell. He always showed that warm smile when he was about to lower the boom.

"The more doctors test, the more they prescribe, and the more they perform, the more they make."

"So, you're saying doctors are incented financially to game the system by doing more whether it's needed or not. Is that right?"

"Bingo. Healthcare has been a volume game for a very long time. It's the key driver of the entire system."

"What happens as a result of doctors being focused on volume?" I knew the answer before Charlie said it.

"It drives the cost up, way up. And it means there is not enough focus on the quality of care. There is less time spent with patients and more time spent on needless tests."

"Volume up equals higher costs and worse care."

Charlie smiled again. "Like I said, bingo."

"What do you propose we do about that Charlie? Got any big ideas?"

"Change the incentives."

"The incentives?"

"Yes, the incentives. Align doctor's pay to quality of care, good outcomes, things that matter. Change it away from the volume game."

"That's brilliant, Charlie, Brilliant! How easy is it to make that kind of change?"

The smile returned.

Charlie had been on the inside his whole career and was

now on the outside able to offer sound criticism of a profession he loved. I looked to other pols for learning but only heard the far right decree the end of Obamacare and saw the left run away from their most significant achievement. No one knew what to do as the new health care model plodded along. Shifting from volume to outcomes seemed a really good place to start.

*****

Chloe

The press was unsure how to handle our campaign in the early days. Was I a Republican pretending to be an Independent? Was I a Democrat afraid to compete in the primaries? Was I a rookie who had no idea what he was doing? There was some truth lurking in all of those questions though I did my best to hide it. After a few weeks it was clear which way the press would lean. They opted to support the devil they knew and test the one they didn't. Chloe was a beat reporter for the big city paper assigned to our campaign. She must have drawn the short straw but it didn't affect her reporting, not one darn bit. She was the same age as Taylor, five foot five with dark brown hair, blue eyes, and always looked hungry. She was smart and savvy, and often used real facts in her dailies. We respected her style and dogged work effort, but I kept getting slammed with the morning news.

"Taylor we need you to handle Chloe," I pleaded one morning after tossing the paper aside.

"Handle Chloe? Seriously Pops, it doesn't work that way."

"Well, what do you propose we do? I'd settle for some unbiased and fair reporting. We don't need any help to win, just a level playing field."

Carla walked in and overheard our back and forth. "It's a good idea. Taylor you can do this."

Taylor was taken aback. Her mentor chose Pops over the kid and that seldom happened. I ate a bite of toast to hide my smile. Once in a while the stars did align. Carla and Taylor left the room to plan their attack. Man, I would not want to face those two on the field, in an alley, heck just about anywhere.

They came up with a terrific plan. I should have known they would play our trump card. They moved me to the sidelines and brought in our closer. The next morning Chloe had an interview with Amy. *Good move kiddo,* I thought to myself. I sat in the background, the deep background and did my best to hear the conversation.

"What's it like to be Coach's wife?"

Amy smiled. She had been asked that question too many times and had grown tired being cast as a tag along. "It's like being married to a movie star surrounded by a wonderful cast, all of them love the bright lights and the stage. They can't get enough adoration from all those fans."

The coffee sprayed out of my mouth as an uncontrollable burst of energy rose inside me. "What the heck …" I began to shout then zipped it up when the stares from Taylor and Carla penetrated my eyeballs.

Chloe hesitated unsure how to respond. She had lofted an easy pitch to get things going and Amy was having none of that. The reporter inside Chloe took over and she dove in. "What kind of film does your husband see himself starring in?"

Amy could not hold back and let out a loud laugh then could not stop the giggles. I set my cup down, grabbed a wet towel and wondered what would happen next. After a few seconds, which felt like five minutes, Amy had calmed herself but had not removed her smile.

"Lately our lives feel a bit like that bar scene from the first *Star Wars* movie. We never know which character will show up next."

Chloe was thrown for another loop. She just stared at Amy then fell into her own giggling attack that would not end. My wife and Chloe laughed and laughed some more and the rest of us joined in. It was a much-needed respite from the day-to-day grind of the trail.

After a few minutes, Amy reached out her hand and touched Chloe on the arm. "Let's go for a walk and have some time alone."

I looked at Taylor and Carla and mouthed "What?" They just shrugged shoulders. They knew and I knew there was no way to control Ames. Two hours later there was still no sign. I was ready to send out the dogs when they rounded the corner and made it back to campaign HQ.

Amy took a chair as Chloe made a hasty escape to put some words on paper. We eagerly surrounded her and asked for some details.

"Chloe's tough."

"She's earned that rep among her peers," said Carla.

"Yes, she is a tough reporter. What I meant to say is she's also a tough kid who's been through a lot in life for such a young age."

We put aside our questions about the interview and took a seat to learn about Chloe. I think we all needed a break from the reality of campaigning.

"That girl ... that young girl put herself through college and took care of a sick father after her mom passed when Chloe was in her early teens. She's been carrying a heavy load for a great many years. They got some help from the church and the state when there was nowhere else to go, and she's been paying it back ever since."

"How does she pay it back?" I asked.

Amy looked at Carla and the light bulb went on. "She pays it back through her writing," said Carla.

Amy nodded. "Chloe is a dream recruit for a biased media that leans left but won't admit it publicly. Her natural inclination is to defend a social viewpoint and she admits that tendency. But she pursues the facts and works hard to draw fair conclusions in her stories."

"You sure can't tell from the headlines she's been tossing out," I said.

"We talked about that. Let's just say Chloe gets a lot of help with the pen from the boys in charge back in the city."

"Why or how did all this come up in the interview?" I asked.

"I told Chloe what I expected and needed from her—a level playing field. Let the facts guide the story, not the boys from the city."

"How did Chloe react, Mom?"

"She went off the record."

"What?" asked Carla.

"Chloe asked for a few minutes off the record." None us said a word we were struck numb at a reporter asking to be off the record.

"Chloe told me in so many words that we were being too nice, playing up the good guy image too much and not working the press hard enough."

"Damn straight," I said.

"She said nice guys finish last in politics because no one believes them, and if no one believes them then no one trusts what they have to say."

"Wait, are you saying the press trusts the crap they get from Nancy and Stevie more than the truth they get from us?"

"It's not that they trust Nancy more; they understand her better. They know to weed through the lies and tricks but they know it's coming. It's expected. Nancy is playing by the rules the press understands."

We were lost in our thoughts trying to figure out what to do with this new insight. I liked the good guy image, I needed the good guy image, and I thrived on it.

"What did you do next, Ames?"

Ames had a serious look, the kind she wore at parent-teacher meetings when Taylor was in school. *Uh oh,* I thought to myself.

"I got out my shovel."

"Your shovel?" asked Carla.

"Yes, my shovel. Bob might need to hold on to that good guy image ... but I don't."

"What...did...you...say...Amy?" I asked.

Her smile returned, the one that said don't worry, I got your back. "You'll see."

"We'll see?"

"Tomorrow morning we can all read the news together. Chloe's on deadline for the morning run so don't contact her."

I woke early for breakfast, as did the whole group. Taylor and Carla were on the net when I sat down at the table. I preferred the real paper but was too impatient that morn.

"What's the headline?"

Tay and Carla giggled. *Was that good or bad?* I wondered.

Taylor slid her iPad over to me, and I read aloud the front-page stunner.

COACH'S WIFE PLAYS BALL

"This can't be good."

Ames walked in and peeked over my shoulder. "Good girl Chloe." That comment drew more laughter from Taylor and Carla who had finished the article. *If they are laughing it can't be that bad, right?* I asked myself.

Amy did not attack Nancy with any dirt, that was not her style. Instead, she asked a number of pointed questions about policies the Congresswoman professed to back and promised to deliver.

"What has Congresswoman Smith accomplished in her 30 plus years in Washington? That's an awful long time to be in the Capitol and not have a memorable result that made a difference for the citizens of Illinois."

Amy also went after the people who support Nancy's campaign.

"You can tell a lot about a person from their friends. Your readers should take a good look at the donors and supporters of Congresswoman Smith's campaign.

"What are you implying about The Guv, Mrs. Newton? He's one of her strongest backers."

"Our governor's don't have a great track record in this state do they? But I'm not saying anything about any one person. I am suggesting the voters of Illinois look at the whole picture of who is backing each candidate. It's very revealing."

The rest of the article was much the same. Amy used her shovel a great deal, questioning the opposition with surgical thrusts to seed doubt in the voter's mind. It was not part of our initial game plan and not something I could do. My wife had my back, our back, and played the game like a pro. She ended the article with our tag line.

"Vote for Coach."

Chapter 41

The Secret

A few days before the election we arranged an exclusive CNN interview in our home. Voter feedback indicated they wanted to know more about the candidate and his family so we put our best foot forward, again. Amy and Chloe had worked out well, so we upped our bet with a biased press at the national level. We were six to seven points behind in the polls and time was running out. We threw a Hail Mary pass and hoped for the best.

I settled into the background as Paul and Carla took charge with some help from Taylor. The three of them schemed, debated talking points and sound bytes for Amy to spout on TV. I laughed at all the planning, knowing full well Amy would say what was on her mind. We would win or lose being the people we were, not fictional characters someone thought the voters preferred. Our house was full as camera crews and lighting fixtures filled the living room and spilled over into any other space they needed. The CNN reporter was known for her challenging yet fair interviews, although she had a reputation for leaning left and I wondered how well she knew Stevie. Paul asked for questions in advance but none were given. We were not expecting any softballs from this pitcher.

The ladies took their seats as I began to pace and tripped on a wire. A camera guy shoved a seat into my legs and I reluctantly obliged. Don't upset the camera dude when he's filming your wife strangely crossed my mind. The lights blared and the temperature in our house rose a degree maybe two. We had the AC on full blast in early November to beat the heat from the CNN team. In the corner of my eye I saw Taylor behind a computer screen. She ran our social media game plan, so it was not unusual to see her scrolling the net. Then I saw her mouth three words that nearly took the life out of me. "Oh my god."

The interview was less than a minute from the starting blocks. I looked at Taylor and she returned my stare. We both eyed Amy, then Taylor leapt from her seat and made a dash through the lights, cameras, and furniture piled in strange places. She settled into a fast walk and reached Amy with thirty seconds to go. Taylor whispered as Amy nodded. It almost looked as if Taylor called a play and Amy said, "Don't worry, I got it."

Taylor circled back through the mess in our house and gave me a look I'd never forget. She seemed to say 'Got your back, you big fool' then went back to the computer screen. It was not the time to rise from my seat and ask what was going on. Instead, I sat still with my focus on Ames. I knew she would look at me just prior to the start of the interview and had to be ready. I would be there for her just like she was always there for me. The director began a countdown from ten going backwards. When he got to five Amy looked over and I said the three words I had planned. "Love you, babe." I got my reward, a big smile from the woman I adored.

The CNN reporter was good, damn good. Fortunately or unfortunately, she was well prepared. Her openers were background questions on our family and life as a coach's wife. Both ladies were at ease during the early rounds, but we all knew it was only a prelude to the real questions to come. Ms. CNN shifted in midstream to some of the mud Stevie had slung and Ames batted it away easily.

"Amy, can you help us understand what really happened with Vince and the accusations tossed around in the campaign?"

Amy gave a warm smile. "Vince is part of our family. I first met him a few feet away in our kitchen. He joined us for Christmas Eve dinner and brought a rose for Taylor and one for me. He was a surprise dinner guest, my husband gave little warning, yet we were happy to share the holiday with such a giving person."

"A giving person? That's not the image being portrayed."

"Of course not. It's the image being painted by desperate people."

"Please share with our audience how Vince, a teen who grew up on the south side streets with no parents in a crime ridden and drug laden neighborhood, can be such a giving person."

"The program my husband ran at the U is a secret weapon. It may be the best social service I know in our state. He built a model that saves kids like Vince from a life of crime. He teaches them how to create a new path for themselves. They just have to work for it and pay it back."

"Pay it back?"

"Yes, pay it back. The reason for all this hoopla is Vince donated large sums of money he collected from signing autographs to help disabled children. He fell in love with those kids."

Amy reached behind her back and pulled out photos of Vince with some of the kids taken when he was QB at the U. Ms. CNN allowed the cameras to take a quick look and moved to a new topic. She was here for a ratings boost and we could all feel the zinger was about to hit.

"Amy my next question might be more difficult for you to address."

Amy looked straight ahead and waited for the serve she knew was coming. She was poised and ready.

"I learned recently that your husband, your forgetful husband, has been accused of attacking his opponent Congresswoman Smith, when they were in college together."

Amy kept her composure and her smile. She had not been asked a question so she waited for it.

"A sorority sister of Congresswoman Smith's has come forward as an eye witness. She saw your husband break into the sorority house through a fire escape then sneak into the Congresswoman's room."

Amy remained cool under fire as Ms. CNN continued her speech. Most people would have interrupted a few times by this point, which would have looked defensive. Not Amy, she was waiting for a serve inside the lines that she could smash back.

Ms. CNN paused for a reaction and got none. Finally she asked a question to get a response. "Are you surprised by this accusation, Amy? I know it's been a long time, but it's a very serious charge."

"I remember like it was yesterday."

Ms. CNN did not expect Amy's retort. "You remember?"

"Oh yes. Though I'd hardly call it an attack. What would you call a two-way attack? We called it a fling back in the day, what do they call it now?"

"A fling? You seem so … so casual about the whole thing."

"College boys." Amy leaned in closer to Ms. CNN. "You know, between you and me…and all your listeners…I'm glad he got that out of his system."

"Out of his system?"

"You know the old saying, set him free and see if he returns. In our case it was true as the wind."

"You're saying that you set Bob free and he came back to you?"

"Yes, that's exactly what I am saying. I broke things off with Bob during senior year. I loved that man so much and still do today, even though he can be forgetful at times." Amy looked over and gave me a wink.

"Nancy stalked him the next week in our favorite bar on campus."

"She stalked him."

"Well, she made the first move. Bob was crying in his beer and feeling sorry for himself. He was an easy target that night and didn't resist very much." Amy looked at me again, this time she was not smiling.

Ms. CNN paused for a beat maybe two. "How do you know all these details, Amy? That's quite remarkable."

"I've known all along. It was my plan to let Bob go in the first place… though being totally honest about it, I had a leash on him the entire time."

"Please tell us more."

"The bartender that night was, and is, a dear friend and he saw the whole thing play out. He gave me plenty of reason to confront Nancy … the former Congresswoman the next day."

"You confronted Nancy, er I mean the Congresswoman the day after?"

"I most certainly did."

"What happened?"

"Let's just say we came to an agreement."

"An agreement?"

"Yes, an agreement. She agreed to meet with Bob that very afternoon and date him properly or get out of the way. You see, Nancy was my test to see if Bob would return. I did not pick Nancy; she was not a preference of mine. Fortunately for me, he came to his senses and returned just like I hoped he would."

Ms. CNN let the cameras roll.

I sat there and looked at my wife, my most amazing best friend. She had known all this time the truth about Nancy and me yet never said a word. *How can anyone be that strong?* I wondered. She knew because Willy told her. That son of a gun broke a solemn oath among men and ran his skinny butt, well not that skinny, right to my ex-girlfriend and blabbed a story. He's the reason Nancy and I met up the next day. He told Amy and she confronted Nancy and our paths had been set. Willy had never said a thing either. The two of them had been in cahoots and kept a secret for more than 33 years.

The dots were now connected. *How did Nancy say it a number of years ago? We were never given a chance ... yeah that's it.* She and Amy had played Thunder Dome after all, and I got the best girl. Amy took Nancy down 33 years ago and had just done it again. I sat in my seat and shook my head wondering if a smile or frown would form. I didn't have to wait very long as the corners of my mouth went high, and I laughed aloud for everyone to hear. *Thank you Willy, you done good. Ames, you were always the strong one.* These were my last two thoughts as Ms. CNN and her crew wrapped it up.

We picked up three points in the overnight polls. The tides were shifting and our only enemy was the clock as Amy had taken out the trash.

Chapter 42

Election Day

The campaign trail had exhausted every fiber in my body. My aching bones screamed pain and I could hear Coach Mac yelling in my head, "Put some ice on it, you big baby." Some memories never fade away and I was thankful for that. I missed my mentor and longed for his sage advice even if it included some ice.

Amy and Taylor went with me to our hotel room, which of course was packed with people, many of them silly drunk by the time we arrived. I acknowledged a few atta boys and pats on the back as we made our way to our only place of privacy, the bedroom where I collapsed on the bed never to wake, never again. Or so I hoped.

Taylor grabbed the TV remote and waited for the signal. Should we look at early polling results or not? Maybe we would look, but only if I could get up out of a prone position, face down on the pillow. It was a struggle as the debate raged in my head.

Rest or TV talking heads?

Rest or talking heads?

Finally, I moved, it was more like a twitch really, and then another. It may have taken five minutes to shift my torso around and face the ladies. Taylor gave me the bent head nod, indicating it was decision time while Amy just shook her head at the crumpled mess of a man splayed on the bed in front of her.

"Ok Tay, go ahead and put it on. Let's get this over with."

In less than a second the TV talking heads were spitting out numbers. It would be a long night for them in many parts of the country, but not Illinois. We were down two points at the start of the day, an improvement of 12 points from the debate. Our trend line was a winner, if only we had more time. But the clock had run out and the final score would be posted soon. *Thank God*, I thought. We could go back to our lives, our happy lives where there was peace, quiet, and my opinion was not questioned, my reputation not pilloried and my family left alone.

"And in Illinois the early results are in for the senate race."

It would be a quick death, a gun to the head and in a second it would all be over. There would be one last speech to thank everyone who worked so hard on a long shot. I could rise up to that challenge.

"Bret, Illinois is too close to call."

Three jaws hit the floor with a thud.

"The Independent candidate, Bob Newton, has pulled even on the last day of the campaign."

"Holy crap," I said.

"Holy crap," Amy said.

We both looked at Taylor as she turned up the volume.

"Holy crap, Pops."

Three holy craps in a row had to be a record, I thought. "Tay let me see that remote." Taylor grudgingly handed over the remote to the one true remote ruler in the family. That's how I saw it anyway. We bounced around to more channels and were mesmerized by the numbers. All news outlets made similar pronouncements, the Illinois Senate race was 'too close to call'.

What the heck was I going to do now? We had planned a graceful exit from politics after spitting out the sour taste it left in our mouths. We hoped our message made an impact for the next brave soul who would climb the hill. We'd cheer for her from the rocking chairs on our front porch and leave our battle scars in the rearview mirror. Our next stop was to see Doc and work on the plan. I put my thoughts and the plan on hold and went back to TV talking heads.

"And in Illinois, the Independent candidate, Bob Newton, is ahead by less than one percent with 15% of counties reporting."

"What the heck do we do now?" I wondered aloud.

Amy rose from her chair, looked around the room and said, "We call a realtor."

Taylor walked toward me, wrapped her arms around my waist and laid her head on my shoulder. She kissed me on the neck then whispered in my ear. "Stay around for a while, Pops, the people want you in the Senate."

Chapter 43

The Oval

Boxes and people filled my new office, a cramped space until some of them went back home, then it would just be a small office, which was okay with me. Carla and Alice had signed on for the move and would have my back...again. Amy and I rented a townhouse and kept our home in Illinois. We were in the Capitol but not in the circle and had no intention of joining the in crowd.

Alice walked into the office with a phone in hand. "It's the Oval."

The small crowd hushed and someone dropped a box to the floor. A few people said, "ouch," as some glass shattered.

"The Oval?" I said.

The next question was the critical one. Who was actually on the phone? The Chief of Staff would signify a meeting to be scheduled. Otherwise, it was a courtesy call, a simple two minute congratulations and then back to business.

Alice cupped her hand around the mouthpiece and whispered for all to hear. "It's the Chief of Staff."

"Holy crap, Pops," Taylor said.

I took the phone and left the room to find a quiet place. It would have taken longer to herd cats out of my office and some probably would have stayed, which I didn't need. My face gave it away upon my return after a short minute. I looked around the silent room and said, "I've been invited to the Oval tomorrow afternoon for 15 minutes."

No one moved or said a word so I broke the trance, "Dinner's at 8:00 p.m., folks, let's wrap things up here and meet at the restaurant."

I had planned one last dinner before Taylor, Amy, and Paul travelled home. It was to be a relaxing and fun evening but now my mind was full of thoughts. *What should I say? What questions to ask? What do I wear?* Amy felt my nervousness and said, "That new suit you bought for the swearing in will look good in the Oval." *Could the woman read me that easily?* I gave Amy a warm smile, one worry down and a bunch to go. I leaned over and whispered in her ear, "I need to stretch, back in a few."

Amy nodded as I made my escape.

"Excuse me folks," I said to the table.

I made my way to the men's room and a small table in the far corner caught my attention. It was Stevie and Nancy. I stopped and stared. My head said walk but my feet stayed put. A few seconds ticked by and I had not moved nor even twitched. I don't remember breathing just standing and staring and wondering how she was doing. Neither one spoke as forks moved dinner around their plates. Nancy set her fork down and slowly turned in my direction. My head yelled move but I remained planted in the middle of the room. Her eyes met mine and we both held our look. I searched her face for a sign, something that would reveal a truth. *Are you angry, Nancy? Are you hurt? Do you have a plan?* I had lost the roadmap and could no longer read the signals. Nancy turned back around and bowed her head. She picked up a napkin and dabbed the corner of one eye.

Stevie looked up as I moved away. I heard a loud thump and knew he rose quickly from the table and was probably headed here to the men's room. I looked in the mirror and waited for the door to swing open. *What did Stevie want? Did he seek revenge? Would he take a swing?* I had no idea what to expect and surrendered my thoughts. *Okay, Stevie whatever it is, bring it.* I turned toward the door and waited. *One one thousand, two…*the door opened much slower than I expected.

Stevie took a step, then another and closed the door behind him. It was a face-off at center ice; all we needed was a puck and some sticks.

"Hello, Coach."

"Stevie."

A couple seconds ticked as I waited for his move. My body tensed and my hands closed. *Come on, dude, let's get this over with*, I thought to myself.

"You set me up."

I nodded.

Stevie chuckled. "It was a good move, one I did not anticipate from you. Nicely played."

Was that a compliment from Slime Guy? I wondered.

My hands opened. There would be no fight, although we weren't done. "How is she?"

Stevie shrugged. "She's all done."

I expected that but felt a deep sadness. "Does she…blame…"

"Yes."

The stab hit home. I closed my eyes and tried to picture Nancy but could not find an image. The deep storage that held all those memories was locked down.

Stevie let a few seconds pass then said, "She also blames herself."

"What will she do?"

Stevie shrugged. "There's always a PAC."

I did not know what else to say and the silence hung between us. Stevie moved along. "I heard you are going to the Oval tomorrow."

How the heck does he know? Did it matter? I nodded.

"It's a different game with the Oval. Call me when you need help, Coach." Stevie stuck out his hand for a shake.

My head screamed, *no chance!* And my gut seconded that vote. My heart suggested it never hurt to have friends in strange places. We all waited for Mr. Ego to weigh in. *Hell no!,* he said and I let Slime Guy hang in the air.

Stevie got the message and turned to leave. "You'll learn, Coach. You will need someone like me if you want to make it in the circle."

The door closed and I let out a deep breath of air. People like Stevie would never understand. I could care less about the circle and never would.

*****

I sat on the couch and looked around the office. *What the heck am I doing here?* I wondered. *I could be at home watching a game and drinking a beer.*

The Oval reminded me of the Guv and I wondered his next move. He had counted a W before time expired and watched in horror as my Hail Mary won the game. His one-way ticket to the circle had been stamped then ripped away by a college football coach who understood Joe Six-Packs better than the political elite. His rep had taken a brutal hit and his calls went unanswered. The Guv was stuck at the state and would not climb another rung. *So much for this ruler of the earth*, I thought.

Alright Bob, get your head in the game, I chided myself. I revisited the game plan for the next fifteen minutes and performed one last check prior to kick-off.

Step One. Go for the easy wins. The Keystone pipeline had significant support from both parties and just made sense. It was more efficient, safer, better for the environment than rail and would generate jobs. Next, repatriate monies trapped overseas, which would spark growth at home and not cost the country a cent. Another easy one if we can get past the politics. Last, get started on Immigration Reform by securing the border and removing objections to a broader bill to release the 13 million stranded inside the country. They have waited long enough.

Step Two. Go long. Get started on tax reform now so a bill could be passed next year. This was a big one that everyone wanted. It only required some negotiation and leadership.

Step Three. Blow up the circle. He might ask about my true purpose, the real reason I ran for office. Was I ready? *Would I tell him?* I wondered. *What would Amy do?* She'd hit him in the gut and call the circle a failure. She'd tell the President how disconnected politicians had become from the folks and the lack of trust people felt. Amy would be respectful yet tear the soul out of the most powerful man in the world. I set that thought aside as the door opened and he walked into the office. I felt the sweat on my back and steadied my hand for a good shake.

"Hello Bob, welcome to Washington." The President stretched out his hand.

What do I call him? Think, Bob, think! "Hello, sir." He had a warm smile and a gentle yet firm shake. It felt good to be near him.

"I watched your campaign especially toward the end when you closed the gap with only a few weeks to go."

"It was a tough battle, sir."

"You beat a very good team. We have great respect for Nancy around here and Stevie seldom loses."

"Thank you."

"That's Stevie's seat you were sitting in by the way."

"Oh, I'm sorry, sir."

The President laughed. He got me.

"Have a seat," he said.

I tried to relax and enjoy the moment but was unsure of the next move. It was a home game for the President a clear advantage in the Oval.

"Bob, there's one thing I did not understand from your campaign. I asked a lot of people and no one gave me a good answer. Nobody seems to know the real reason you are here in the Capitol."

I gulped. *So much for step one and two. He's going right to step three.*

"What's your motivation, Bob? Why are you really in D.C.?"

I breathed in deep, looked the man in the eyes and thought of Jerrod. *Okay, buddy, I'm in the Oval with the man. Should I speak truth and reveal our plan, the one we worked on all those years ago?*

I gulped.

The Independent

What would Jerrod do?

"I'm here to start a third party, sir."

The President nodded.

Chapter 44

I sat at my new desk and reflected back on the night that changed everything. The vote had surprised me. I tossed out the idea as a ruse, something to lighten the day and remove some of the burden we all wore as the campaign had wound down. Yet, part of me hoped the voters would go for it. We could not close the 5-6 point gap no matter what we did or said, and my team had worked damn hard. Time was running out, there were just a few days remaining in the campaign. I gathered our small group together for a team vote. We did this a lot during the campaign to break ties or see how each other felt about an issue.

I looked at their tired faces, Amy and Taylor sat as straight as their worn bodies would allow. Paul was ready for much needed sleep and Carla finished a call so we could begin. She was always working the phones with an endless energy that boosted everyone around her. This was our group, the power team, the voting block I cared most about. I loved everyone at the table. We had become a well-oiled machine and were just starting to click. We overcame a late entry and some bad goofs by the candidate to make it a close race. Nancy was breathing hard and looking over her shoulder as she ran ahead in her red spikes. I was trailing and eating her dust but coming up fast, much faster than she thought possible. She looked worried, nervous and scared. I had never seen Nancy scared and it encouraged me greatly. That's how I pictured it in my head, running very close behind Nancy and she wearing the red.

"Alright, time for some truth talk." I opened the late night meeting. "We need a new play, a Hail Mary pass, something that will shock the voters into action, wake them up."

The voting block groaned in unison.

"Who has an idea? Come on throw it out on the table and we'll kick it around. Anyone?"

Two heads hit the table while Carla answered another call. It was Amy and me left sitting tall in our chairs, the two of us together. "Got any big ideas?"

Amy shook her head. She looked a bit sad though she tried hard not to show it. Even the strongest among us was wearing thin I thought to myself. Carla returned and I knew now was the time.

"Ok, I have an idea. It's not a real good one but it will get us started."

The two heads on the table righted themselves as eight eyes stared at me and pleaded for a real Hail Mary, not some fake.

"The CNN interview is two days from now. Our best player will be on the small screen in front of the voters. We need to create a reason, some reason for the reporter to bait Amy and then my dear you hit the ball out of the park."

"What's the bait, Pops?" Asked Taylor.

The room went silent as they waited for the bait. They had no idea what I was thinking, what a good man can do when his back is against the wall. All it takes is some justification. If my opponent can play tricks and makes up lies then I had to do something about it. It took me a while to figure out the quandary, how to play dirty against Stevie without soiling my hands. Instead of going negative against Nancy … I would go negative against myself.

"There was a Sorority girl the night I spent in Nancy's room. Her name is Ellen and she saw me come through the fire escape."

The End

Acknowledgements

What makes a good coach? I have been thinking about this question a lot the past two years as I wrote two books with Coach Bob as the hero. In my life there have been many coaches who influenced me, taught me and showed me how to be better. Some coaches worked in athletics - football, basketball, hockey and baseball were the passions of my youth. Other coaches had business careers and some were friends from school or work, and a long time ago the Catholic Church. Each of them left an impression on me when I listened and heeded their advice, whether spoken or shown.

There are many common traits in a good coach. He (or she) commands respect, teaches through behaviors more than words and instills discipline, humility and character in students. A good coach brings diverse talents together into a team with common goals. A great coach inspires his pupils to achieve more than they thought possible. The best coaches impact the trajectory of a student's life whether they realize it or not, at the time.

I decided to build Coach Bob around these themes and chose two attributes to define him. Coach Bob shows others how to "earn it" and he helps players define a "path in life" after the last whistle has blown. These two attributes are my best attempt at describing what constitutes a good coach and they are drawn from the many men and women who have helped shape the person I have become. To all you coaches who have impacted me, I say thank you!

I'd also like to thank politicians that run clean campaigns, use real facts to back up their views and serve in office to support their fellow citizens. It seems there are fewer of you each year and your voices are not being heard. Please turn up the volume.

To Mindy Reed and Danielle Hartman Acee from The Authors' Assistant, my heartfelt thanks for editing and designing another one.

Any endeavor of mine over the past 36 years has not been a solo performance. My wife Kim has been at my side providing support and love in her unique way. She makes everything better and for that I am grateful.